Wilfred Whitten

London in Song

Wilfred Whitten

London in Song

ISBN/EAN: 9783337008413

Printed in Europe, USA, Canada, Australia, Japan

Cover: Foto ©Andreas Hilbeck / pixelio.de

More available books at **www.hansebooks.com**

LONDON
IN
SONG
Compiled
By
Wilfred Whitten
PUBLISHED BY GRANT RICHARDS
9 HENRIETTA STREET COVENT GARDEN

TO
MY WIFE

INTRODUCTION

THIS book is for the lover of London. The love and knowledge of London, in poets and in readers, have given me my principle of selection ; and my own love and knowledge of London, such as they are, have given me my impulse. London therefore, not Literature, is primarily exhibited in these pages. Fine poems, inspired by London, will be found in profusion, but mingled with these are many London poems which are only witty, or only curious, or only sincere. London is a mighty mingling; and this book answers to London.

I have taken more than two hundred poems, or sets of verses, the oldest by Chaucer, the newest by living poets, and have placed them in three groups. In the first and largest group, London as a whole is contemplated, and the great brilliant "Town" displays its fashions and bric-à-brac. In the last group are placed poems of the City—the market of the world. Dick Whittington and Bow Bells, and the Lord Mayor in his coach, and the Cockney, wistful of Cheapside while he hears the lark—are there. Joining and harmonising these two Londons is "London River";

and with the silent river I associate the silence of the Abbey.

It seemed well to suggest a chronological order of the poems, however faintly. Therefore the date of each poem appears under its title, enabling the reader, I hope, to adjust his mind quickly to variations of time. Notes will be found at the end of the book; these could easily have been extended, but I trust they will be deemed sufficient.

The question must be asked: What is the general character of London verse? I think that London-inspired verse may be divided into three bodies: the Poetry of Pageants and Occasions; the Poetry of Town Life and Manners; the Poetry of Vision and Reflection.

This order is almost chronological. Pageantry and the keeping of festivals, having nearly vanished from London life, no longer inspire our poets. The notion of hailing and celebrating London on high occasions seems alien to modern ideas. One may regret this; one may regret that the opportunities of last year were not taken, and that of the many poets who apostrophised the Empire and England a few did not glorify London, the heart of both.

The poetry of town life and manners was born later and lasted longer; it is still heard. But it was native to the seventeenth and eighteenth centuries, when the very word "town" took its more human significance. London was then a snug city, and an easy theme. Now, there are many Londons, not to name the suburbs, and the "town" poet is jostled into silence.

The poetry of vision and reflection, the third class of London-inspired verse, is of our own time. It is odd, but London seems to have inspired such poetry in proportion as she has become herself prosaic. London gives more lovely themes to poets, now that she is vast and smoky, than she did when milkmaids carried milk to Fleet Street from the fields, and strawberries were picked in Holborn. When Wordsworth, standing on Westminster Bridge on the morning of September 3, 1802, breathed his sonnet, he began this new poetry of London.

> " Silent, bare,
> Ships, towers, domes, theatres, and temples lie
> Open unto the fields, and to the sky."

Long enough (and far more so) had London lain open to the fields and sky; but the thing had not been said, or much felt. Yet our poets are bettering Wordsworth's teaching. He could venture to show poor Susan only an imaginary and pasteboard Spring—"a mountain ascending, a vision of trees," a river in Cheapside. To-day the very Spring is exquisitely found in our streets, and the filial bond between London and Nature is perceived. Not the less is London's human spectacle felt and studied. Poets, therefore, are ceasing to write of London under chance and partial inspirations; they are beginning to see London steady and whole, and to make volumes where their predecessors made single poems.

The justification of this book may be that it forms a hopeful commentary on this new Poetry of London—by displaying, in a general view, the thoughts which London has awakened in her poets and citizens during six centuries. But I leave the critical usefulness of this collection to be considered by others: my hope is that it may deepen in a few minds—as it has done in my own—the happiness of living in London.

WILFRED WHITTEN.

1st June 1898.

CONTENTS

LONDON CITY

CONTENTS XV

LONDON TOWN

GEMME of all joy, jasper of jocunditie,
    Most myghty carbuncle of vertue and valour,
Strong Troy in vigour and in strenuytie ;
    Of royall cities rose and geraflour ;
    Emperesse of townes, exalt in honour,
In beautie berying the crone imperiall ;
    Swete paradise, precelling in pleasure ;
London, thou art the Flour of Cities all.

DUNBAR.

L ONDON ; that great sea whose ebb and flow
    At once is deaf and loud, and on the shore
Vomits its wrecks, and still howls on for more.
Yet in its depth what treasures !
Percy Bysshe Shelley : Letter to Maria Gisborne.

The Glory of the Earth

1784

WHERE finds Philosophy her eagle eye,
    With which she gazes at yon burning disk
Undazzled, and detects and counts his spots?
In London: where her implements exact,
With which she calculates, computes, and scans,
All distance, motion, magnitude, and now
Measures an atom, and now girds a world?
In London.   Where has commerce such a mart,
So rich, so throng'd, so drain'd, and so supplied,
As London—opulent, enlarg'd, and still
Increasing London?   Babylon of old
Not more the glory of the Earth than she,
A more accomplish'd world's chief glory now.
William Cowper : The Sofa.

The Flour of Cities All

1501

LONDON, thou art of townes *A per se*.
   Soveraign of cities, semeliest in sight,
Of high renoun, riches, and royaltie;
   Of lordis, barons, and many goodly knyght;
   Of most delectable lusty ladies bright;
Of famous prelatis, in habitis clericall;
   Of merchauntis full of substaunce and myght:
London, thou art the Flour of Cities all.

Gladdith anon thou lusty Troynovaunt,
   Citie that some tyme cleped was New Troy,
In all the erth, imperiall as thou stant,
   Pryncesse of townes, of pleasure and of joy,
   A richer restith under no Christen roy;
For manly power, with craftis naturall,
   Fourmeth none fairer sith the flode of Noy:
London, thou art the Flour of Cities all.

Gemme of all joy, jasper of jocunditie,
   Most myghty carbuncle of vertue and valour,
Strong Troy in vigour and in strenuytie;
   Of royall cities rose and geraflour;
   Emperesse of townes, exalt in honour,
In beautie berying the crone imperiall;
   Swete paradise, precelling in pleasure;
London, thou art the Flour of Cities all.

Aboue all ryuers thy Ryuer hath renowne,
  Whose beryall stremys, pleasant and preclare,
Under thy lusty wallys renneth down,
  Where many a swanne doth swymme with wingis fare ;
  Where many a barge doth saile, and row with are,
Where many a ship doth rest with toppe-royall.
  O ! towne of townes, patrone and not compare :
London, thou art the Flour of Cities all.

Upon thy lusty Brigge of pylers white
  Been merchauntis full royall to behold ;
Upon thy stretis goeth many a semely knyght
  (Arrayit) in velvet gownes and cheynes of gold.
  By Julyus Cesar thy Tour founded of old
May be the Hous of Mars victoryall,
  Whos artillary with tonge may not be told :
London, thou art the Flour of Cities all.

Strong be thy wallys that about thee standis ;
  Wise be the people that within thee dwellis ;
Fresh is thy ryuer with his lusty strandis ;
  Blith be thy churches, wele sownyng thy bellis ;
  Riche be thy merchauntis in substaunce that excellis ;
Fair be their wives, right lovesom, white and small ;
  Clere be thy virgyns, lusty under kellis :
London, thou art the Flour of Cities all.

Thy famous Maire, by pryncely governaunce,
  With swerd of justice the ruleth prudently.
No Lord of Paris, Venyce, or Floraunce
  In dygnitie or honoure goeth to hym nye.

He is exampler, loodë-ster, and guye,
Principall patrone and roose orygynalle,
Above all Maires as maister moost worthy :
London, thou art the Flour of Cities all.
William Dunbar : Collected Poems.

Hail, London !

1739

HAIL, London ! justly queen of cities crown'd,
　　For freedom, wealth, extent, and arts renown'd ;
No need of fables to enhance thy praise,
No wand'ring demi-god thy walls to raise :
Let Rome imperial claim an elder date,
And boast her kindred to the Dardan state,
Thy ancient heroes palms as glorious grace,
Thy British founders, and thy Saxon race.
　　Our ancestors, in architecture rude,
Built their first towns of rough unchisel'd wood ;
No veiny marble yet, no Parian stone,
Nor sculptor's art, nor joiner's skill was known ;
These by our Roman visitors were taught,
Which they from Greece, and Greece from Egypt brought.
Soon Thames along her rising shores admires
Her stony battlements, and lofty spires ;
Sublime Augusta rais'd her tow'ry head,
Her Albion's pride, and envying neighbour's dread.
Since founded first, a thousand years twice told,
Two thousand suns have annual circles roll'd ;
Perpetual growth has stretch'd her ample bound,
'Till scarce sev'n leagues can mete her circuit round.

A hundred temples for devotion rise,
A hundred steeples glitter in the skies.
Lo! in the midst Wren's wond'rous pile appears,
Which, like a mountain, its huge bulk uprears;
Such sure to sailors on a distant stream,
The lofty pike of Teneriffe must seem.
Muse, mount with easy flight th' aspiring dome,
And let thy eyes o'er the wide prospect roam.
See how the Thames with dimpling motion smiles,
And from all climes presents Augusta spoils :
Eastward behold! a thousand vessels ride,
Which like a floating city crowd her tide.
See the strong bridge connect the distant shores;
The flood beneath thro' strait'ning arches roars :
(Above, amazing sight! two length'ning rows
Of lofty buildings a fair street compose),
Still farther east, large as a town, is seen
The Tow'r, a strong and copious magazine;
There, in becoming order, rang'd remain
Arms oft victorious on the hostile plain;
Drums, cannon, swords and bombs inactive sleep,
And thunders brood which Britain's foes shall weep.
Look all around, and note the bustling throng,
How thro' each street, like waves, they press along.
There stands Th' Exchange ('tis now the busy time),
Resort of merchants drawn from ev'ry clime;
Far west remark our monarch's regal seat,
See there the dome where pow'rful senates meet :
There, Rufus' ancient hall resounds with law !
And there the Abbey strikes religious awe !
Thus London shines in fame the first and best,
May all who labour for her peace be blest !

Anon. : Gentleman's Magazine, 1739.

London

1894

A THWART the sky a lowly sigh
   From west to east the sweet wind carried;
The sun stood still on Primrose Hill;
   His light in all the city tarried:
The clouds on viewless columns bloomed
Like smouldering lilies unconsumed.

"Oh sweetheart, see! how shadowy,
   Of some occult magician's rearing,
Or swung in space of heaven's grace
   Dissolving, dimly reappearing,
Afloat upon ethereal tides
St. Paul's above the city rides!"

A rumour broke through the thin smoke
   Enwreathing abbey, tower, and palace,
The parks, the squares, the thoroughfares,
   The million-peopled lanes and alleys,
An ever-muttering prisoned storm,
The heart of London beating warm.

John Davidson: Ballads and Songs.

London Town

1897

LET others chaunt a country praise,
    Fair river walks and meadow ways ;
Dearer to me my sounding days
      In London Town :
To me the tumult of the street
Is no less music, than the sweet
Surge of the wind among the wheat,
      By dale or down.

Three names mine heart with rapture hails,
With homage : *Ireland, Cornwall, Wales :*
Lands of lone moor, and mountain gales,
      And stormy coast :
Yet London's voice upon the air
Pleads at mine heart, and enters there ;
Sometimes I wellnigh love and care
      For London most.

Listen upon the ancient hills :
All silence ! save the lark, who trills
Through sunlight, save the rippling rills :
      There peace may be.
But listen to great London ! loud,
As thunder from the purple cloud,
Comes the deep thunder from the crowd,
      And heartens me.

O gray, O gloomy skies! What then?
Here is a marvellous world of men;
More wonderful than Rome was, when
                The world was Rome!
See the great stream of life flow by!
Here thronging myriads laugh and sigh,
Here rise and fall, here live and die:
                In this vast home.

In long array they march toward death,
Armies, with proud or piteous breath:
Forward! the spirit in them saith,
                Spirit of life:
Here the triumphant trumpets blow;
Here mourning music sorrows low:
Victors and vanquished, still they go
                Forward in strife.

Who will not heed so great a sight?
Greater than marshalled stars of night,
That move to music and with light:
                For these are men!
These move to music of the soul;
Passions, that madden or control:
These hunger for a distant goal,
                Seen now and then.

Is mine too tragical a strain,
Chaunting a burden full of pain,
And labour, that seems all in vain?
                I sing but truth.

Still, many a merry pleasure yet,
To many a merry measure set,
Is ours, who need not to forget
         Summer and youth.

Do London birds forget to sing?
Do London trees refuse the spring?
Is London May no pleasant thing?
         Let country fields,
To milking maid and shepherd boy,
Give flowers, and song, and bright employ:
Her children also can enjoy,
         What London yields.

Gleaming with sunlight, each soft lawn
Lies fragrant beneath dew of dawn;
The spires and towers rise, far withdrawn,
         Through golden mist:
At sunset, linger beside Thames:
See now, what radiant lights and flames!
That ruby burns: that purple shames
         The amethyst.

Winter was long, and dark, and cold:
Chill rains! grim fogs, black fold on fold,
Round street, and square, and river rolled!
         Ah, let it be:
Winter is gone!   Soon comes July,
With wafts from hayfields by and by:
While in the dingiest courts you spy
         Flowers fair to see.

Take heart of grace : and let each hour
Break gently into bloom and flower :
Winter and sorrow have no power
       To blight all bloom.
One day, perchance, the sun will see
London's entire felicity :
And all her loyal children be
       Clear of all gloom.

A dream ?   Dreams often dreamed come true :
Our world would seem a world made new
To those, beneath the churchyard yew
       Laid long ago !
When we beneath like shadows bide,
Fair London, throned upon Thames' side,
May be our children's children's pride :
       And we shall know.
       Lionel Johnson : Ireland, with other Poems.

Urbanus Loquitur

1894

LET others sing the country's charm :
   The whispering trees, the tangled lane,
The perfume-burdened air, the trills
   Of lark and nightingale ; the wain,
That homeward brings the scented hay,
When evening's peace absorbs the day.

Let others laud those primal cares,
   Which fill the country hours with bliss :

The timely rest; clear eyes, that greet
   Earth waking 'neath Aurora's kiss;
The easy, sauntering, walk; the toil,
That waits upon the bounteous soil.

Let others paint with fresh delight
   The country maiden's cheek of rose;
Her lover's artless, amorous, gifts,
   Which pure affection's heart enclose;
The children nestling round their sire
At night-fall, by the winter fire.

For me, for me, another world's
   Enchantments hold my heart in thrall:
These London pavements, low'ring sky,
   Store secrets, on mine eyes that fall,
More curious far, than earth or air
By country paths can make appear.

The stern reformer scowls aghast,
   'Mid the doomed city's trackless woe:
Apelles veils his shuddering gaze,
   Its ugliness "offends him so":
The dainty-eared musician dies
In torment, of its raucous cries.

Yet are there souls of coarser grain,
   Or else more flexible, who find
Strange, infinite, allurements lurk,
   Undreamed of by the simpler mind,
Along these streets, within the walls
Of *cafés*, shops, and music halls.

'Twixt jar of tongues, at endless strife
On art, religion, social needs,
How many a keen thought springs to birth
In him, this dubious book that reads !
For curious eyes no hours are spent,
That bring not interest, content.

I'll call not these the best, nor those ;
The country fashions, or the town :
On each descend heaven's bounteous rains,
On each the impartial sun looks down.
Why should we gird and argue, friend ;
Not follow, where our natures tend ?

The secret's this : where'er our lot,
To read, mark, learn, digest them well,
The devious paths we mortals take,
To gain, at length, our heaven or hell :
Alike in some still, rural, scene,
Or Regent Street and Bethnal Green.

Selwyn Image : Poems and Carols.

To London

1822

O LONDON, comprehensive word !
Whose sound, though scarce in whispers heard,
Breathes independence !—if I share
That first of blessings, I can bear
Ev'n with thy fogs and smoky air.

Of leisure fond, of freedom fonder,
O grant me in thy streets to wander ;
Grant me thy cheerful morning walk,
Thy dinner and thy evening talk.
What though I'm forced my doors to make fast ?
What though no cream be mine for breakfast ?
Though knaves around me cheat and plunder,
And fires can scarcely be kept under,
Though guilt in triumph stalks abroad
By Bow and Marlborough-street unawed,
And many a rook finds many a pigeon
In law, and physic, and religion,
Eager to help a thriving trade on,
And proud and happy to be preyed on ?—
What signify such paltry blots ?
The glorious sun himself has spots.

London, within thy ample verge
What crowds lie sheltered, or emerge
Buoyant in every shape and form,
As smiles the calm or drives the storm ;
Blest if they reach the harbour free
Of golden Mediocrity !
Here, ev'n the dwellings of the poor
And lonely are, at least, obscure,
And, in obscurity, exempt
From poverty's worst plague, contempt.
Unmarked the poor man seeks his den ;
Unheeded issues forth again ;
Wherefore appears he ? None inquires,
Nor why nor whither he retires.
All that his pride would fain conceal,
All that shame blushes to reveal,

The petty shifts, the grovelling cares
To which the sons of Want are heirs,
Those ills, which, grievous to be borne,
Call forth—not sympathy but scorn,
Here lost, elude the searching eye
Of callous Curiosity.

And what though Poverty environ
Full many a wretch with chains of iron?
These in no stricter bondage hold
Their slaves than manacles of gold.
The costliest fetters are as strong
As common ones, and last as long.
Whom gall they most?—'Tis doubtful which,
The very poor, or very rich;
Those scourged by wants and discontents,
Or these by their establishments;
Victims, from real evils free,
To nerves, *cui bono?* and ennui.

.   .   .   .

What though to rail or laugh at money
Be over-dull, or over-funny,
(Since who would ridicule employment,
Or cry down power, or quiz enjoyment,)
London is, surely, to a tittle
The place for those who have but little.
Here I endure no throbs, no twitches
Of envy at another's riches,
But, smiling, from my window see
A dozen twice as rich as he;
And, if I stroll, am sure to meet
A dozen more in every street.

None are distinguished, none are rare
From wealth which hundreds round them share,
But, neutralized by one another
Whene'er they think to raise a pother,
Be they kind-hearted, or capricious,
Vain, prodigal, or avaricious,
Proud, popular, or what they will,
Are elbowed by their rivals still.

Should one among them dare be dull,
Or prose, because his purse is full ;
Should he, in breach of all decorum,
Make the least mention of the Quorum ;
Drop but a hint of what transgressions
Are punished at the Quarter-sessions ;
Or murmur at those vile encroachers
On rural privilege—the poachers ;
Soon would a general yawn or cough
From such a trespass warn him off,
Spite of his India-bonds, and rents,
His acres, and his three-per-cents,
None would endure such parish-prate,
Were half the island his estate ;
Though he in ready cash were sharing
The wealth, without the sense, of Baring.

A village is a hive of glass.
There nothing undescried can pass,
There all may study at their ease
The forms and motions of the bees ;
What wax or honey each brings home
To swell the treasures of the comb,
Upon his loaded thighs and wings ;

And which are drones, and which have stings;
Whether in consequence be higher
The Rector, or the neighbouring Squire,
Or he, the Attorney of the place,
With knocker brazen as his face.

But count the motes or specks who can
On this our huge Leviathan!
Or note, with curious pencil, down
The motions of this monster-town!
Weak is the voice of Slander here;
Not half her venom taints the ear.
Few feel the fulness of her power,
" Her iron scourge, or torturing hour ";
And yet, so general is the scrape,
Few from her malice quite escape.
All, in a common fate confounded,
Are slightly scratched, none deeply wounded.
Such is the Town !—Do right or wrong,
None will abuse or praise you long.
The moments you enjoy or bear
Soon pass, and then—you've had your share.

Henry Luttrell: Letters to Julia.

London Poets

1889

THEY trod the streets and squares where now I tread,
With weary hearts, a little while ago;
When, thin and grey, the melancholy snow
Clung to the leafless branches overhead;

Or when the smoke-veiled sky grew stormy-red
In autumn; with a re-arisen woe
Wrestled, what time the passionate spring winds blow;
And paced scorched stones in summer:—they are dead.

The sorrow of their souls to them did seem
As real as mine to me, as permanent.
To-day, it is the shadow of a dream,
The half-forgotten breath of breezes spent.
So shall another soothe his woe supreme—
"No more he comes, who this way came and went."

Amy Levy: A London Plane Tree,
and other Poems.

The Poet's London

1845

L ONDON, I take thee to a Poet's heart!
    For those who seek, a Helicon thou art.
Let schoolboy Strephons bleat of flocks and fields,
Each street of thine a loftier Idyl yields;
Fed by all life, and fann'd by every wind,
There, burns the quenchless poetry—*Mankind!*
Yet not for me the Olympiad of the gay,
The recking Season's dusty holiday:—
Soon as its summer pomp the mead assumes,
And Flora wanders through her world of blooms,
Vain the hot field-days of the vex'd debate,
When Sirius reigns,—let Tapeworm rule the state!
Vain Devon's cards, and Lansdowne's social feast,
Wit but fatigues, and Beauty's reign hath ceast.
His mission done, the monk regains his cell;

Nor even Douro's matchless face can spell.
Far from Man's works, escaped to God's, I fly,
And breathe the luxury of a smokeless sky.
Me, the still " London," not the restless " Town "
(The light plume fluttering o'er the helmëd crown),
Delights ;—for there, the grave Romance hath shed
Its hues ; and air grows solemn with the Dead.
If, where the Lord of Rivers parts the throng,
And eastward glides by buried halls along,
My steps are led, I linger, and restore
To the changed wave the poet-shapes of yore ;
See the gilt barge, and hear the fated king
Prompt the first mavis of our Minstrel Spring ;
Or mark, with mitred Nevile, the array
Of arms and craft alarm " the Silent Way,"
The Boar of Gloucester, hungering, scents his prey !
Or, landward, trace, where thieves their festive hall
Hold by the dens of Law (worst thief of all !)
The antique Temple of the armëd Zeal
That wore the cross a mantle to the steel ;
Time's dreary void the kindling dream supplies,
The walls expand, the shadowy towers arise,
And forth, as when by Richard's lion side,
For Christ and Fame, the Warrior-Phantoms ride !
Or if, less grave with thought, less rich with lore,
The later scenes, the lighter steps explore,
If through the haunts of living splendour led—
Has the quick Muse no empire but the Dead ?
In each keen face, by Care or Pleasure worn,
Grief claims her sigh, or Vice invites her scorn ;
And every human brow that veils a thought
Conceals the Castaly which Shakespeare sought.

Lord Lytton : The New Timon.

On London Stones

1876

ON London stones I sometimes sigh
  For wider green and bluer sky;—
Too oft the trembling note is drowned
In this huge city's varied sound;—
" Pure song is country-born "—I cry.

Then comes the spring,—the months go by,
The last stray swallows seaward fly;
    And I—I too!—no more am found
            On London stones!

In vain !—the woods, the fields deny
That clearer strain I fain would try;
    Mine is an urban Muse, and bound
    By some strange law to paven ground;
Abroad she pouts;—she is not shy
            On London stones!
            Austin Dobson: Old World Idylls.

The Contrast

1798

IN London I never know what I'd be at,
  Enraptured with this, and enchanted with that;
I'm wild with the sweets of variety's plan,
And Life seems a blessing too happy for man.

But the country, Lord help me! sets all matters right,
So calm and composing from morning to night;
Oh! it settles the spirits when nothing is seen
But an ass on a common, a goose on a green.

In town, if it rain, why it damps not our hope,
The eye has her choice, and the fancy her scope;
What harm though it pour whole nights or whole days?
It spoils not our prospects, or stops not our ways.

In the country what bliss, when it rains in the fields,
To live on the transports that shuttlecock yields;
Or go crawling from window to window, to see
A pig on a dunghill, or crow on a tree.

In London, if folks ill together are put,
A bore may be dropt, and a quiz may be cut;
We change without end; and if lazy or ill,
All wants are at hand, and all wishes at will.

In the country you're nail'd, like a pale in the park,
To some *stick* of a neighbour that's cramm'd in the ark;
And 'tis odd, if you're hurt, or in fits tumble down,
You reach death ere the doctor can reach you from town.

In London how easy we visit and meet,
Gay pleasure's the theme, and sweet smiles are our treat:
Our morning's a round of good-humour'd delight,
And we rattle, in comfort, to pleasure at night.

In the country, how sprightly! our visits to make
Through ten miles of mud, for Formality's sake;
With the coachman in drink, and the moon in a fog,
And no thought in our head but a ditch or a bog.

In London the spirits are cheerful and light,
All places are gay and all faces are bright ;
We've ever new joys, and revived by each whim,
Each day on a fresh tide of pleasure we swim.

But how gay in the country ! what summer delight
To be waiting for winter from morning to night !
Then the fret of impatience gives exquisite glee
To relish the sweet rural subjects we see.

In town we 've no use for the skies overhead,
For when the sun rises then we go to bed ;
And as to that old-fashion'd virgin the moon,
She shines out of season, like satin in June.

In the country these planets delightfully glare
Just to show us the object we want isn't there ;
O, how cheering and gay, when their beauties arise,
To sit and gaze round with the tears in one's eyes !

But 'tis in the country alone we can find
That happy resource, that relief of the mind,
When, drove to despair, our last effort we make,
And drag the old fish-pond, for novelty's sake :

Indeed I must own, 'tis a pleasure complete
To see ladies well draggled and wet in their feet ;
But what is all that to the transport we feel
When we capture, in triumph, two toads and an eel ?

I have heard tho', that love in a cottage is sweet,
When two hearts in one link of soft sympathy meet :
That's to come—for as yet I, alas ! am a swain
Who require, I own it, more links to my chain.

Your magpies and stock-doves may flirt among trees,
And chatter their transports in groves, if they please :
But a house is much more to my taste than a tree,
And for groves, O ! a good grove of chimneys for me.

In the country, if Cupid should find a man out,
The poor tortured victim mopes hopeless about ;
But in London, thank Heaven ! our peace is secure,
Where for one eye to kill, there's a thousand to cure.

I know love's a devil, too subtle to spy,
That shoots through the soul, from the beam of an eye ;
But in London these devils so quick fly about,
That a new devil still drives an old devil out.

In town let me live then, in town let me die,
For in truth I can't relish the country, not I.
If one must have a villa in summer to dwell,
O, give me the sweet shady side of Pall Mall.
Captain Charles Morris : Lyra Urbanica.

London Lycpeny.

About 1450

TO London once, my stepps I bent,
    Where trouth in no wyse should be faynt :
To Westmynster ward I forthwith went,
To a man of law to make complaynt.
I sayd, "for Mary's love, that holy saynt !
Pity the poore that would proceede ";
But for lack of mony I cold not spede.

And as I thrust the prese amonge,
By froward chaunce my hood was gone ;
Yet for all that I stayd not longe,
Tyll to the Kyngs bench I was come.
Before the judge I kneled anon,
And prayd hym for God's sake to take heede ;
But for lack of mony I myght not spede.

Beneath them sat clarkes a great rout,
Which fast dyd wryte by one assent ;
There stoode up one and cryed about,
Rychard, Robert, and John of Kent ;
I wyst not wele what this man ment ;
He cryed so thycke there indede ;
But he that lackt mony myght not spede.

Unto the common place I yode thoo,
Where sat one with a sylken hoode ;
I dyd hym reverence, for I ought to do so,
And told my case as well as I cold,
How my goods were defrauded me by falsehood.
I gat not a mum of his mouth for my meed,
And for lack of mony I myght not spede.

Unto the Rolls I gat me from thence,
Before the clarkes of the chauncerye,
Where many I found earnyng of pence,
But none at all once regarded mee ;
I gave them my playnt uppon my knee ;
They lyked it well when they had it reade,
But lackyng mony I cold not be sped.

In Westmynster hall I found out one,
Which went in a long gown of raye;
I crouched and kneled before hym anon:
For Maryes love, of help I hym praye.
"I wot not what thou meanest," gan he say;
To get me thence he dyd me bede,
For lack of mony I cold not spede.

Within this hall, neithere ryche nor yett poor,
Wold do for me ought, although I shold dye;
Which seeing, I gat me out of the doore,
Where Flemynges began on me for to cry,
"Master, what will you copen or by,
Fyne felt hatts, or spectacles to reede?
Lay down your sylver, and here you may spede."

Then to Westmynster gate I presently went,
When the sonn was at hyghe pryme;
Cokes to me, they tooke good entent,
And profered me bread with ale and wyne,
Rybbs of befe both fat and ful fyne;
A fayre cloth they gan for to sprede;
But wantyng mony I myght not then spede.

Then unto London I did me hye,
Of all the land it beareth the pryse;
Hot pescods one began to crye,
Straberry rype, and cherryes in the ryse:
One bad me come nere, and by some spyce,
Peper and sayforne, they gan me bede;
But for lacke of mony I myght not spede.

Then to the Chepe I began me drawne,
Where mutch people I sawe for to stande;

One offred me velvet, sylke, and lawne,
And other he taketh me by the hande,
"Here is Parys thred, the fynest in the lande,"
I never was used to such thyngs indede,
And wantyng mony I myght not spede.

Then went I forth by London stone,
Throughout all Canwyke strecte;
Drapers mutch cloth me offred anone:
Then comes me one, cryde hot shepes feete,
One cryde makerell, ryshes grene, another gan greete,
One bad me by a hood to cover my head;
But for want of mony I myght not be sped.

Then I hyed me into Estchepe;
One cryes rybbs of befe, and many a pye;
Pewter potts they clattered on a heape,
There was harpe, pype, and mynstrelsye;
"Yea by cock!" "nay by cock!" some began crye,
Some songe of Jenken and Julyan for there mede;
But for lack of mony I myght not spede.

Then into Cornhyll anon I yode,
Where was much stolen gere amonge;
I saw where honge myne owne hoode,
That I had lost amonge the thronge;
To by my own hood I thought it wronge,
I knew it well as I dyd my crede;
But for lack of mony I cold not spede.

The Taverner took me by the sleve;
"Sir," sayth he, "wyll you our wyne assay?"
I answered, that can not mutch me greve,

A peny can do no more than it may :
I dranke a pynt, and for it dyd pay ;
Yet sore a hungerd from thence I yede,
And wantyng my mony I cold not spede.

Then hyed I me to Belynsgate ;
And one cryed "hoo, go we hence !"
I prayd a barge man for Gods sake,
That he wold spare me my expence.
"Thou scapst not here," quod he, "under ij pence,
I lyst not yet bestow my almes dede" :
Thus lacking mony I cold not spede.

Then I convayed me into Kent ;
For of the law wold I meddle no more,
Because no man to me tooke entent,
I dyght me to do as I dyd before.
Now Jesus that in Bethlem was bore,
Save London, and send trew lawyers there mede,
For who so wants mony with them shall not spede.

John Lydgate : Minor Poems.

Return to London

1648

FROM the dull confines of the drooping West,
    To see the day spring from the pregnant East,
Ravish'd in spirit, I come, nay, more, I fly
To thee, blest place of my nativity !
Thus, thus, with hallow'd foot I touch the ground,
With thousand blessings by thy fortune crown'd.

O fruitful Genius! that bestowest here
An everlasting plenty, year by year;
O place! O people! manners! framed to please
All nations, customs, kindreds, languages!
I am a free-born Roman; suffer then
That I amongst you live a citizen.
London my home is; though by hard fate sent
Into a long and irksome banishment;
Yet since call'd back, henceforward let me be,
O native country, repossess'd by thee!
For, rather than I'll to the West return,
I'll beg of thee first here to have mine urn.
Weak I am grown, and must in short time fall;
Give thou my sacred relics burial.

Robert Herrick: Hesperides.

The May-Lord

1611

LONDON, to thee I do present
　　The merry month of May;
Let each true subject be content
To hear me what I say:
For from the top of Conduit-Head,
As plainly may appear,
I will both tell my name to you,
And wherefore I came here.
My name is Ralph, by due descent
Though not ignoble I,
Yet far inferior to the flock
Of gracious grocery;

And by the common counsel of
My fellows in the Strand,
With gilded staff and crossed scarf,
The May-Lord here I stand.
Rejoice, O English hearts, rejoice !
Rejoice, O lovers dear !
Rejoice, O city, town, and country !
Rejoice eke every shere !

.   .   .   .   .   .

Now little fish on tender stone
Begin to cast their bellies,
And sluggish snails, that erst were mew'd,
Do creep out of their shellies ;
The rumbling rivers now do warm,
For little boys to paddle ;
The sturdy steed now goes to grass,
And up they hang his saddle.
The heavy hart, the bellowing buck,
The rascal, and the pricket,
Are now among the yeoman's pease,
And leave the fearful thicket.

And be like them, O you, I say,
Of this same noble Town,
And lift aloft your velvet heads,
And slipping off your gown,
With bells on legs, and napkins clean
Unto your shoulders tied,
With scarfs and garters as you please,
And "Hey for our town !" cried,
March out and show your willing minds,
By twenty and by twenty,
To Hogsdon, or to Newington,

Where ale and cakes are plenty !
And let it ne'er be said for shame,
That we, the youths of London,
Lay thrumming of our caps at home,
And left our custom undone.
    Up then, I say, both young and old,
    Both man and maid a-Maying,
    With drums and guns that bounce aloud,
    And merry tabor playing !
    Which to prolong, God save our King,
    And send his country peace,
    And root out treason from the land !
    And so, my friends, I cease.

*Beaumont and Fletcher : The Knight
of the Burning Pestle.*

The Milkmaids' Dance

1825

IN London, thirty years ago,
  When pretty milkmaids went about,
It was a goodly sight to see
  Their May-Day Pageant all drawn out :—

Themselves in comely colours drest,
  Their shining garland in the middle,
A pipe and tabor on before,
  Or else the foot-inspiring fiddle.

They stopt at houses, where it was
  Their custom to cry " Milk below ! "
And, while the music play'd, with smiles,
  Join'd hands, and pointed toe to toe.

Thus they tripp'd on, till—from the door
  The hop'd-for annual present sent—
A signal came, to curtsey low,
  And at that door cease merriment.

Such scenes and sounds once blest my eyes,
  And charm'd my ears—but all have vanish'd !
On May-Day, now, no garlands go,
  For milkmaids, and their dance, are banish'd.

Anon. : Hone's Every-Day Book.

The May Pole in the Strand

1619

FAIRLY we marched on, till our approach
    Within the spacious passage of the Strand,
Objected to our sight a summer broach
    Yclept a May Pole, which in all our land,
      No city, town, nor street, can parallel,
      Nor can the lofty spire of Clerkenwell,
      Although he have the advantage of a rock,
      Perch up more high his turning weather-cock.

Stay, quoth my muse, and here behold a sign
    Of harmless mirth and honest neighbourhood,
Where all the parish did in one combine
    To mount the rod of peace, and none withstood ;
      Where no capricious constables disturb them,
      Nor justice of the peace did seek to curb them,
      Nor peevish puritan, in railing sort,
      Nor over-wise church-warden, spoil'd the sport.

Happy the age, and harmless were the days
  (For then true love and amity were found,)
When every village did a May-Pole raise,
   And Whitson-ales and May-games did abound,
    And all the lusty yonkers, in a rout,
    With merry lasses danc'd the rod about,
    Then friendship to their banquets bid the guests,
    And poor men far'd the better for their feasts.

    .   .   .   .   .

Then lords of castles, manors, towns and towers
  Rejoiced when they beheld the farmer's flourish,
And would come down into the summer-bowers
  To see the country gallants dance the morrice.

    .   .   .   .

But since the summer poles were overthrown,
  And all good sports and merriments decay'd
How times and men are chang'd, so well is known,
  It were but labour lost if more were said.

    .   .   .   .   .

But I do hope once more the day will come,
  That you shall mount and perch your cocks as high
As e'er you did, and that the pipe and drum
  Shall bid defiance to your enemy :
    And that all fiddlers, which in corners lurk,
    And have been almost starved for want of work,
    Shall draw their crowds, and, at your exaltation,
    Play many a fit of merry recreation.
Pasquil's Palinodia and Progress
to the Tavern.

Vanished London

1798

ALL sublunary things of death partake !
  What alteration does a cent'ry make !
Kings and comedians all are mortal found,
Cæsar and Pinkethman are under ground.
What's not destroy'd by Time's devouring hand ?
Where's Troy, and where's the May-pole in the Strand?
Pease, cabbages, and turnips once grew where
Now stands new Bond Street, and a newer square ;
Such piles of buildings now rise up and down
London itself seems going out of town.

James Bramston : The Art of Politicks.

A May Morning in London

1840

GOLD above, and gold below,
  The earth reflected the golden glow,
From river, and hill, and valley ;
Gilt by the golden light of morn,
The Thames—it look'd like the Golden Horn,
And the barge, that carried coal or corn,
  Like Cleopatra's Galley !

Bright as clusters of golden-rod
Suburban poplars began to nod,
  With extempore splendour furnish'd ;

While London was bright with glittering clocks,
Golden dragons, and golden cocks,
      And above them all,
      The dome of St. Paul,
With its Golden Cross and its Golden Ball
   Shone out as if newly burnish'd !

> *Thomas Hood : Miss Kilmansegg*
> *and Her Precious Leg.*

A Song of London

1895

THE sun's on the pavement,
      The current comes and goes,
And the grey streets of London
      They blossom like the rose.

Crowned with the spring sun,
      Vistas fair and free ;
What joy that waits not ?
      What that may not be ?

The blue-bells may beckon,
      The cuckoo call—and yet—
The grey streets of London
      I never may forget.

O fair shines the gold moon
      On blossom-clustered eaves,
But bright blinks the gas-lamp
      Between the linden-leaves.

And the green country meadows
Are fresh and fine to see,
But the grey streets of London
They're all the world to me.

Rosamund Marriott Watson : Vespertilia.

London from Shooter's Hill

1823

A MIGHTY mass of brick, and smoke, and shipping,
    Dirty and dusky, but as wide as eye
Could reach, with here and there a sail just skipping
    In sight, then lost amidst the forestry
Of masts ; a wilderness of steeples peeping
    On tiptoe through their sea-coal canopy ;
A huge, dun cupola, like a foolscap crown
On a fool's head—and there is London Town !

But Juan saw not this : each wreath of smoke
    Appear'd to him but as the magic vapour
Of some alchymic furnace, from whence broke
    The wealth of worlds (a wealth of tax and paper) :
The gloomy clouds, which o'er it as a yoke
    Are bow'd, and put the sun out like a taper,
Were nothing but the natural atmosphere,
Extremely wholesome, though but rarely clear.

Lord Byron : Don Juan.

Don Juan in London

1823

HAIL! Thames, hail!   Upon thy verge it is
    That Juan's chariot, rolling like a drum
In thunder, holds the way it can't well miss,
Through Kennington and all the other " tons,"
Which make us wish ourselves in town at once ;—

Through groves, so call'd as being void of trees,
    (Like *lucus* from *no* light) ; through prospects named
Mount Pleasant, as containing nought to please,
    Nor much to climb ; through little boxes framed
Of bricks, to let the dust in at your ease,
    With " To be let," upon their doors proclaim'd ;
Through " Rows " most modestly call'd " Paradise,"
Which Eve might quit without much sacrifice ;—

Through coaches, drays, choked turnpikes, and a whirl
    Of wheels, and roar of voices, and confusion ;
Here taverns wooing to a pint of " purl,"
    There mails fast flying off like a delusion ;
There barbers' blocks with periwigs in curl
    In windows ; here the lamplighter's infusion
Slowly distill'd into the glimmering glass
(For in those days we had not got to gas—) ;

Through this, and much, and more, is the approach
    Of travellers to mighty Babylon :
Whether they come by horse, or chaise, or coach,
    With slight exceptions, all the ways seem one.
I could say more, but do not choose to encroach

Upon the Guide-book's privilege.   The sun
Had set some time, and night was on the ridge
Of twilight, as the party cross'd the bridge.

That's rather fine, the gentle sound of Thamis—
    Who vindicates a moment, too, his stream—
Though hardly heard through multifarious "dammes."
    The lamps of Westminster's more regular gleam,
The breadth of pavement, and yon shrine where fame is
    A spectral resident—whose pallid beam
In shape of moonshine hovers o'er the pile—
Make this a sacred part of Albion's isle.

The Druids' groves are gone—so much the better :
    Stonehenge is not—but what the devil is it ?—
But Bedlam still exists with its sage fetter,
    That madmen may not bite you on a visit ;
The Bench, too, seats or suits full many a debtor ;
    The Mansion House, too (though some people quiz it),
To me appears a stiff yet grand erection ;
But then the Abbey's worth the whole collection.

The line of lights, too, up to Charing Cross,
    Pall Mall, and so forth, have a coruscation
Like gold as in comparison to dross,
    Match'd with the Continent's illumination,
Whose cities Night by no means deigns to gloss.
    The French were not as yet a lamp-lighting nation,
And then they grew so—on their new-found lantern,
Instead of wicks, they made a wicked man turn.

        .   .   .   .

Over the stones still rattling, up Pall Mall,
    Through crowds and carriages, but waxing thinner

As thunder'd knockers broke the long seal'd spell
   Of doors 'gainst doors, and to an early dinner
Admitted a small party as night fell,—
   Don Juan, our young diplomatic sinner,
Pursued his path, and drove past some hotels,
St. James's Palace and St. James's " Hells."

     .   .   ,

              —O my gentle Juan !
   Thou art in London—in that pleasant place,
Where every kind of mischief's daily brewing,
   Which can await warm youth in its wild race.
'Tis true, that thy career is not a new one ;
   Thou art no novice in the headlong chase
Of early life ; but this is a new land,
Which foreigners can never understand.
                 Lord Byron : Don Juan.

Ye Flags of Piccadilly

1862

YE flags of Piccadilly,
   Where I posted up and down,
And wished myself so often
   Well away from you and town—

Are the people walking quietly
   And steady on their feet,
Cabs and omnibuses plying
   Just as usual in the street ?

Do the houses look as upright
    As of old they used to be,
And does nothing seem affected
    By the pitching of the sea?

Through the Green Park iron railings
    Do the quick pedestrians pass?
Are the little children playing
    Round the plane-tree in the grass?

This squally wild north-wester
    With which our vessel fights,
Does it merely serve with you to
    Carry up some paper kites?

Ye flags of Piccadilly,
    Which I hated so, I vow
I could wish with all my heart
    You were underneath me now!
       Arthur Hugh Clough: Songs in Absence.

Fair Pall Mall

1716

O BEAR me to the paths of fair Pall Mall,
    Safe are thy pavements, grateful is thy smell!
At distance rolls along the gilded coach,
Nor sturdy carmen on thy walks encroach;
No lets would bar thy ways were chairs deny'd
The soft supports of laziness and pride;
Shops breathe perfume, thro' sashes ribbons glow,
The mutual arms of ladies, and the beau.
       John Gay: Trivia.

St. James's Street

1867

ST. James's Street, of classic fame,
    For Fashion still is seen there:
St. James's Street? I know the name,
    I almost think I've been there!
Why, that's where Sacharissa sigh'd
    When Waller read his ditty;
Where Byron lived, and Gibbon died,
    And Alvanley was witty.

A famous Street! To yonder Park
    Young Churchill stole in class-time;
Come, gaze on fifty men of mark,
    And then recall the past time.
The *plats* at White's, the play at *Crock's*,
    The bumpers to Miss Gunning;
The *bonhomie* of Charley Fox,
    And Selwyn's ghastly funning.

The dear old Street of clubs and *cribs*,
    As north and south it stretches,
Still seems to smack of Rolliad squibs,
    And Gillray's fiercer sketches;
The quaint old dress, the grand old style,
    The *mots*, the racy stories;
The wine, the dice, the wit, the bile—
    The hate of Whigs and Tories.

At dusk, when I am strolling there,
    Dim forms will rise around me ;
Lepel flits past me in her chair,—
    And Congreve's airs astound me !
And once Nell Gwynne, a frail young Sprite,
    Look'd kindly when I met her ;
I shook my head, perhaps,—but quite
    Forgot to quite forget her.

The Street is still a lively tomb
    For rich, and gay, and clever ;
The crops of dandies bud and bloom,
    And die as fast as ever.
Now gilded youth loves cutty pipes,
    And slang that's rather *scaring* ;
It can't approach its prototypes
    In taste, or tone, or bearing.

In Brummell's day of buckle shoes,
    Lawn cravats and roll collars,
They'd fight, and woo, and bet—and lose
    Like gentlemen and scholars :
I'm glad young men should go the pace,
    I half forgive *Old Rapid* ;
These louts disgrace their name and race—
    So vicious and so vapid !

Worse times may come. *Bon ton*, indeed,
    Will then be quite forgotten,
And all we much revere will speed
    From ripe to worse than rotten :
Let grass then sprout between yon stones,
    And owls then roost at Boodle's,

For Echo will hurl back the tones
  Of screaming *Yankee Doodles.*

I love the haunts of old Cockaigne,
    Where wit and wealth were squander'd ;
The halls that tell of hoop and train,
    Where grace and rank have wander'd ;
Those halls where ladies fair and leal
    First ventured to adore me !
Something of that old love I feel
    For this old Street before me.
          Frederick Locker-Lampson : London Lyrics.

Bond Street

1831

D EAR Street !—where at a certain hour
    Man's follies bud forth into flower !
Where the gay minor sighs for fashion ;
Where majors live that minor's cash on ;
Where each who wills may suit his wish,
Here choose a Guido—there his fish :—
Or where, if woman's love beguiles,
The ugliest dog is sure of smiles.
Dear street of noise, of crowds, of wealth,
Of all earth's thousand joys, save health ;
Of plate, of books—and (I incline a
Little that way) of old Sevres China.
Of all, in short, by which pursuing
We glide entranced to our undoing !
          Lord Lytton : The Siamese Twins.

A Song of Hyde Park

1671

COME all you noble, you that are neat ones,
    Hyde Park is now both fresh and green.
Come all you gallants that are great ones,
    And are desirous to be seen :
        Would you a wife or mistress rare,
        Here are the best of England fair ;
        Here you may choose, also refuse,
        As you your judgments please to use.

Come all you courtiers in your neat fashions,
    Rich in your new unpaid-for silk :
Come you brave wenches, and court your stations,
    Here in the bushes the maids do milk :
        Come then and revel, the Spring invites
        Beauty and youth for your delights,
        All that are fair, all that are rare,
        You shall have license to compare.

Here the great ladies all of the land are,
    Drawn with six horses at the least :
Here are all that of the Strand are,
    And to be seen now at the best.
        Westminster Hall, who is of the Court,
        Unto his place doth now all resort :
        Both high and low here you may know,
        And all do come themselves to show.

The merchants' wives that keep their coaches,
    Here in the Park do take the air ;

They go abroad to avoid reproaches,
  And hold themselves as ladies fair :
    For whilst their husbands gone are to trade
    Unto their ships by sea or land :
    Who will not say, why may not they
    Trade, like their own husbands, in their own way!

Here from the country come the girls flying
  For husbands, though of parts little worth,
They at th' Exchange have been buying
  The last new fashion that came forth ;
    And are desirous to have it seen,
    As if before it ne'er had been ;
    So you may see all that may be
    Had in the town or country.

Here come the girls of the rich City,
  Aldermen's daughters fair and proud,
Their jealous mothers come t' invite ye,
  For fear they should be lost i' the crowd :
    Who for their breeding are taught to dance,
    Their birth and fortune to advance :
    And they will be as frolic and free,
    As you yourself expect to see.

Anon. : Westminster Drolleries.

Rotten Row

1867

I HOPE I'm fond of much that's good,
  As well as much that's gay ;
I'd like the country if I could ;
  I love the Park in May :

And when I ride in Rotten Row,
I wonder why they call'd it so.

A lively scene on turf and road ;
    The crowd is bravely drest :
The Ladies' Mile has overflow'd,
    The chairs are in request :
The nimble air, so soft, so clear,
Can hardly stir a ringlet here.

I'll halt beneath those pleasant trees,—
    And drop my bridle-rein,
And, quite alone, indulge at ease
    The philosophic vein :
I'll moralise on all I see—
Yes, it was all arranged for me !

Forsooth, and on a lovelier spot
    The sunbeam never shines.
Fair ladies here can talk and trot
    With statesmen and divines :
Could I have chosen, I'd have been
A Duke, a Beauty, or a Dean.

What grooms !   What gallant gentlemen !
    What well-appointed hacks !
What glory in their pace, and then
    What beauty on their backs !
My Pegasus would never flag
If weighted as my Lady's nag.

But where is now the courtly troop
    That once rode laughing by ?

I miss the curls of Cantilupe,
  The laugh of Lady Di :
They all could laugh from night to morn,
And Time has laugh'd them all to scorn.

I then could frolic in the van
  With dukes and dandy earls ;
Then I was thought a *nice* young man
  By rather *nice* young girls !
I've half a mind to join Miss Browne,
And try one canter up and down.

Ah, no—I'll linger here awhile,
  And dream of days of yore ;
For me bright eyes have lost the smile,
  The sunny smile they wore :—
Perhaps they say, what I'll allow,
That I'm not quite so handsome now.

F. Locker-Lampson : London Lyrics.

The Jilt

1813

S AY, Lucy, what enamour'd spark
  Now sports thee through the gazing Park
  In new barouche or tandem ;
And, as infatuation leads,
Permits his reason and his steeds
  To run their course at random ?

Fond youth, those braids of ebon hair,
Which to a face already fair
    Impart a lustre fairer ;
Those locks which now invite to love,
Soon unconfin'd and false shall prove,
    And changeful as the wearer.

Unpractised in a woman's guile,
Thou think'st, perchance, her halcyon smile
    Portends unruffled quiet :
That, ever charming, fond and mild,
No wanton thoughts, or passions wild,
    Within her soul can riot.

Alas ! how often shalt thou mourn,
(If nymphs like her, so soon forsworn,
    Be worth a moment's trouble,)
How quickly own, with sad surprise,
The paradise that bless'd thine eyes
    Was painted on a bubble.

In her accommodating creed
A lord will always supersede
    A commoner's embraces :
His lordship's love contents the fair,
Until enabled to ensnare
    A nobler prize—his Grace's !

Unhappy are the youths who gaze,
Who feel her beauty's maddening blaze,
    And trust to what she utters !
For me, by sad experience wise,
At rosy cheeks or sparkling eyes,
    My heart no longer flutters.

Chamber'd in Albany, I view
On every side a jovial crew
   Of Benedictine neighbours.
I sip my coffee, read the news,
I own no mistress but the muse,
   And she repays my labours.
                    James and Horace Smith :
                    Horace in London.

Willy-Nilly in Piccadilly
1840

THE horse that carried Miss Kilmansegg,
   And a better never lifted leg,
   Was a very rich bay, call'd Banker—
A horse of a breed and a mettle so rare,—
By Bullion out of an Ingot mare,—
That for action, the best of figures, and air,
   It made many good judges hanker.

    .   .   .   .

Mayhap 'tis the trick of such pamper'd nags
To shy at the sight of a beggar in rags,—
   But away, like the bolt of a rabbit,—
Away went the horse in the madness of fright,
And away went the horsewoman mocking the sight—
Was yonder blue flash a flash of blue light,
   Or only the skirt of her habit?

    .   .   .   .

She'll lose her life! She is losing her breath!
A cruel chase, she is chasing Death!
   As female shriekings forewarn her:
And now—as gratis as blood of Guelph—

She clears that gate, which has clear'd itself
    Since then, at Hyde Park Corner!
Alas! for the hope of the Kilmanseggs!
For her head, her brain, her body, and legs,
    Her life's not worth a copper!
Willy-nilly in Piccadilly,
A hundred hearts turn sick and chilly,
    A hundred voices cry, "Stop her!"
And one old gentleman stares and stands,
Shakes his head and lifts his hands,
    And says, "How very improper!"

On and on!—what a perilous run!
The iron rails seem all mingling in one,
    To shut out the Green Park scenery!
And now the Cellar its dangers reveals,
She shudders—she shrieks—she's doom'd, she feels
To be torn by powers of horses and wheels,
    Like a spinner by steam machinery.

Sick with horror she shuts her eyes,
But the very stones seem uttering cries,
    As they did to that Persian daughter,
When she climb'd up the steep vociferous hill,
Her little silver flagon to fill
    With the magical golden water!

" Batter her! shatter her!
Throw and scatter her!"
Shouts each stony-hearted chatterer!
    " Dash at the heavy Dover!
Spill her! kill her! tear and tatter her!
Smash her! crash her!" (the stones didn't flatter her!)
" Kick her brains out! let her blood spatter her!
    Roll on her over and over!"

For so she gather'd the awful sense
Of the street in its past unmacadamised tense,
    As the wild horse overran it,—
His four heels making the clatter of six,
Like a Devil's tatto, play'd with iron sticks
    On a kettle-drum of granite !

On ! still on ! she's dazzled with hints
Of oranges, ribbons, and colour'd prints,
A kaleidoscope jumble of shapes and tints,
    And human faces all flashing,
Bright and brief as the sparks from the flints,
    That the desperate hoof keeps dashing.

On and on ! still frightfully fast !
Dover-street, Bond-street, all are past !
But—yes—no—yes ! they're down at last !
    The Furies and Fates have found them !
Down they go with sparkle and crash,
Like a bark that's struck by the lightning flash—
    There's a shriek—and a sob—
    And the dense dark mob
Like a billow closes round them !

Thomas Hood : Poems.

Kensington Gardens

1722

WHERE Kensington high o'er the neighbouring lands
    'Midst greens and sweets, a regal fabric, stands,
And sees each spring, luxuriant in her bowers,
A snow of blossoms, and a wild of flowers,

The dames of Britain oft in crowds repair
To gravel walks, and unpolluted air.
Here, while the town in damps and darkness lies,
They breathe in sunshine, and see azure skies ;
Each walk, with robes of various dyes bespread,
Seems from afar a moving tulip-bed,
Where rich brocades and glossy damasks glow,
And chintz, the rival of the showery bow.

Here England's daughter, darling of the land,
Sometimes, surrounded with her virgin band,
Gleams through the shades.　She, towering o'er the rest,
Stands fairest of the fairer kind confess'd,
Form'd to gain hearts, that Brunswick's cause deny'd,
And charm a people to her father's side.

Thomas Tickell : Kensington-Garden.

A Woman of Fashion

About 1777

THEN, behind, all my hair is done up in a plat,
　　And so, like a cornet's tuck'd under my hat,
Then I mount on my palfrey as gay as a lark,
And, follow'd by John, take the dust in High Park.
In the way I am met by some smart macaroni
Who rides by my side on a little bay pony—
No sturdy Hibernian, with shoulders so wide,
But as taper and slim as the ponies they ride ;
Their legs are as slim, and their shoulders no wider,
Dear sweet little creatures, both pony and rider !

But sometimes, when hotter, I order my chaise,
And manage, myself, my two little greys:
Sure never were seen two such sweet little ponies,
Other horses are clowns, and these macaronis,
And to give them this title, I'm sure isn't wrong,
Their legs are so slim, and their tails are so long.

In Kensington Gardens to stroll up and down,
You know was the fashion before you left town,
The thing's well enough, when allowance is made
For the size of the trees and the depth of the shade ;
But the spread of their leaves such a shelter affords
To those noisy impertinent creatures call'd birds,
Whose ridiculous chirruping ruins the scene,
Brings the country before me, and gives me the spleen.

Yet, though 'tis too rural—to come near the mark,
We all herd in *one* walk, and that, nearest the Park,
Where with ease we may see, as we pass by the wicket,
The chimneys of Knightsbridge, and—footmen at cricket.
I must, though, in justice, declare that the grass,
Which, worn by our feet, is diminish'd apace,
In a little time more will be brown and as flat
As the sand of Vauxhall, or as Ranelagh mat.
Improving thus fast, perhaps, by degrees
We may see rolls and butter spread under the trees,
With a small pretty band in each seat of the walk,
To play little tunes and enliven our talk.

Richard Brinsley Sheridan : Posthumous Verses.

Lines written in Kensington Gardens

1852

IN this lone, open glade I lie,
    Screen'd by deep boughs on either hand;
And at its end, to stay the eye,
Those black-crown'd, red-boled pine-trees stand!

Birds here make song, each bird has his,
Across the girdling city's hum.
How green under the boughs it is!
How thick the tremulous sheep-cries come!

Sometimes a child will cross the glade
To take his nurse his broken toy;
Sometimes a thrush flit overhead
Deep in her unknown day's employ.

Here at my feet what wonders pass,
What endless, active life is here!
What blowing daisies, fragrant grass!
An air-stirr'd forest, fresh and clear.

Scarce fresher is the mountain-sod
Where the tired angler lies, stretch'd out,
And, eased of basket and of rod,
Counts his day's spoil, the spotted trout.

In the huge world, which roars hard by,
Be others happy if they can!
But in my helpless cradle I
Was breathed on by the rural Pan.

I, on men's impious uproar hurl'd,
Think often, as I hear them rave,
That peace has left the upper world
And now keeps only in the grave.

Yet here is peace for ever new!
When I who watch them am away,
Still all things in this glade go through
The changes of their quiet day.

Then to their happy rest they pass!
The flowers upclose, the birds are fed,
The night comes down upon the grass,
The child sleeps warmly in his bed.

Calm soul of all things! make it mine
To feel, amid the city's jar,
That there abides a peace of thine,
Man did not make, and cannot mar.

The will to neither strive nor cry,
The power to feel with others give!
Calm, calm me more! nor let me die
Before I have begun to live.

Matthew Arnold: Lyric Poems.

In Kensington Gardens

1892

UNDER the almond tree,
   Room for my love and me!
  Over our heads the April blossom ;
April-hearted are we.

Under the pink and white,
Love in her eyes alight ;
  Love and the Spring and Kensington Gardens :
Hey for the heart's delight !

              Arthur Symons : Silhouettes.

A New Song of the Spring Garden

1885

COME hither ye gallants, come hither ye maids,
  To the trim gravelled walks, to shady arcades ;
Come hither, come hither, the nightingales call ;—
Sing *Tantarara,*—Vauxhall ! Vauxhall !

Come hither, ye cits, from your Lothbury hives !
Come hither, ye husbands, and look to your wives !
For the sparks are as thick as the leaves in the Mall ;—
Sing *Tantarara,*—Vauxhall ! Vauxhall !

Here the 'prentice from Aldgate may ogle a Toast !
Here his Worship must elbow the knight of the post !

For the wicket is free to the great and the small ;—
Sing *Tantarara,*—Vauxhall ! Vauxhall !

Here Betty may flaunt in her mistress's sack !
Here Trip wear his master's brocade on his back !
Here a hussy may ride, and a rogue take the wall ;—
Sing *Tantarara,*—Vauxhall ! Vauxhall !

Here Beauty may grant, here Valour may ask !
Here the plainest may pass for a Belle (in a mask) !
Here a domino covers the short and the tall ;—
Sing *Tantarara,*—Vauxhall ! Vauxhall !

'Tis a type of the world, with its drums and its din ;
'Tis a type of the world, for when you come in
You are loth to go out ; like the world 'tis a ball ;—
Sing *Tantarara,*—Vauxhall, Vauxhall !

Austin Dobson : At the Sign of the Lyre.

Farmer Colin at Vauxhall

1720

O MARY ! soft in feature,
    I've been at dear Vauxhall ;
  No Paradise is sweeter,
  Not that they Eden call.

At night such new vagaries,
    Such gay and harmless sport ;
All looked like giant-fairies
    At this their monarch's court.

Methought, when first I entered,
   Such splendours round me shone,
Into a world I'd ventured
   Where shone another sun :

While music never cloying,
   As skylarks sweet, I hear ;
Their sounds I'm still enjoying,
   They'll always soothe my ear.

Here paintings sweetly glowing
   Where'er our glances fall ;
Here colours, life bestowing,
   Bedeck the Greenwood Hall.

The king there dubs a farmer,
   There John his doxy loves ;
But my delight's the charmer
   Who steals a pair of gloves.

As still amazed I'm straying
   O'er this enchanted grove,
I spy a harper playing
   All in his proud alcove.

I doff my hat, desiring
   He'll tune up " Buxom Joan " ;
But what was I admiring ?
   Odzooks ! a man of stone !

But now, the tables spreading,
   They all fall to with glee ;
Not e'en at squire's fine wedding
   Such dainties did I see.

I longed (poor country rover !)
　　But none heed country elves.
These folk, with lace daubed over,
　　Love only their dear selves.

Thus whilst 'mid joys abounding,
　　As grasshoppers they're gay,
At distance crowds surrounding
　　The Lady of the May.

The man i' th' moon tweer'd shyly
　　Soft twinkling through the trees,
As though 'twould please him highly
　　To taste delights like these.

Anon. : Old Song-Books.

At Shining Vauxhall

1817

COME, come, I am very
　　Disposed to be merry—
So hey ! for a wherry
　　I beckon and bawl !
'Tis dry, not a damp night,
And pleasure will tramp light
To music and lamp-light
　　At shining Vauxhall !

Ay, here's the dark portal—
The check-taking mortal

I pass, and turn short all
   At once on the blaze—
Names famous in story,
Lit up *con amore*,
All flaming in glory,
   Distracting the gaze !

Oh *my* name lies fallow—
Fame never will hallow
In red light and yellow
   Poetical toil—
I've long tried to write up
My name, and take flight up ;
But ink will not light up
   Like cotton and oil !

But sad thoughts, keep under !—
The painted Rotund*er*
Invites me.   I wonder
   Who's singing so clear ?
'Tis Sinclair, high flying,
Scotch ditties supplying ;
But some hearts are sighing
   For Dignum, I fear !

How bright is the lustre,
How thick the folks muster,
And eagerly cluster,
   On bench and in box,—
Whilst Povey is waking
Sweet sounds, or the taking
Kate Stephens is shaking
   Her voice and her locks !

What clapping attends her !—
The white doe befriends her—
How Braham attends her
    Away by the hand,
For Love to succeed her ;
The Signor doth heed her,
And sigheth to lead her
    Instead of the band !

Then out we all sally—
Time's ripe for the Ballet,
Like bees they all rally
    Before the machine !—
But I am for tracing
The bright walks and facing
The groups that are pacing
    To see and be seen.

How motley they mingle—
What men might one single,
And names that would tingle
    Or tickle the ear—
Fresh Chinese contrivers
Of letters—survivors
Of pawnbrokers—divers
    Beau Tibbses appear !

Such little and great men,
And civic and state men—
Collectors and rate-men—
    How pleasant to nod
To friends—to note fashions,
To make speculations

On people and passions—
   To laugh at the odd !

To sup on true slices
Of ham—with fair prices
For fowl—while cool ices
   And liquor abound—
To see Blackmore wander,
A small salamander,
Adown the rope yonder,
   And light on the ground !

Oh, the fireworks are splendid ;
But darkness is blended—
Bright things are soon ended,
   Fade quickly, and fall !
There goes the last rocket !—
Some cash out of pocket,
By stars in the socket
   I go from Vauxhall !
                    Thomas Hood : Collected Poems.

St. James's Prayers

1719

L AST Sunday at St. James's prayers,
   The prince and princess by,
I, drest in all my whale-bone airs,
   Sat in a closet nigh.
I bow'd my knees, I held my book,
   Read all the answers o'er ;

But was perverted by a look,
    Which pierced me from the door.
High thoughts of Heaven I came to use,
    With the devoutest care,
Which gay young Strephon made me lose,
    And all the raptures there.
He stood to hand me to my chair,
    And bow'd with courtly grace ;
But whisper'd love into my ear,
    Too warm for that grave place.
" Love, love," said he, " by all adored,
    My tender heart has won."
But I grew peevish at the word,
    And bade he would be gone.
He went quite out of sight, while I
    A kinder answer meant ;
Nor did I for my sins that day
    By half so much repent.

Anon. : Wit and Mirth.

Love or London?

1737

FROM Lincoln to London rode forth our young squire,
    To bring down a wife whom the swains might admire :
But, in spite of whatever the mortal could say,
The goddess objected the length of the way !

To give up the opera, the park, and the ball,
For to view the stag's horns in an old country hall ;
To have neither China nor Indian to see !
Nor a laceman to plague in a morning—not she !

To forsake the dear play-house, Quin, Garrick, and Clive,
Who by dint of mere humour had kept her alive;
To forego the full box for his lonesome abode,
O Heavens! she should faint, she should die on the road.

To forego the gay fashions and gestures of France,
And leave dear Auguste in the midst of the dance,
And Harlequin too!—'twas in vain to require it;
And she wonder'd how folks had the face to desire it.

To be sure she could breathe nowhere else but in town;
Thus she talk'd like a wit, and he look'd like a clown;
But the while honest Harry despair'd to succeed,
A coach with a coronet trail'd her to 'Tweed.

William Shenstone : Collected Poems.

St. George's, Hanover Square

1856

SHE pass'd up the aisle on the arm of her sire,
  A delicate lady in bridal attire,
    Fair emblem of virgin simplicity;
Half London was there, and, my word, there were few
That stood by the altar, or hid in a pew,
    But envied Lord Nigel's felicity.

Beautiful bride!—So meek in thy splendour,
So frank in thy love, and its trusting surrender,
    Departing you leave us the town dim!

May happiness wing to thy bower, unsought,
And may Nigel, esteeming his bliss as he ought,
Prove worthy thy worship,—confound him !
F. Locker-Lampson : London Lyrics.

On St. James's Park

AS LATELY IMPROVED BY HIS MAJESTY

1661

OF the first Paradise there's nothing found,
   Plants set by Heaven are vanish'd, and the ground;
Yet the description lasts : who knows the fate
Of lives that shall this Paradise relate.
   Instead of rivers rolling by the side
Of Eden's garden, here flows in the tide :
The sea, which always serv'd his empire, now
Pays tribute to our prince's pleasure too.
Of famous cities we the founders know ;
But rivers, old as seas to which they go,
Are Nature's bounty : 'tis of more renown
To make a river, than to build a town.

For future shade, young trees upon the banks
Of the new stream appear in even ranks :
The voice of Orpheus, or Amphion's hand,
In better order could not make them stand.
May they increase as fast, and spread their boughs,
As the high fame of their great owner grows !
May he live long enough to see them all
Dark shadows cast, and as his palace tall !

F

Methinks I see the love that shall be made,
The lovers walking in that amorous shade :
The gallants dancing by the river side ;
They bathe in summer, and in winter slide.
Methinks I hear the music in the boats,
And the loud echo which returns the notes :
While, overhead, a flock of newsprung fowl
Hangs in the air, and does the sun controul ;
Dark'ning the sky, they hover o'er, and shroud
The wanton sailors with a feather'd cloud.
Beneath, a shoal of silver fishes glides,
And plays about the gilded barges' sides :
The ladies angling in the crystal lake,
Feast on the waters with the prey they take :
At once victorious with their lines and eyes,
They make the fishes and the men their prize.
A thousand Cupids on the billows ride,
And sea-nymphs enter with the swelling tide :
From Thetis sent as spies to make report,
And tell the wonders of her sovereign's court.
All that can, living, feed the greedy eye,
Or dead, the palate, here you may descry ;
The choicest things that furnish'd Noah's ark,
Or Peter's sheet, inhabiting this Park :
All with a border of rich fruit-trees crown'd,
Whose loaded branches hide the lofty mound.
Such various ways the spacious alleys lead,
My doubtful Muse knows not what path to tread.

Yonder, the harvest of cold months laid up,
Gives a fresh coolness to the royal cup :
There ice, like crystal, firm, and never lost,
Tempers hot July with December's frost ;

Winter's dark prison, whence he cannot fly,
'Though the warm Spring, his enemy, draws nigh.
Strange ! that extremes should thus preserve the snow,
High on the Alps, and in deep caves below.

Here a well-polish'd Mall gives us the joy,
To see our prince his matchless force employ ;
His manly posture, and his graceful mien,
Vigour and youth in all his motions seen ;
His shape so lovely, and his limbs so strong,
Confirm our hopes we shall obey him long.
No sooner had he touch'd the flying ball,
But 'tis already more than half the Mall,
And such a fury from his arm has got,
As from a smoking culverin 'twere shot.
May that ill fate his enemies befall,
To stand before his anger or his ball !

Near this my Muse, what most delights her, sees
A living gallery of aged trees ;
Bold sons of Earth, that thrust their arms so high,
As if once more they would invade the sky.
In such green palaces the first kings reign'd,
Slept in their shades, and angels entertain'd ;
With such old counsellors they did advise,
And, by frequenting sacred groves, grew wise,
Free from th' impediments of light and noise,
Man, thus retir'd, his nobler thoughts employs.
Here Charles contrives the ordering of his states,
Here he resolves his neighbouring princes' fates :
What nation shall have peace, where war be made
Determin'd is in this oraculous shade ;
The world, from India to the frozen North,
Concern'd in what this solitude brings forth.

His fancy objects from his view receives ;
The prospect thought and contemplation gives.
That seat of empire here salutes his eye,
To which three kingdoms do themselves apply ;
The structure by a prelate rais'd, Whitehall,
Built with the fortune of Rome's capitol :
Both, disproportion'd to the present state
Of their proud founders, were approv'd by Fate.
From hence he does that antique Pile behold
Where royal heads receive the sacred gold :
It gives them crowns and does their ashes keep ;
There made like gods, like mortals there they sleep :
Making the circle of their reign complete,
Those suns of empire ! where they rise they set.
When others fell, this, standing, did presage
The crown should triumph over pop'lar rage :
Hard by that House, where all our ills were shap'd,
Th' auspicious temple stood, and yet escap'd.
So, snow on Etna does unmelted lie,
Whence rolling flames and scatter'd cinders fly ;
The distant country in the ruin shares,
What falls from Heaven the burning mountain spares.
Next, that capacious Hall he sees, the room
Where the whole nation does for justice come ;
Under whose large roof flourishes the gown,
And judges grave on high tribunals frown.

Here, like the people's pastor, he does go,
His flock subjected to his view below :
On which reflecting in his mighty mind,
No private passion does indulgence find :
The pleasures of his youth suspended are,
And made a sacrifice to public care.

Here, free from court compliances, he walks,
And with himself, his best adviser, talks:
How peaceful olive may his temples shade,
For mending laws, and for restoring trade:
Or, how his brows may be with laurel charg'd,
For nations conquer'd, and our bounds enlarg'd.
Of ancient prudence here he ruminates,
Of rising kingdoms, and of falling states:
What ruling arts gave great Augustus fame,
And how Alcides purchas'd such a name.
His eyes, upon his native Palace bent,
Close by, suggests a greater argument:
His thoughts rise higher, when he does reflect
On what the world may from that star expect,
Which at his birth appear'd; to let us see,
Day, for his sake, could with the night agree:
A prince, on whom such different light did smile,
Born the divided world to reconcile!
Whatever Heaven, or high-extracted blood,
Could promise, or foretell, he will make good;
Reform these nations, and improve them more,
Than this fair Park, from what it was before.

Edmund Waller: Collected Poems.

West London

1867

CROUCH'D on the pavement close by Belgrave Square
      A tramp I saw, ill, moody, and tongue-tied;
A babe was in her arms, and at her side
A girl; their clothes were rags, their feet were bare.

Some labouring men, whose work lay somewhere there,
Pass'd opposite ; she touch'd her girl, who hied
Across, and begg'd, and came back satisfied.
The rich she had let pass with frozen stare.

Thought **I** : Above her state this spirit towers ;
She will not ask of aliens, but of friends,
Of sharers in a common human fate.

She turns from that cold succour, which attends
The unknown little from the unknowing great,
And points us to a better time than ours.

Matthew Arnold: Collected Poems.

East London.

1867

'TWAS August, and the fierce sun overhead
    Smote on the squalid streets of Bethnal Green,
  And the pale weaver, through his windows seen
In Spitalfields, look'd thrice dispirited ;

I met a preacher there I knew, and said :
    "Ill and o'erwork'd, how fare you in this scene ?"
    "Bravely !" said he ; "for I of late have been
Much cheer'd with thoughts of Christ, *the living bread.*"

O human soul ! as long as thou canst so
Set up a mark of everlasting light,
Above the howling senses' ebb and flow,

To cheer thee, and to right thee if thou roam,
Not with lost toil thou labourest through the night!
Thou mak'st the heaven thou hop'st indeed thy home.
                    Matthew Arnold: Collected Poems.

The Poet of Fashion

1822

HIS book is successful, he's steeped in renown;
        His lyric effusions have tickled the town;
Dukes, dowagers, dandies, are eager to trace
The fountain of verse in the verse-maker's face;
While, proud as Apollo, with peers *tête-à-tête*,
From Monday till Saturday dining off plate,
His heart full of hope, and his head full of gain,
The Poet of Fashion dines out in Park Lane.

Now lean-jointured widows who seldom draw corks,
Whose tea-spoons do duty for knives and for forks,
Send forth, vellum-covered, a six o'clock card,
And get up a dinner to peep at the bard;
Veal, sweetbread, boiled chickens, and tongue crown the
        cloth,
And soup, *à la reine*, little better than broth;
While, past his meridian, but still with some heat,
The Poet of Fashion dines out in Sloane Street.

Enrolled in the tribe who subsist by their wits,
Remember'd by starts, and forgotten by fits,
Now artists and actors, the bardling engage,
To squib in the journals, and write for the stage.

Now soup *à la reine* bends the knee to ox-cheek,
And chickens and tongue bow to bubble and squeak—
While, still in translation employ'd by "the Row,"
The Poet of Fashion dines out in Soho.

Pushed down from Parnassus to Phlegethon's brink,
Toss'd, torn, and trunk-lining, but still with some ink,
Now squab city misses their albums expand,
And woo the worn rhymer for "something off-hand";
No longer with stilted effrontery fraught,
Bucklersbury now seeks what St. James's once sought,
And (O, what a classical haunt for a bard!)
The Poet of Fashion dines out in Barge-yard.

James Smith: Comic Miscellanies.

Good-Night to the Season

1827

GOOD-NIGHT to the Season!   'Tis over!
    Gay dwellings no longer are gay;
The courtier, the gambler, the lover,
    Are scattered like swallows away;
There's nobody left to invite one,
    Except my good uncle and spouse;
My mistress is bathing at Brighton,
    My patron is sailing at Cowes;
For want of a better employment,
    Till Ponto and Don can get out,
I'll cultivate rural enjoyment,
    And angle immensely for trout.

Good-night to the Season !—the lobbies,
    Their changes and rumours of change,
Which startled the rustic Sir Bobbies,
    And made all the Bishops look strange ;
The breaches, and battles, and blunders,
    Performed by the Commons and Peers ;
The Marquis's eloquent blunders,
    The Baronet's eloquent ears ;
Denouncings of Papists and treasons,
    Of foreign dominions and oats ;
Misrepresentations of reasons,
    And misunderstandings of notes.

Good-night to the Season !—the buildings
    Enough to make Inigo sick ;
The paintings, and plasterings, and gildings
    Of stucco, and marble, and brick ;
The orders deliciously blended
    From love of effect into one ;
The club-houses only intended,
    The palaces only begun ;
The hell, where the fiend in his glory
    Sits staring at putty and stones,
And scrambles from story to story,
    To rattle at midnight his bones.

Good-night to the Season !—the dances,
    The fillings of hot little rooms,
The glancings of rapturous glances,
    The fancyings of fancy costumes ;
The pleasures which fashion makes duties,
    The praisings of fiddles and flutes,
The luxury of looking at Beauties,
    The tedium of talking to mutes ;

The female diplomatists, planners
　　Of matches for Laura and Jane,
The ice of her Ladyship's manners,
　　The ice of his Lordship's champagne.

Good-night to the Season !—the rages
　　Led off by the chiefs of the throng,
The Lady Matilda's new pages,
　　The Lady Eliza's new song ;
Miss Fennel's macaw, which at Boodle's
　　Was held to have something to say ;
Mrs. Splenetic's musical poodles,
　　Which bark "Batti ! Batti !" all day ;
The pony Sir Araby sported,
　　As hot and as black as a coal,
And the lion his mother imported,
　　In bearskins and grease, from the Pole.

Good-night to the Season !—the Toso,
　　So very majestic and tall ;
Miss Ayton, whose singing was so-so,
　　And Pasta, divinest of all ;
The labour in vain of the ballet,
　　So sadly deficient in stars ;
The foreigners thronging the Alley,
　　Exhaling the breath of cigars ;
The *loge* where some heiress (how killing !)
　　Environed with exquisites sits,
The lovely one out of her drilling,
　　The silly ones out of their wits.

Good-night to the Season !—the splendour
　　That beamed in the Spanish Bazaar ;

Where I purchased—my heart was so tender—
　　A card-case, a pasteboard guitar,
A bottle of perfume, a girdle,
　　A lithographed Riego, full-grown,
Whom bigotry drew on a hurdle
　　That artists might draw him on stone ;
A small panorama of Seville,
　　A trap for demolishing flies,
A caricature of the Devil,
　　And a look from Miss Sheridan's eyes.

Good-night to the Season !—the flowers
　　Or the grand horticultural fête,
When boudoirs were quitted for bowers,
　　And the fashion was—not to be late ;
When all who had money and leisure
　　Grew rural o'er ices and wines,
All pleasantly toiling for pleasure,
　　All hungrily pining for pines,
And making of beautiful speeches,
　　And marring of beautiful shows,
And feeding on delicate peaches,
　　And treading on delicate toes.

Good-night to the Season !—another
　　Will come with its trifles and toys,
And hurry away, like its brother,
　　In sunshine, and odour, and noise.
Will it come with a rose or a briar ?
　　Will it come with a blessing or curse ?
Will its bonnets be lower or higher ?
　　Will its morals be better or worse ?

Will it find me grown thinner or fatter,
      Or fonder of wrong or of right,
Or married—or buried?—no matter :
      Good-night to the Season—good-night !
                    Winthrop Mackworth Praed :
                          Collected Poems.

Phil Porter's Farewell to Town, when Dying

1661

FAREWELL *Three Kings*, where I have spent
      Full many an idle hour ;
Where oft I won, but never lost,
      If 'twere within my power.

Farewell my dearest Piccadilly,
      Notorious for great dinners ;
Oh what a Tennis Court was there !
      Alas !—too good for sinners.

Farewell the glory of Hyde Park,
      Which was to me so dear ;
Ah, since I can't enjoy it more,
      Would I were buried there !

Farewell tormenting creditors,
      Whose scores did so perplex me ;
Well !   Death I see for something's good,
      For now they'll cease to vex me.

Farewell true brethren of the Sword,
   All martial men and stout;
Farewell dear Drawer at the *Fleece*,
   I cannot leave thee out.

My time draws on, I now must go,
   From this beloved light;
Remember me to pretty Sue,
   And so, dear friends, Good-Night!
                    Anon: Wit and Drollery.

Mr. Pope's Farewell to London

1715

DEAR, damn'd, distracting town, farewell!
   Thy fools no more I'll tease;

   .   .   .   .

To drink and droll be Rowe allow'd
   Till the third watchman's toll;
Let Jarvis gratis paint, and Frowde
   Save threepence and his soul.

Farewell, Arbuthnot's raillery
   On every learned sot;
And Garth, the best good Christian he,
   Although he knows it not.

Lintot, farewell! thy bard must go;
   Farewell, unhappy Tonson!
Heaven gives thee for thy loss of Rowe
   Lean Philips and fat Johnson.

Why should I stay?   Both parties rage ;
    My vixen mistress squalls ;
The wits in envious feuds engage ;
    And Homer (damn him !) calls.

The love of arts lies cold and dead
    In Halifax's urn ;
And not one Muse of all he fed
    Has yet the grace to mourn.

.   .   .   .   .

Why make I friendships with the great,
    When I no favours seek ?
Or follow girls, seven hours in eight ?
    I us'd but once a week.

Still idle, with a busy air,
    Deep whimsies to contrive ;
The gayest valetudinaire,
    Most thinking rake, alive.

Solicitous for others' ends,
    Though fond of dear repose ;
Careless or drowsy with my friends,
    And frolic with my foes.

Luxurious lobster-nights, farewell,
    For sober, studious days !
And Burlington's delicious meal,
    For salads, tarts, and pease !

Adieu to all but Gay alone,
  Whose soul, sincere and free,
Loves all mankind, but flatters none,
  And so may starve with me.
                    Alexander Pope: Collected Poems.

To Mr. MacAdam

1826

THY first great trial in this mighty town
    Was, if I rightly recollect, upon
  That gentle hill which goeth
Down from " The County " to the Palace gate,
    And, like a river, thanks to thee, now floweth
Past the Old Horticultural Society—
The chemist Cobb's, the house of Howell and James,
Where ladies play high shawl and satin games—
        A little *Hell* of lace !
And past the Athenæum, made of late,
        Severs a sweet variety
Of milliners and booksellers who grace
        Waterloo Place,
Making division, the Muse fears and guesses,
'Twixt Mr. Rivington's and Mr. Hessey's.
Thou stood'st thy trial Mac ! and shaved the road
From Barber Beaumont's to the King's abode
So well, that paviours threw their rammers by,
Let down their tucked shirt sleeves, and with a sigh
Prepared themselves, poor souls, to chip or die !
Next from the palace to the prison, thou
  Didst go, the highway's watchman, to thy beat—

Preventing though the *rattling* in the street,
      Yet kicking up a row
Upon the stones—ah ! truly watchman-like,
Encouraging thy victims all to strike,
      To further thy own purpose, Adam, daily ;—
Thou hast smoothed, alas, the path to the Old Bailey !
      And to the stony bowers
Of Newgate, to encourage the approach,
      By caravan or coach—
Hast strewed the way with flints as soft as flowers.
                    Thomas Hood : Ode to Mr. MacAdam.

London Misnomers

1813.

FROM Park Land to Wapping, by day and by night,
      I've many a year been a roamer,
And find that no lawyer can London indict,
      Each street, ev'ry lane's a misnomer.
I find Broad Street, St. Giles's, a poor narrow nook,
      Battle Bridge is unconscious of slaughter,
Duke's Place cannot muster the ghost of a duke,
      And Brook Street is wanting in water.

I went to Cornhill for a bushel of wheat,
      And sought it in vain ev'ry shop in,
The Hermitage offered a tranquil retreat
      For the jolly Jack hermits of Wapping.
Spring Gardens, all wintry, appear on the wane,
      Sun Alley's an absolute blinder,
Mount Street is a level, and Bearbinder Lane
      Has neither a bear nor a binder.

No football is kicked up and down in Pall Mall,
    Change Alley, alas ! never varies,
The Serpentine river's a straitened canal,
    Milk Street is denuded of dairies.
Knight's bridge, void of tournaments, lies calm and still,
    Butcher Row cannot boast of a cleaver,
And (tho' it abuts on his garden) Hay Hill
    Won't give Devon's duke the hay fever.

The Cockpit's the focus of law, not of sport,
    Water Lane is affected with dryness,
And, spite of its gorgeous approach, Prince's Court
    Is a sorry abode for his Highness.
From Baker Street North all the bakers have fled,
    So, in verse not quite equal to Homer,
Methinks I have proved what at starting I said,
    That London's one mighty misnomer.
                James Smith : Comic Miscellanies.

Queen Elinor and the
Charing Cross

1593

LET Spanish steeds, as swift as fleeting wind,
    Convey these princes to their funeral :
Before them let a hundred mourners ride.
In every time of their enforc'd abode,
Rear up a cross in token of their worth,
Whereon fair Elinor's picture shall be plac'd.

Arriv'd at London, near our palace-bounds,
Inter my lovely Elinor, late deceas'd;
And, in remembrance of her royalty,
Erect a rich and stately carvèd cross,
Whereon her stature shall with glory shine,
And henceforth see you call it Charing Cross;
For why the chariest and the choicest queen
That ever did delight my royal eyes,
There dwells in darkness.
George Peele: King Edward the First.

On the Statue of King Charles I.
at Charing Cross

1674

THAT the first Charles does here in triumph ride,
   See his son reign'd where he a martyr died,
And people pay that rev'rence as they pass,
(Which then he wanted) to the sacred brass,
Is not th' effect of gratitude alone,
To which we owe the statue and the stone;
But Heav'n this lasting monument has wrought,
That mortals may eternally be taught,
Rebellion, though successful, is but vain,
And kings so kill'd rise conquerors again.
This truth the royal image does proclaim,
Loud as the trumpet of surviving Fame.
Edmund Waller: Collected Poems.

A Ballad upon a Wedding

About 1635

I TELL thee, Dick, where I have been,
  Where I the rarest sights have seen :
    Oh things without compare !
Such sights again cannot be found
In any place on English ground,
    Be it at wake, or fair.

At Charing Cross, hard by the way
Where we (thou know'st) do sell our hay,
    There is a house with stairs ;
And there did I see coming down
Such folks as are not in our town,
    Forty at least, in pairs.

Amongst the rest, one pest'lent fine,
(His beard no bigger though than thine)
    Walk'd on before the rest :
Our landlord looks like nothing to him :
The king (God bless him) 'twould undo him ;
    Shou'd he go still so drest.

At Course-a-park, without all doubt,
He should have first been taken out
    By all the maids i' th' town :
Though lusty Roger there had been,
Our little George upon the green,
    Or Vincent of the crown.

But wot you what? the youth was going
To make an end of all his wooing;
　　The parson for him staid:
Yet by his leave, for all his haste,
He did not so much wish all past
　　(Perchance) as did the maid.

The maid—and thereby hangs a tale—
For such a maid no Whitson ale
　　Could ever yet produce:
No grape that's kindly ripe, could be
So round, so plump, so soft as she,
　　Nor half so full of juice.

Her finger was so small, the ring
Wou'd not stay on which they did bring,
　　It was too wide a peck:
And to say truth (for out it must)
It look'd like the great collar (just)
　　About our young colt's neck.

Her feet beneath her petticoat,
Like little mice stole in and out,
　　As if they fear'd the light:
But oh! she dances such a way!
No sun upon an Easter Day
　　Is half so fine a sight.

Her cheeks so rare a white was on,
No daisy makes comparison,
　　(Who sees them is undone)
For streaks of red were mingled there,
Such as are on a Katherine pear,
　　The side that's next the sun.

Her lips were red, and one was thin
Compar'd to that was next her chin,
  Some bee had stung it newly.
But (Dick) her eyes so guard her face,
I durst no more upon them gaze,
  Than on the sun in July.

Her mouth so small when she does speak,
Thoud'st swear her teeth her words did break,
  That they might passage get,
But she so handled still the matter,
They came as good as ours, or better,
  And are not spent a whit.

Passion o' me ! how I run on !
There's that that would be thought upon,
  I trow, besides the bride.
The bus'ness of the kitchen's great,
For it is fit that men should eat ;
  Nor was it there deny'd.

When all the meat was on the table,
What man of knife, or teeth, was able
  To stay to be entreated :
And this the very reason was,
Before the parson could say grace,
  The company was seated.

How hats fly off, and youths carouse ;
Healths first go round, and then the house,
  The bride's came thick and thick ;
And when 'twas nam'd another's health,
Perhaps he made it hers by stealth,
  And who could help it, Dick ?

O th' sudden up they rise and dance;
Then sit again, and sigh and glance:
   Then dance again and kiss.
Thus sev'ral ways the time did pass,
Whilst ev'ry woman wish'd her place,
   And ev'ry man wish'd his.

By this time all were stol'n aside
To counsel and undress the bride;
   But that he must not know:
But yet 'twas thought he guest her mind,
And did not mean to stay behind
   Above an hour or so.

Sir John Suckling : Collected Poems.

The Downfall of Charing-Cross

1647

UNDONE, undone the lawyers are,
   They wander about the town,
Nor can find the way to Westminster,
   Now Charing-Cross is down:
At the end of the Strand, they make a stand,
   Swearing they are at a loss,
And chaffing say, that's not the way,
   They must go by Charing-Cross.

The Parliament to vote it down
   Conceived it very fitting,
For fear it should fall, and kill them all,
   In the house as they were sitting.

They were told, god-wot, it had a plot,
   Which made them so hard-hearted,
To give command, it should not stand,
   But be taken down and carted.

Men talk of plots, this might have been worse
   For any thing I know,
Than that Tomkins and Chaloner,
   Were hang'd for long ago.
Our Parliament did that prevent,
   And wisely them defended,
For plots they will discover still,
   Before they were intended.

But neither man, woman, nor child,
   Will say, I'm confident,
They ever heard it speak one word
   Against the Parliament,
An informer swore, it letters bore,
   Or else it had been freed;
I'll take, in troth, my Bible oath,
   It could neither write, nor read,

The Committee said, that verily
   To Popery it was bent;
For aught I know, it might be so,
   For to church it never went.
What with excise, and such device,
   The kingdom doth begin
To think you'll leave them ne'er a cross,
   Without doors nor within.

Methinks the common-council shou'd
  Of it have taken pity,
'Cause, good old Cross, it always stood
  So firmly to the city.
Since crosses you so much disdain,
  Faith, if I were as you,
For fear the king should rule again,
  I'd pull down Tyburn too.

Anon: Percy's Reliques of Ancient
English Poetry.

Sonnet

ON HEARING ST. MARTIN'S BELLS ON MY WAY HOME
FROM A SPARRING MATCH AT THE FIVES-COURT

1820

BEAUTIFUL bells ! that on this airy eve
  Swoon with such deep and mellow cadences,—
Filling,—then leaving empty the rapt breeze ;—
Pealing full voic'd,—and seeming now to grieve
In distant dreaming sweetness !—ye bereave
  My mind of worldly care by dim degrees ;—
Dropping the balm of falling melodies
Over a heart that yearneth to receive.
Oh, doubly soft ye seem !—since even but now
  I've left the Fives-Court rush,—the flash,—the rally,—
  The noise of "Go it Jack,"—the stop—the blow,—
The shout—the chattering hit—the check—the sally ;—
  Oh, doubly sweet y'e seem to come and go ;—
  Like peasants' pipes, at peace time, in a valley !

John Hamilton Reynolds: The Fancy.

Trafalgar Square

1892

. . . .

TRAFALGAR Square
  (The fountains volleying golden glaze)
Shines like an angel-market.   High aloft
Over his couchant Lions in a haze
Shimmering and bland and soft,
A dust of chrysoprase,
Our Sailor takes the golden gaze
Of the saluting sun, and flames superb
As once he flamed it on his ocean round.
The dingy dreariness of the picture-place,
Turned very nearly bright,
Takes on a luminous transiency of grace,
And shows no more a scandal to the ground.
The very blind man pottering on the kerb,
Among the posies and the ostrich feathers,
And the rude voices touched with all the weathers
Of the long, varying year,
Shares in the universal alms of light.
The windows, with their fleeting, flickering fires,
The height and spread of frontage shining sheer,
The quiring signs, the rejoicing roofs and spires—
'Tis El Dorado—El Dorado plain,
The Golden City!   And when a girl goes by,
Look ! as she turns her glancing head,
A call of gold is floated from her ear !
Golden, all golden !   In a golden glory,
Long-lapsing down a golden coasted sky,

The day not dies but seems
Dispersed in wafts and drifts of gold, and shed
Upon a past of golden song and story
And memories of gold and golden dreams.
William Ernest Henley: London Voluntaries.

Ballade of Summer

1884

WHEN strawberry pottles are common and cheap,
    Ere elms be black, or limes be sere,
When midnight dances are murdering sleep,
Then comes in the sweet o' the year!
And far from Fleet Street, far from here,
The Summer is Queen in the length of the land,
And moonlit nights they are soft and clear,
When fans for a penny are sold in the Strand!

When clamour that doves in the lindens keep
Mingles with musical plash of the weir,
Where drowned green tresses of crowsfoot creep,
Then comes in the sweet o' the year!
And better a crust and a beaker of beer,
With rose-hung hedges on either hand,
Than a palace in town and a prince's cheer,
When fans for a penny are sold in the Strand!

When big trout late in the twilight leap,
When cuckoo clamoureth far and near,
When glittering scythes in the hayfield reap,
Then comes in the sweet o' the year!

And it's oh to sail, with the wind to steer,
Where kine knee-deep in the water stand,
On a Highland loch, or a Lowland mere,
When fans for a penny are sold in the Strand!

ENVOY

Friend, with the fops while we dawdle here,
Then comes in the sweet o' the year!
And the Summer runs out, like grains of sand,
When fans for a penny are sold in the Strand!

Andrew Lang: Rhymes à la Mode.

A London Plane-Tree

1893

GREEN is the plane-tree in the square,
    The other trees are brown;
They droop and pine for country air;
    The plane-tree loves the town.

Here from my garret-pane, I mark
    The plane-tree bud and blow,
Shed her recuperative bark,
    And spread her shade below.

Among her branches, in and out,
    The city breezes play;
The dun fog wraps her round about;
    Above, the smoke curls grey.

Others the country take for choice,
And hold the town in scorn ;
But she has listened to the voice
Of city breezes borne.

Amy Levy : A London Plane-Tree,
and other Poems.

Bloomsbury

1893

FOR me, for me, these old retreats
    Amid the world of London streets !
My eye is pleased with all it meets
        In Bloomsbury.

I know how prim is Bedford Park,
At Highgate oft I've heard the lark,
Not these can lure me from my ark
        In Bloomsbury.

I know how green is Peckham Rye,
And Syd'nham, flashing in the sky,
But did I dwell there I should sigh
        For Bloomsbury.

I know where Maida Vale receives
The night dews on her summer leaves,
Not less my settled spirit cleaves
        To Bloomsbury.

Some love the Chelsea river gales,
And the slow barges' ruddy sails,
And these I'll woo when glamour fails
        In Bloomsbury.

Enough for me in yonder square
To see the perky sparrows pair,
Or long laburnum gild the air
                    In Bloomsbury.

Enough for me in midnight skies
To see the moons of London rise,
And weave their silver fantasies
                    In Bloomsbury.

Oh, mine in snows and summer heats,
These good old Tory brick-built streets!
My eye is pleased with all it meets
                    In Bloomsbury.

Anon.

The Farmer in London

1803

'TIS not for the unfeeling, the falsely refined,
    The squeamish in taste, and the narrow of mind,
And the small critic wielding his delicate pen,
That I sing of old Adam, the pride of old men.

He dwells in the centre of London's wide Town;
His staff is a sceptre—his grey hairs a crown;
And his bright eyes look brighter, set off by the streak
Of the unfaded rose that still blooms on his cheek.

'Mid the dews, in the sunshine of morn—'mid the joy
Of the fields, he collected that bloom, when a boy;
That countenance there fashioned, which, spite of a stain
That his life hath received, to the last will remain.

A Farmer he was ; and his house far and near
Was the boast of the country for excellent cheer :
How oft have I heard in sweet Tilsbury Vale
Of the silver-rimmed horn whence he dealt his mild ale !

Yet Adam was far as the farthest from ruin,
His fields seemed to know what their master was doing ;
And turnips, and corn-land, and meadow, and lea,
All caught the infection—as generous as he.

Yet Adam prized little the feast and the bowl,—
The fields better suited the case of his soul :
He strayed through the fields like an indolent wight,
The quiet of nature was Adam's delight.

For Adam was simple in thought ; and the poor,
Familiar with him, made an inn of his door :
He gave them the best that he had ; or, to say
What less may mislead you, they took it away.

Thus thirty smooth years did he thrive on his farm :
The Genius of plenty preserved him from harm :
At length, what to most is a season of sorrow,
His means are run out,—he must beg, or must borrow.

To the neighbours he went,—all were free with their money ;
For his hive had so long been replenished with honey,
That they dreamt not of dearth ;—he continued his rounds,
Knocked here—and knocked there, pounds adding to
        pounds.

He paid what he could with his ill-gotten pelf,
And something, it might be, reserved for himself :
Then (what is too true) without hinting a word,
Turned his back on the country—and off like a bird.

You lift up your eyes !—but I guess that you frame
A judgment too harsh of the sin and the shame;
In him it was scarcely a business of art,
For this he did all in the *ease* of his heart.

To London—a sad emigration I ween—
With his grey hairs he went from the brook and the green;
And there, with small wealth but his legs and his hands,
As lonely he stood as a crow on the sands.

All trades, as need was, did old Adam assume,—
Served as stable-boy, errand-boy, porter, and groom;
But nature is gracious, necessity kind,
And, in spite of the shame that may lurk in his mind,

He seems ten birthdays younger, is green and is stout;
Twice as fast as before does his blood run about;
You would say that each hair of his beard was alive,
And his fingers are busy as bees in a hive.

For he's not like an old man that leisurely goes
About work that he knows, in a track that he knows;
But often his mind is compelled to demur,
And you guess that the more then his body must stir.

In the throng of the town like a stranger is he,
Like one whose own country's far over the sea;
And Nature, while through the great city he hies,
Full ten times a day takes his heart by surprise.

This gives him the fancy of one that is young,
More of soul in his face than of words on his tongue;

Like a maiden of twenty he trembles and sighs,
And tears of fifteen will come into his eyes.

What's a tempest to him, or the dry parching heats?
Yet he watches the clouds that pass over the streets;
With a look of such earnestness often will stand,
You might think he'd twelve reapers at work in the Strand.

Where proud Covent Garden, in desolate hours
Of snow and hoar frost, spreads her fruits and her flowers,
Old Adam will smile at the pains that have made
Poor winter look fine in such strange masquerade.

'Mid coaches and chariots, a waggon of straw,
Like a magnet, the heart of old Adam can draw;
With a thousand soft pictures his memory will teem,
And his hearing is touched with the sounds of a dream.

Up the Haymarket hill he oft whistles his way,
Thrusts his hands in a waggon, and smells at the hay,
He thinks of the fields he so often hath mown,
And is happy as if the rich freight were his own.

But chiefly to Smithfield he loves to repair,—
If you pass by at morning, you'll meet with him there.
The breath of the cows you may see him inhale,
And his heart all the while is in Tilsbury Vale.

Now farewell, old Adam! when low thou art laid,
May one blade of grass spring up over thy head;
And I hope that thy grave, wheresoever it be,
Will hear the wind sigh through the leaves of a tree.

William Wordsworth: Poems
Referring to Old Age.

A London Rose

1894

DIANA, take this London rose,
   Of crimson grace for your pale hand,
Who love all loveliness that grows :
A London rose—ah, no one knows,
   A penny bought it in the Strand !

But not alone for hearts' delight;
   The crimson has a deeper stain
For your kind eyes that, late by night,
Grew sad at London's motley sight
   Beneath the gaslit driving rain.

And now again I fear you start
   To find that sorry comedy
Re-written on a rose's heart :
'Tis yours alone to read apart,
   Who have such eyes to weep and see.

Soon rose and rhyme must die forgot,
   But this, Diana—ah, who knows !
May die, yet live on in your thought
Of London's fate, and his, who bought
   For love of you a London rose.

Ernest Rhys: A London Rose and other Rhymes.

H

Holy Thursday

1789

'TWAS on a holy Thursday, their innocent faces clean,
　　The children walking two and two, in red, and blue,
　　　　and green:
Grey-headed beadles walked before, with wands as white as
　　snow,
Till into the high dome of St. Paul's they like Thames
　　waters flow.

O what a multitude they seemed, these flowers of London
　　town!
Seated in companies they sit, with radiance all their own.
The hum of multitudes was there, but multitudes of lambs,
Thousands of little boys and girls raising their innocent
　　hands.

Now like a mighty wind they raise to heaven the voice of
　　song,
Or like harmonious thunderings the seats of heaven among:
Beneath them sit the aged men, wise guardians of the poor.
Then cherish pity, lest you drive an angel from your door.

William Blake: Songs of Innocence.

London Weather

1716

WHEN sleep is first disturb'd by morning cries;
 From sure prognostics learn to know the skies,
Lest you of rheums and coughs at night complain;
Surpris'd in dreary fogs or driving rain.
When suffocating mists obscure the morn,
Let thy worst wig, long us'd to storms, be worn;
This knows the powder'd footman, and with care,
Beneath his flapping hat secures his hair.
Be thou, for every season, justly drest,
Nor brave the piercing frost with open breast;
And when the bursting clouds a deluge pour,
Let thy surtout defend the drenching show'r.

The changing weather certain signs reveal,
Ere winter sheds her snow, or frosts congeal.
You'll see the coals in brighter flame aspire,
And sulphur tinge with blue the rising fire:
Your tender shins the scorching heat decline,
And at the dearth of coals the poor repine;
Before her kitchen hearth, the nodding dame
In flannel mantle wrapt, enjoys the flame;
Hov'ring, upon her feeble knees she bends,
And all around the grateful warmth ascends.
Nor do less certain signs the town advise,
Of milder weather and serener skies.
The ladies gaily dress'd, the Mall adorn
With various dyes, and paint the sunny morn;

The wanton fawns with frisking pleasure range,
And chirping sparrows greet the welcome change:
Not that their minds with greater skill are fraught,
Endu'd by instinct, or by reason taught,
The seasons operate on ev'ry breast,
'Tis hence that fawns are brisk, and ladies drest.
When on his box the nodding coachman snores,
And dreams of fancy'd fares; when tavern-doors
The chairmen idly crowd; then ne'er refuse
To trust thy busy steps in thinner shoes.

But when the swinging signs your ears offend
With creaking noise, then rainy floods impend;
Soon shall the kennels swell with rapid streams,
And rush in muddy torrents to the Thames.
The bookseller, whose shop's an open square,
Foresees the tempest, and with early care
Of learning strips the rails; the rowing crew
To tempt a fare, clothe all their tilts in blue:
On hosiers' poles depending stockings tied,
Flag with the slacken'd gale from side to side;
Church-monuments foretell the changing air;
Then Niobe dissolves into a tear,
And sweats with sacred grief: you'll hear the sounds
Of whistling winds, ere kennels break their bounds;
Ungrateful odours common-sewers diffuse,
And dropping vaults distil unwholesome dews,
Ere the tiles rattle with the smoking show'r,
And spouts on heedless men their torrents pour.

All superstition from thy breast repel.
Let cred'lous boys, and prattling nurses tell,

How, if the festival of Paul be clear,
Plenty from lib'ral horn shall strow the year;
When the dark skies dissolve in snow or rain,
The lab'ring hind shall yoke the steer in vain;
But if the threat'ning winds in tempests roar,
Then war shall bathe her wasteful sword in gore.
How, if on Swithin's feast the welkin low'rs,
And ev'ry penthouse streams with hasty show'rs,
Twice twenty days shall clouds their fleeces drain,
And wash the pavements with incessant rain.
Let not such vulgar tales debase thy mind;
Nor Paul nor Swithin rule the clouds and wind.

If you the precepts of the Muse despise,
And slight the faithful warning of the skies,
Others you'll see, when all the town's afloat,
Wrapt in th' embraces of a kersey coat,
Or double-bottom'd frieze; their guarded feet
Defy the muddy dangers of the street,
While you with hat unloop'd, the fury dread
Of spouts high streaming, and with cautious tread
Shun ev'ry dashing pool, or idly stop,
To seek the kind protection of a shop.
But bus'ness summons; now with hasty scud
You jostle for the wall; the spatter'd mud
Hides all thy hose behind; in vain you scour,
Thy wig, alas! uncurl'd, admits the show'r.
So fierce Alecto's snaky tresses fell,
When Orpheus charm'd the rig'rous powers of hell,
Or thus hung Glaucus' beard, with briny dew
Clotted and straight, when first his am'rous view
Surpris'd the bathing fair; the frighted maid
Now stands a rock, transform'd by Circe's aid.

Good housewives all the winter's rage despise,
Defended by the riding-hood's disguise :
Or underneath th' umbrella's oily shed,
Safe thro' the wet on clinking pattens tread.
Let Persian dames th' umbrella's ribs display,
To guard their beauties from the sunny ray ;
Or sweating slaves support the shady load,
When eastern Monarchs show their state abroad.
Britain in winter only knows its aid,
To guard from chilly show'rs the walking maid.

John Gay : Trivia.

A Winter Song

1600

AUTUMN hath all the summer's fruitful treasure ;
    Gone is our sport, fled is our Croyden's pleasure !
Short days, sharp days, long nights come on apace :
Ah, who shall hide us from the winter's face ?
Cold doth increase, the sickness will not cease,
And here we lie, God knows, with little ease.
From winter, plague, and pestilence, good Lord, deliver us !

London doth mourn, Lambeth is quite forlorn !
Trades cry, woe worth that ever they were born !
The want of term is town and city's harm ;
Close chambers we do want to keep us warm.
Long banishèd must we live from our friends :
This low-built house will bring us to our ends.
From winter, plague, and pestilence, good Lord, deliver us !

Thomas Nashe : Summer's Last Will
and Testament.

Morning in London

1709

NOW hardly here and there a hackney-coach
   Appearing, show'd the ruddy morn's approach,
Now Betty from her master's bed had flown,
And softly crept to discompose her own;
The slip-shod 'prentice from his master's door
Had pared the dirt, and sprinkled round the floor;
Now Moll had whirl'd her mop with dext'rous airs,
Prepared to scrub the entry and the stairs.
The youth with broomy stumps began to trace
The kennel's edge, where wheels had worn the place.
The small-coal man was heard with cadence deep,
Till drown'd in shriller notes of chimney-sweep:
Duns at his lordship's gate began to meet;
And brick-dust Moll had scream'd through half the street.
The turnkey now his flock returning sees,
Duly let out a-nights to steal for fees:
The watchful bailiffs take their silent stands,
And school-boys lag with satchels in their hands.

Jonathan Swift : Collected Poems.

A London Fog

1822

FIRST, at the dawn of lingering day,
   It rises, of an ashy grey;
Then deepening with a sordid stain
Of yellow, like a lion's mane,

Vapour importunate and dense,
It wars at once with every sense ;
Invades the eyes, is tasted, smelt,
And, like Egyptian darkness, felt.
The ears escape not.   All around
Returns a dull unwonted sound.
Loath to stand still, afraid to stir,
The chilled and puzzled passenger,
Oft blundering from the pavement fails
To feel his way along the rails,
Or at the crossings, in the roll
Of every carriage dreads the pole.

.　　　.　　　.　　　.

Scarce an eclipse with pall so dun
Blots from the face of heaven the sun.
But soon a thicker, darker cloak
Wraps all the town.   Behold, the smoke,
Which steam-compelling trade disgorges
From all her furnaces and forges
In pitchy clouds, too dense to rise,
Descends rejected from the skies ;
Till struggling day, extinguished quite,
At noon gives place to candle-light.

Oh, Chemistry, attractive maid,
Descend, in pity, to our aid !
Come with thy all-pervading gases,
Thy crucibles, retorts, and glasses,
Thy fearful energies and wonders,
Thy dazzling lights and mimic thunders ;
Let Carbon in thy train be seen,
Dark Azote and fair Oxygene,

And Wollaston and Davy guide
The car that bears thee at thy side,
If any power can, anyhow,
Abate these nuisances, 'tis thou ;
And see, to aid thee in the blow,
The bill of Michael Angelo,
O join (success a thing of course is)
Thy heavenly to his mortal forces ;
Make all chimneys chew the cud
Like hungry cows, as chimneys should !

Henry Luttrell: Letters to Julia.

In the Rain

1895

RAIN in the glimmering street—
  Murmurous, rhythmical beat ;
Shadows that flicker and fly ;
Blue of wet road, of wet sky,
(Grey in the depths and the heights) ;
Orange of numberless lights,
Shapes fleeting on, going by.

Figures, fantastical, grim—
Figures, prosaical, tame,
Each with chameleon-stain,
Dun in the crepuscle dim,
Red in the nimbus of flame—
Glance through the veil of the rain.

Rain in the measureless street—
Vistas of orange and blue ;
Music of echoing feet,
Pausing, and pacing anew.

Rain, and the clamour of wheels,
Splendour, and shadow, and sound ;
Coloured confusion that reels
Lost in the twilight around.

  .   .   .   .   .

When I lie hid from the light,
Stark, with the turf overhead,
Still, on a rainy Spring night,
I shall come back from the dead.

Turn then and look for me here
Stealing the shadows along ;
Look for me—I shall be near,
Deep in the heart of the throng :

Here, where the current runs rife,
Careless, and doleful, and gay,
Moving, and motley, and strong,
Good in its sport, in its strife.

  .   .   .   .   .

Ah, might I be—might I stay—
Only for ever and aye,
Living and looking on life !

Rosamond Marriott Watson : A Summer Night.

To a London Sparrow

1883

AT dawn thy voice is loud—a merry voice
    When other sounds are few and faint.   Before
The muffled thunders of the Underground
Begin to shake the houses, and the noise
Of eastward traffic fills the thoroughfares,
Thy voice then welcomes day.   Oh, what a day !—
How foul and haggard-faced !   See, where she comes
In garments of the chill discoloured mists
Stealing unto the west with noiseless foot
Through dim forsaken streets.   Is she not like,
As sister is to sister, unto her
Whose stainèd cheeks the nightly rains have wet
And made them grey and seamed and desolate,
Beneath the arches of the bitter bridge ?
And thou, O Sparrow, from the windy ledge
Where thou dost nestle—creaking chimney-pots
For softly-sighing branches ; sooty slates
For leafy canopy ; rank steam of slums
For flowery fragrance ; and for star-lit woods
This waste that frights, a desert desolate
Of fabrics gaunt and grim and smoke-begrimed,
By goblin misery haunted ; scowling towers
Of cloud and stone, gigantic tenements
And castles of despair, by spectral gleams
Of fitful lamps illumined ;—from such place
Canst thou, O Sparrow, welcome day so foul ?
Ay, not more blithe of heart in forests dim
The golden-throated thrush awakes what time

The leaves atremble whisper to the breath,
The flowery breath, of morning azure-eyed !

Never a morning comes but I do bless thee,
Thou brave and faithful Sparrow, living link
That binds us to the immemorial past ;
O blithe heart in a house so melancholy,
And keeper for a thousand gloomy years
Of many a gay tradition ; heritor
Of Nature's ancient cheerfulness, for thee
'Tis ever Merry England !   Never yet
In thy companionship of centuries
With man in lurid London didst regret
Thy valiant choice ;—yea, even from the time
When all its low-roofed rooms were sweet with scents
From summer fields, where shouting children plucked
The floating lily from the reedy Fleet,
Scaring away the timid water-hen.

W. H. Hudson : Merry England.

The Common Cries of London

17th Century

MY masters all, attend you,
    If mirth you love to hear,
And I will tell you what they cry
    In London all the year.
I'll please you if I can ;
    I will not be too long :
I pray you all attend awhile
    And listen to my song.

The fish-wife first begins :
    Any mussels lily white !
Herrings, sprats, or plaice,
    Or cockles for delight.
Any welflet oysters !
    Then she doth change her note :
She had need to have her tongue be greas'd
    For she rattles in the throat.

    ·   ·   ·   ·   ·

Mark but the waterman
    Attending for his fare,
Of hot and cold, of wet and dry,
    He always takes his share :
He carrieth bonnie lasses
    Over to the plays,
And here and there he gets a bit
    And that his stomach stays.

    ·   ·   ·   ·

Ripe, cherry ripe !
    The costermonger cries ;
Pippins fine or pears !
    Another after hies,
With basket on his head
    His living to advance,
And in his purse a pair of dice
    For to play at mumchance.

Hot pippin pies !
    To sell unto my friends,
Or pudding pies in pans,
    Well stuft with candle ends.

Will you buy any milk?
  I heard a wench that cries:
With a pail of fresh cheese and cream,
  Another after hies.

Oh! the wench went neatly;
  Methought it did me good,
To see her cherry cheeks
  So dimpled o'er with blood:
Her waistcoat washed white
  As any lily flower;
Would I had time to talk with her
  The space of half-an-hour.

Anon.: Roxburghe Ballads.

The Same

19th Century

JUST fresh from the market my cresses are,
  Come buy, come buy of me,
My fine brown water-cresses,
For breakfast or for tea.

Here's your sweet lavender,
Sixteen sprigs a penny,
Which you will find my ladies,
Will smell as sweet as any.

Here's 'taters hot, my little chap,
Now just lay out a copper,
I'm known all up and down the Strand,
You'll not find any hotter.

Here's two-a-penny oranges
The real St. Michael sort,
They are the sweetest oranges,
Ladies, you ever bought.

Any old pots or kettles,
Or any old brass to mend ;
Come my pretty maids all,
To me your aid must lend.

Here's door mats of every sort,
Just look into my store,
Here's one for the parlour, and one for the kitchen,
And one for the back-door.

This man from Covent Garden comes
With his green wares early,
Singing out Carrots and Turnips oh !
Making a hurly-burly.

Have you got any old knives to grind ?
And scissors I grind too ;
Bring them out, my pretty dears,
I'll make them look like new.

Strawberries gather'd on a fine morning,
Dear ladies only see,
And only sixpence for a pottle,
Come buy, come buy of me.

Hearthstones, my pretty,
I sell them four a penny ;
Hearthstones come buy,
As long as I have any.

Here's brooms and brushes of every kind,
For cleaning of the floor,
You can't find better anywhere,
So pick one from my store.

Muffins oh! crumpets oh!
Come buy, come buy of me;
Muffins and crumpets, muffins
For breakfast or for tea.

Sprats alive, oh! sprats alive,
Just up from Billingsgate;
Come buy some sprats of me, my dear,
For yourself, or for your mate.

Bonnet-boxes, and cap-boxes,
The best that e'er was seen,
They are so very nicely made,
They'll keep your things so clean.

This man you'll know from all the rest,
Because he cries old clothes,
And you will know that he's a Jew,
By looking at his nose.

Now ladies, here's roots for your gardens,
Come buy some of me, if you please;
Here's tulips, hearts-ease, and roses,
Sweet Williams and sweet peas.

Dust or ash this chap calls out,
With all his might and main,
He's got a mighty cinder heap,
Somewhere near Gray's Inn Lane.

Any old chairs to men'?
Any old chairs to seat?
I'll make them quite as good as new,
And make them look so neat.

With heart so light, and cans so bright
This man comes from the dairy,
Milk, my pretty maids, below,
Come, get your jugs, do, Mary.

Here's cherries oh! my pretty,
My cherries round and sound,
Whitehearts, Kentish, or Blackhearts,
And only two-pence a pound.

Here I am with my rabbits,
Hanging on my pole,
The finest Hampshire rabbits,
That e'er crept from a hole.

This young man goes tripping along,
And his eyes they twinkle, twinkle,
As he cries, Come, dears, and buy
My shrimps and perry winkle winkle.

This man looks so very fine,
And with his barrow neat,
Calls at all old ladies' doors
To leave his cats' and dogs' meat.

Sweep, soot oh! sweep,
This little boy does cry;
Early each morn he is sent out
Whether it's wet or dry.

Anon. : The Cries of London.

I

The Mermaid

About 1610

WHAT things have we seen
    Done at the Mermaid ! heard words that have been
So nimble, and so full of subtile flame,
As if that every one from whence they came
Had meant to put his whole wit in a jest,
And had resolved to live a fool the rest
Of his dull life ; then when there hath been thrown
Wit able enough to justify the town
For three days past ; wit that might warrant be
For the whole city to talk foolishly
Till that were cancell'd ; and when that was gone,
We left an air behind us, which alone
Was able to make the two next companies
Right witty ; though but downright fools, more wise.
       Francis Beaumont : Letter to Ben Jonson.

The Mermaid Tavern

1818

SOULS of Poets dead and gone,
    What Elysium have ye known,
Happy field or mossy cavern,
Choicer than the Mermaid Tavern ?
Have ye tippled drink more fine
Than mine host's Canary wine ?
Or are fruits of Paradise
Sweeter than those dainty pies

Of venison?   O generous food!
Drest as though bold Robin Hood
Would, with his maid Marian,
Sup and bowse from horn and can.

I have heard that on a day
Mine host's sign-board flew away,
Nobody knew whither, till
An astrologer's old quill
To a sheep-skin gave the story,—
Said he saw you in your glory,
Underneath a new old-sign
Sipping beverage divine,
And pledging with contented smack
The Mermaid in the Zodiac.

Souls of Poets dead and gone,
What Elysium have ye known,
Happy field or mossy cavern,
Choicer than the Mermaid Tavern?
John Keats: Collected Poems.

Verses

PLACED OVER THE DOOR AT THE ENTRANCE INTO THE
APOLLO ROOM AT THE DEVIL TAVERN

1624

WELCOME all who lead or follow,
  To the Oracle of Apollo—
Here he speaks out of his pottle,
Or the tripos, his tower bottle:

All his answers are divine,
Truth itself doth flow in wine.
Hang up all the poor hop-drinkers,
Cries old Sim, the king of skinkers;
He the half of life abuses,
That sits watering with the Muses.
Those dull girls no good can mean us;
Wine it is the milk of Venus,
And the poet's horse accounted:
Ply it, and you all are mounted.
'Tis the true Phœbian liquor,
Cheers the brain, makes wit the quicker,
Pays all debts, cures all diseases,
And at once three senses pleases.
Welcome all who lead or follow,
To the Oracle of Apollo.

Ben Jonson: Collected Poems.

An Ode to Ben Jonson

1625

AH Ben!
    Say how or when
Shall we thy guests,
Meet at those lyric feasts,
    Made at the Sun,
The Dog, the Triple Tun?
Where we such clusters had,
As made us nobly wild, not mad;
    And yet each verse of thine
Out-did the meat, out-did the frolic wine.

My Ben!
Or come again
Or send to us
Thy wit's great overplus;
But teach us yet
Wisely to husband it,
Lest we that talent spend;
And having once brought to an end
That precious stock,—the store
Of such a wit the world should have no more.

Robert Herrick: Hesperides.

The Coffee-House

1675

YOU that delight in wit and mirth,
    And love to hear such news
As comes from all parts of the earth,
    Dutch, Danes, and Turks, and Jews;
I'll send ye to a rendezvous,
    Where it is smoking new;
Go hear it at a Coffee-house,
    It cannot but be true.

There battles and sea-fights are fought,
    And bloody plots display'd;
They know more things than e'er was thought,
    Or ever was betray'd:
No money in the Minting-house,
    Is half so bright and new;
And coming from a Coffee-house,
    It cannot but be true.

Before the navies fell to work,
    They knew who should be winner;
They there can tell ye what the Turk
    Last Sunday had to dinner.
Who last did cut De Ruyter's corns,
    Amongst his jovial crew;
Or who first gave the devil horns,
    Which cannot but be true.

A fisherman did boldly tell,
    And strongly did avouch,
He caught a shoal of mackerel,
    They parley'd all in Dutch;
And cry'd out *Yaw, yaw, yaw, mine hare*,
    And as the draught they drew,
They shook for fear that Monk was there:
    This sounds as if 'twere true.

There's nothing done in all the world,
    From monarch to the mouse,
But every day or night 'tis hurl'd
    Into the Coffee-house:
What Lilly or what Booker could
    By art not bring about,
At Coffee-house you'll find a brood,
    Can quickly find it out.

.   .   .   .

They know all that is good or hurt,
    To damn ye or to save ye;
There is the college and the court,
    The country, camp, and navy.

So great an university,
   I think there ne'er was any,
In which you may a scholar be,
   For spending of a penny.

Here men do talk of everything,
   With large and liberal lungs,
Like women at a gossiping,
   With double tire of tongues;
They'll give a broadside presently,
   'Soon as you are in view,
With stories that you'll wonder at,
   Which they will swear are true.

You shall know there what fashions are,
   How perriwigs are curl'd;
And for a penny you shall hear
   All novels in the world;
Both old and young, and great and small,
   And rich and poor you'll see;
Therefore let's to the coffee all,
   Come all away with me.
          Thomas Jordan : Triumphs of London.

The Wits' Coffee-House

1687

AS I remember, said the sober Mouse,
   I've heard much talk of the Wits' Coffee-house.
Thither, says Brindle, thou shalt go and see
Priests sipping coffee, sparks and poets tea;

Here rugged frieze, there quality well drest,
These baffling the grand Seignior ; those the Test,
And hear shrew'd guesses made, and reasons given,
That humane laws were never made in Heaven.
But above all, what shall oblige thy sight,
And fill thy eye-balls with a vast delight,
Is the poetic judge of sacred wit,
Who do's i' th' darkness of his glory sit ;
And as the Moon who first receives the light,
With which she makes these nether regions bright ;
So does he shine, reflecting from afar,
The rays he borrow'd from a better star :
For rules which from Corneille and Rapin flow,
Admir'd by all the scribbling herd below.
From French tradition while he does dispense
Unerring truths, 'tis schism, a damm'd offence,
To question his, or trust your private sense.
        Prior and Montagu : The Hind and Panther Reversed.

The Farmer's Return from London

1762

Enter WIFE [*hastily*].

WHERE are you my children ?—Why Sally, Dick,
        Ralph ?

Enter CHILDREN *running*.

Your father is come !—Heaven bless him ! and safe.

Enter FARMER.

O Jahn ! my heart dances with joy thou art come.

FARMER.

And troth so does mine, for I love thee and whoam.

[Kisses.]

WIFE.

Now kiss all your children—and now me agen.

[Kisses.]

O bless thy sweet feace !—for one kiss, gi' me ten !

FARMER.

Keep some for anon, Dame—you quoite stop my breath :
You kill me wi' koindness—you buss me to death :
Enough, Love !—enough is as good as a feeast :
Let's ha' some refreshment for me and my beeast.
Dick, get me a poipe. [Exit D.] Ralph, go to the mare ;
Gi' poor wench some oaats. [Exit R.] Dame, reach me a
        chair !
Sal, draw me some aal to wash the dirt down. [Exit Sal.]

.   .   .   .   .

WIFE.

But London, dear Jahn !

FARMER.

Is a fine hugeous City !
Where the geese are all swans, and the fools are all witty.

WIFE.

Did you see ony Wits ?

FARMER.

I looked up and down,
But 'twas labour in vain—they were all out of town.

I ask'd for the maakers o' news, and such things !
Who know all the secrets of kingdoms, and kings !
So busy were they, and such matters about,
That six days in the seven they never stir out.
Koind souls ! with our freedom they maake such a fuss,
That they lose it themselves to bestow it on us,

WIFE.

But was't thou at Court, Jahn?   What there hast thou seen?

FARMER.

I saw 'em—Heav'n bless 'em !—you know whom I mean.
I heard their healths pray'd for—agen and agen,
With provoiso that one may be sick now and then.
Some looks speak their hearts, as it were with a tongue—
O Dame !—I'll be damn'd, if they e'er do us wrong ;
Here's to 'em—bless 'em boath—do you take the jug ;
Woud't do their hearts good—I'd swallow the mug.
[Drinks.]
Come, pledge me, my boy. [To DICK.]—Hold, lad, hast
    nothing to say ?

DICK.

Here, Daddy,—Here's to 'em !   [Drinks.]

FARMER.

Well said, Dick, boy !

DICK.

Huzza !

WIFE.

What more did'st thou see, to beget admiraation ?

FARMER.

The City's fine show,—but first the crownation !
'Twas tho' all the world had been there with their spouses ;
There's was street within street, and houses on houses !
I thought from above (when the folk fill'd the pleaces),
The streets pav'd with heads, and the walls made of feaces !
Such justling and bustling !—'twas worth all the pother.
—I hope, from my soul, I shall ne'er see another.

SAL.

Dad, what did you see at the pleays, and the shows ?

FARMER.

What did I see at the pleays and the shows ?
Why bouncing and grinning, and a pow'r of fine cloaths :
From top to the bottom 'twas all 'chanted ground !
Gold, painting, and music, and blaazing all round !
Above 'twas like Bedlam, all roaring and rattling !
Below, the fine folk were all curts'ying and prattling :
Strange jumble together—Turks, Christians, and Jews !
—At the Temple of Folly, all crowd to the pews.
Here too doizen'd out, were those same freakish ladies,
Who keep open market,—tho' smuggling their trade is.
I saw a new pleay too—they call'd it *The School*—
I thought it pure stuff—but I thought like a fool—
'Twas *The School of*—pize on it !—my mem'ry is naught—
The greaat ones dislik'd it—they heate to be taught :
The cratticks too grumbled—I'll tell you for whoy,
They wanted to laugh—and were ready to croy.

WIFE.

Pray what are your *cratticks ?*

FARMER.

Like watchmen in town,
Lame, feeble, half-blind, yet they knock poets down.
Like old Justice Wormwood,—a crattick's a man
That can't sin himself,—and he heates those that can.
I ne'er went to Opras!—I thought it too grand,
For poor folk to like what they don't understand.
The top joke of all, and what pleas'd me the moast,
Some wise ones and I sat up with a Ghoast.

WIFE AND CHILDREN.

A Ghoast! [*Starting.*]

FARMER.

Yes, a Ghoast!

WIFE.

I shall swoond away, Love!

FARMER.

Odzooks!—thou'rt as bad as thy betters above!
With her nails, and her knuckles, she answer'd so noice!
For *Yes* she knock'd once, and for *No* she knock'd twoice.

.   .   .   .   .   .

They may talk of the country, but, I say, in town,
Their throats are much woider, to swallow things down.
I'll uphold, in a week,—by my troth I don't joke—
That our little Sal—shall fright all the town folk—
Come, get me some supper—but first let me peep
At the rest of my children—my calves, and my sheep.
                                        [*Going.*]

WIFE.

Ah! Jahn!

David Garrick: The Farmer's Return.

In the Temple

1892

THE grey and misty night,
   Slim trees that hold the night among
  Their branches, and, along
The vague Embankment, light on light.

The sudden, racing lights !
   I can just hear, distinct, aloof,
  The gaily chattering hoof
Beating the rhythm of festive nights.

The gardens to the weeping moon
   Sigh back the breath of tears.
   O the refrain of years on years
'Neath the weeping moon !

Arthur Symons : Silhouettes.

The Red Rose and White

About 1590

SUFFOLK. Within the Temple Hall we were too loud :
  The garden here is more convenient.

      .   .   .

Plantagenet. Let him that is a true-born gentleman
And stands upon the honour of his birth,
If he suppose that I have pleaded truth,
From off this brier pluck a white rose with me.
Somerset. Let him that is no coward nor no flatterer,
But dare maintain the party of the truth,

Pluck a red rose from off this thorn with me.

.   .   .

Plantagenet. Hath not thy rose a canker, Somerset ?
Somerset. Hath not thy rose a thorn, Plantagenet ?

.   .   .

Warwick. . . . Here I prophesy : this brawl to-day,
Grown to this faction in the Temple Garden,
Shall send between the red rose and the white
A thousand souls to death and deadly night.

Shakespeare : 1 *Henry VI.*

Holborn

About 1594

*G*LOUCESTER. My Lord of Ely !
  Ely. My lord?
  Gloucester.   When I was last in Holborn,
I saw good strawberries in your garden there :
I do beseech you send for some of them.
  Ely. Marry, and will, my lord, with all my heart.

Shakespeare : King Richard III.

My Lodging is in Leather Lane

1810

MY lodging is in Leather Lane
    A parlour that's next to the sky ;
'Tis exposed to the wind and the rain,
    But the wind and the rain I defy :
Such love warms the coldest of spots,
    As I feel for Scrubinda the fair ;

Oh, she lives by the scouring of pots,
   In Dyot Street, Bloomsbury Square.

Oh, were I a quart, pint, or gill,
   To be scrubb'd by her delicate hands,
Let others possess what they will
   Of learning, and houses, and lands ;
My parlour that's next to the sky
   I'd quit, her blest mansion to share ;
So happy to live and to die
   In Dyot Street, Bloomsbury Square.

And oh, would this damsel be mine,
   No other provision I'd seek ;
On a look I could breakfast and dine,
   And feast on a smile for a week.
But ah ! should she false-hearted prove,
   Suspended, I'll dangle in air ;
A victim to delicate love
   In Dyot Street, Bloomsbury Square.

     William Barnes Rhodes : Bombastes Furioso.

Street Companions

1847

WHENE'ER through Gray's Inn porch I stray,
   I meet a spirit by the way ;
He wanders with me all alone,
And talks with me in undertone.

The crowd is busy seeking gold,
It cannot see what I behold ;
I and the spirit pass along
Unknown, unnoticed, in the throng.

While on the grass the children run,
And maids go loitering in the sun,
I roam beneath the ancient trees,
And talk with him of mysteries.

The dull brick houses of the square,
The bustle of the thoroughfare,
The sounds, the sights, the crush of men,
Are present, but forgotten then.

I see them, but I heed them not,
I hear, but silence clothes the spot ;
All voices die upon my brain
Except that spirit's in the lane.

He breathes to me his burning thought,
He utters words with wisdom fraught,
He tells me truly what I am—
I walk with mighty Verulam.

He goes with me through crowded ways,
A friend and mentor in the maze,
Through Chancery Lane to Lincoln's Inn,
To Fleet Street, through the moil and din.

I meet another spirit there,
A blind old man with forehead fair,
Who ever walks the right hand side
Toward the fountain of St. Bride.

Amid the peal of jangling bells,
Or people's roar that falls and swells,
The whir of wheels and tramp of steeds,
He talked to me of noble deeds.

I hear his voice above the crush,
As to and fro the people rush ;
Benign and calm, upon his face
Sits melancholy, robed in grace.

He hath no need of common eyes,
He sees the fields of Paradise ;
He sees and pictures unto mine
A gorgeous vision, most divine.

He tells the story of the Fall,
He names the fiends in battle-call,
And shows my soul, in wonder dumb,
Heaven, Earth, and Pandemonium.

He tells of Lycidas the good,
And the sweet lady in the wood,
And teaches wisdom, high and holy,
In mirth and heavenly melancholy.

And oftentimes, with courage high,
He raises Freedom's rallying cry ;
And, ancient leader of the van,
Asserts the dignity of man—

Asserts the rights with trumpet tongue
That Justice from Oppression wrung,
And poet, patriot, statesman, sage,
Guides by his own a future age.

With such companions at my side
I float on London's human tide;
An atom on its billows thrown,
But lonely never, nor alone.

Charles Mackay: Town Lyrics.

Clever Tom Clinch

GOING TO BE HANGED

1727

AS clever Tom Clinch, while the rabble was bawling,
  Rode stately through Holborn to die in his calling,
He stopt at the George for a bottle of sack,
And promised to pay for it when he came back.
His waistcoat, and stockings, and breeches, were white,
His cap had a new cherry ribbon to tie't.
The maids to the doors and the balconies ran,
And said, "Lack-a-day, he's a proper young man!"
But as from the windows the ladies he spied,
Like a beau in the box, he bow'd low on each side!
And when his last speech the loud hawkers did cry,
He swore from his cart, "It was all a damn'd lie!"
The hangman for pardon fell down on his knee;
Tom gave him a kick in the guts for his fee:
Then said, "I must speak to the people a little;
But I'll see you all damn'd before I will whittle.
My honest friend Wild (may he long hold his place)
He lengthen'd my life with a whole year of grace:
Take courage, dear comrades, and be not afraid,
Nor slip this occasion to follow your trade;

My conscience is clear, and my spirits are calm,
And thus I go off, without prayer-book or psalm;
Then follow the practice of clever Tom Clinch,
Who hung like a hero, and never would flinch.

Jonathan Swift : Collected Poems.

A Chamber in Grub Street

1758

WHERE the Red Lion, staring o'er the way,
    Invites each passing stranger that can pay;
Where Calvert's butt and Parson's black champagne
Regale the drabs and bloods of Drury Lane;
There in a lonely room, from bailiffs snug,
The Muse found Scroggen stretched beneath a rug;
A window, patched with paper, lent a ray
That dimly showed the state in which he lay;
The sanded floor, that grits beneath the tread;
The humid wall with paltry pictures spread;
The royal game of goose was there in view,
And the twelve rules the Royal Martyr drew;
The *Seasons*, framed with listing, found a place,
And brave Prince William show'd his lamp-black face;
The morn was cold; he views with keen desire
The rusty grate unconscious of a fire:
With beer and milk arrears the frieze was scor'd,
And five crack'd teacups dress'd the chimney-board;
A nightcap deck'd his brows instead of bay,
A cap by night—a stocking all the day!

Oliver Goldsmith : Collected Poems.

Time Was!

1772

TIME was, when satin waistcoats and scratch wigs,
    Enough distinguish'd all the City prigs,
Whilst every sunshine Sunday saw them run
To club their sixpences, at Islington;
When graver citizens, in suits of brown,
Lin'd ev'ry dusty avenue to town,
Or led the children and the loving spouse,
To spend two shillings at White-Conduit House:
But now, the 'prentices, in suits of green,
At Richmond or at Windsor may be seen;
Where in mad parties they run down to dine,
To play at gentlefolks, and drink bad wine:
Whilst neat post-chariots roll their masters down
To some snug box, a dozen miles from town.

.   .   .   .   .

Time was, when tradesmen laid up what they gain'd,
And frugally a family maintain'd;
When they took stirring housewives for their spouses,
To keep up prudent order in their houses;
Who thought no scorn at night to sit them down,
And make their children's clothes, or mend their own;
Would Polly's coat to younger Bess transfer,
And make their caps without a milliner:
But now, a-shopping half the day they're gone,
To buy five hundred things, and pay for none;
While Miss despises all domestic rules,
But lisps the French of Hackney boarding-schools;

And ev'ry lane around Whitechapel Bars
Resounds with screaming notes, and harsh guitars.

Time was, too, when the prudent dames would stay
Till Christmas holidays to see a play,
And met at cards, at that glad time alone,
In friendly sets of loo or cheap pope-Joan;
Now, ev'ry lady writes her invitations
For weekly routs, to all her wise relations:
And ev'ry morning teems with fresh delights;
They run the City over, seeing sights;
Then hurry to the play as night approaches,
And spend their precious time in hackney-coaches.

Hence spring assemblies with such uncouth names,
As Deptford, Wapping, Rotherhithe, and Shad-Thames,
Where ev'ry month the powder'd white-glov'd sparks,
Spruce haberdashers, pert attorneys' clerks,
With deep-enamour'd 'prentices prefer
Their suit to many a sighing milliner:
In scraps of plays their passions they impart,
With all the awkward bows they learn from Hart.
'Tis here they learn their genius to improve,
And throw by *Wingate* for the *Art of Love;*
They frame th' acrostic deep and rebus terse,
And fill the day-book with enamour'd verse;
Ev'n learned Fenning on his vacant leaves,
The ill-according epigram receives,
And Cocker's margin hobbling sonnets grace
To Delia, measuring out a yard of lace.

'Tis true, my friend; and thus throughout the nation
Prevails this general love of dissipation:

It matters little where their sports begin,
Whether at Arthur's, or the Bowl and Pin;
Whether they tread the gay Pantheon's round,
Or play at skittles at St. Giles's pound,
The self-same idle spirit drags them on,
And peer and porter are alike undone:
Whilst thoughtless imitation leads the way,
And laughs at all the grave or wise can say.

Charles Jenner: Town Eclogues.

Consolation

1895

AS I walked through London,
     The fresh wound burning in my breast,
As I walked through London,
Longing to have forgotten, to harden my heart, and to rest,
A sudden consolation, a softening light
Touched me: the streets alive and bright,
With hundreds each way thronging, on their tide
Received me, a drop in the stream, unmarked, unknown.
And to my heart I cried:
Here can thy trouble find shelter, thy wound be eased!
For see, not thou alone,
But thousands, each with his smart,
Deep-hidden, perchance, but felt in the core of the heart!
And as to a sick man's feverish veins
The full sponge warmly pressed,
Relieves with its burning the burning of forehead and hands,
So I, to my aching breast

Gathered the griefs of those thousands, and made them my
    own ;
My bitterest pains
Merged in a tenderer sorrow, assuaged and appeased.
Laurence Binyon: Lyric Poems.

The Streets by Night

1896

COME let us forth, and wander the rich, the murmuring
    night !
The shy, blue dusk of summer trembles above the street ;
On either side uprising glimmer houses pale :
But me the turbulent babble and voice of crowds delight ;
For me the wheels make music, the mingled cries are sweet ;
Motion and laughter call : we hear, we will not fail.

For see, in secret vista, with soft, retiring stars,
With clustered suns, that stare upon the throngs below,
With pendent dazzling moons, that cast a noonday white,
The full streets beckon : Come, for toil has burst his bars,
And idle eyes rejoice, and feet unhasting go.
O let us out and wander the gay and golden night.
Laurence Binyon: London Visions, First Series.

In the Train

1892

THE train through the night of the town,
    Through a blackness broken in twain
    By the sudden finger of streets ;

Lights, red, yellow, and brown,
From curtain and window-pane,
The flashing eyes of the streets.

Night, and the rush of the train,
A cloud of smoke through the town,
Scaring the life of the streets;
And the leap of the heart again,
Out into the night, and down
The dazzling vista of streets!

Arthur Symons: Silhouettes.

The Midnight Pomp of London's Artillery

1616

WHAT mighty musters, and what brave arrays,
Of martial shows, in use to keep our arms,
Hast thou—O London !—made against all harms?

.   .   .   .   .

When Mars did seem in triumph down descending,
To stoop from heaven upon thee, and commending
Thy then triumphant march and martial sport,
Decked in his richest coat of steel, did court
Peace in thy streets, conducting through the same
A warlike troop, that, by that yearly game,
The noise of arms (made common to thy ears)
Might at no time disturb thee with vain fears;
When drums' and trumpets' sounds, which do delight
A cheerful heart, waking the drowsy night,

Did fright the wandering Moon, who from her sphere,
Beholding Earth beneath, looked pale with fear,
To see the air appearing all on flame,
Kindled by thy bon-fires, and from the same
A thousand sparks dispersed throughout the sky,
Which like to wand'ring stars about did fly ;
Whose wholesome heat, purging the air, consumes
The Earth's unwholesome vapours, fogs, and fumes.
The wakeful shepherd, laid by his flock in field,
With wonder at that time far off beheld
The wanton shine of thy triumphant fires
Playing upon the tops of thy tall spires.

Thy goodly buildings, that till then did hide
Their rich array, open'd their windows wide,
Where Kings, great peers, and many a noble dame,
Whose bright pearl-glittering robes did mock the flame
Of the Night's burning lights, did sit to see,
How every Senator in his degree,
Adorn'd with shining gold and purple weeds,
And stately-mounted on rich-trapp'd steeds,
Their guard attending, through the streets did ride.

   .   .   .   .   .

While in the streets the stickelers to and fro,
To keep decorum, still did come and go ;
When tables set were plentifully spread,
And at each door neighbour with neighbour fed ;
Where modest mirth, attendant at the feast,
With plenty, gave content to every guest ;
Where true good-will crown'd cups with fruitful wine,
And neighbours in true love did fast combine ;
Where the Law's pick-purse, strife 'twixt friend and friend,
By reconcilement happily took end :

A happy time !—when men knew how to use
The gifts of happy peace, yet not abuse
Their quiet rest with rust of ease, so far
As to forget all discipline of War !

Richard Nicolls : London's Artillery.

War

1842

.   .   .   .   .

THE sentinel on Whitehall gate
   Looked forth into the night,
And saw, o'erhanging Richmond Hill
The streak of blood-red light.
The bugle's note and cannon's roar
The deathlike silence broke,
And with one start, and with one cry,
The royal city woke.
At once on all her stately gates
Arose the answering fires ;
At once the wild alarum clashed
From all her reeling spires ;
From all the batteries of the Tower
Pealed forth the voice of fear ;
And all the thousand masts of Thames
Sent back a louder cheer :
And from the furthest wards was heard
The rush of hurrying feet,
And the broad stream of pikes and flags,
Rushed down each roaring street ;
And broader still became the blaze,

And louder still the din,
As fast from every village round
The horse came spurring in :
And eastward straight from wild Blackheath
The warlike errand went,
And roused in many an ancient hall
The gallant squires of Kent.
Southward from Surrey's pleasant hills
Flew those bright couriers forth ;
High on bleak Hampstead's swarthy moor
They started for the north.

 . . . . .

Lord Macaulay : The Spanish Armada.

Night-Walking

1716

WHEN Night first bids the twinkling stars appear,
 Or with her cloudy vest enwraps the air,
Then swarms the busy street ; with caution tread,
Where the shop-windows falling threat thy head ;
Now lab'rers home return and join their strength
To bear the tott'ring plank, or ladder's length ;
Still fix thy eyes intent upon the throng,
And, as the passes open, wind along.

Where the fair columns of St. Clement stand,
Whose straiten'd bounds encroach upon the Strand ;
Where the low penthouse bows the walker's head,
And the rough pavement wounds the yielding tread ;
Where not a post protects the narrow space,
And, strung in twines, combs dangle in thy face ;
Summon at once thy courage, rouse thy care,

Stand firm, look back, be resolute, beware.
Forth issuing from steep lanes, the collier's steeds
Drag the black load ; another cart succeeds,
'Team follows team, crowds heap'd on crowds appear,
And wait impatient till the road grow clear.
Now all the pavement sounds with trampling feet,
And the mix'd hurry barricades the street.
Entangled here, the waggon's lengthen'd team
Cracks the tough harness ; here a ponderous beam
Lies overturn'd athwart ; for slaughter fed
Here lowing bullocks raise their horned head.
Now oaths grow loud, with coaches coaches jar,
And the smart blow provokes the sturdy war ;
From the high box they whirl the thong around,
And with the twining lash their shins resound :
Their rage ferments, more dangerous wounds they try,
And the blood gushes down their painful eye.
And now on foot the frowning warriors light,
And with their ponderous fists renew the fight ;
Blow answers blow, their cheeks are smear'd with blood
Till down they fall, and grappling roll in mud.

.   .   .   .   .   .

Where the mob gathers, swiftly shoot along,
Nor idly mingle in the noisy throng :
Lur'd by the silver hilt, amid the swarm,
The subtle artist will thy side disarm.
Nor is thy flaxen wig with safety worn ;
High on the shoulder, in a basket borne,
Lurks the sly boy, whose hand, to rapine bred,
Plucks off the curling honours of thy head.
Here dives the skulking thief, with practis'd sleight,

And unfelt fingers, make thy pocket light.
Where's now thy watch, with all its trinkets, flown?
And thy late snuff-box is no more thy own.
But lo! his bolder thefts some tradesman spies,
Swift from his prey the scudding lurcher flies;
Dext'rous he 'scapes the coach with nimble bounds,
Whilst every honest tongue "Stop thief!" resounds.
So speeds the wily fox, alarm'd by fear,
Who lately filch'd the turkey's callow care;
Hounds following hounds grow louder as he flies,
And injur'd tenants join the hunters' cries.
Breathless, he stumbling falls.   Ill-fated boy!
Why did not honest work thy youth employ?
Seiz'd by rough hands, he's dragged amid the rout,
And stretch'd beneath the pump's incessant spout:
Or, plung'd in miry ponds, he gasping lies,
Mud chokes his mouth, and plaisters o'er his eyes.

Let not the ballad-singer's shrilling strain
Amid the swarm thy listening ear detain:
Guard well thy pocket; for these Syrens stand
To aid the labours of the diving hand;
Confed'rate in the cheat, they draw the throng,
And cambric handkerchiefs reward the song.
But soon as coach or cart drives rattling on,
The rabble part, in shoals they backward run.
So Jove's loud bolts the mingled war divide,
And Greece and Troy retreat on either side.

If the rude throng pour on with furious pace,
And hap to break thee from a friend's embrace,
Stop short; nor struggle through the crowd in vain,

But watch with careful eye the passing train.
Yet I (perhaps too fond), if chance the tide
'Tumultuous bear my partner from my side,
Impatient venture back; despising harm,
I force my passage where the thickest swarm.

.   .   .   .   .

That walker who, regardless of his pace,
Turns oft to pore upon the damsel's face,
From side to side by thrusting elbows tost,
Shall strike his aching breast against a post;
Or water, dash'd from fishy stalls, shall stain
His hapless coat with spirts of scaly rain.
But, if unwarily he chance to stray
Where twirling turnstiles intercept the way,
The thwarting passenger shall force them round
And beat the wretch half breathless to the ground.

Let constant vigilance thy footsteps guide,
And wary circumspection guard thy side;
Then shalt thou walk, unharm'd, the dangerous night,
Nor need th' officious linkboy's smoky light;
Thou never will attempt to cross the road,
Where ale-house benches rest the porter's load,
Grievous to heedless shins; no barrow's wheel,
That bruises oft the truant school-boy's heel,
Behind thee rolling, with insidious pace,
Shall mark thy stocking with a miry trace.
Let not thy vent'rous steps approach too nigh,
Where, gaping wide, low steepy cellars lie.
Should thy shoe wrench aside, down, down you fall,
And overturn the scolding huckster's stall;

The scolding huckster shall not o'er thee moan,
But pence exact for nuts and pears o'erthrown.

Though you through cleanlier allies wind by day,
To shun the hurries of the public way,
Yet ne'er to those dark paths by night retire ;
Mind only safety, and contemn the mire.
Then no impervious courts thy haste detain,
Nor sneering alewives bid thee turn again.

Where Lincoln's-inn, wide space, is rail'd around,
Cross not with vent'rous step ; there oft is found
The lurking thief, who, while the day-light shone,
Made the walls echo with his begging tone :
That crutch, which late compassion mov'd, shall wound
Thy bleeding head, and fell thee to the ground.

Though thou art tempted by the link-man's call,
Yet trust him not along the lonely wall ;
In the mid way he'll quench the flaming brand,
And share the booty with the pilf'ring band.
Still keep the public street, where oily rays,
Shot from the crystal-lamp o'erspread the ways.

John Gay: Trivia.

"Don't You Smell Fire?"

1820

RUN !—run for St. Clement's engine !
    For the Pawnbroker's all in a blaze,
And the pledges are frying and singeing—
    Oh ! how the poor pawners will craze !

Now where can the turncock be drinking?
   Was there ever so thirsty an elf?—
But he still may tope on, for I'm thinking
   That the plugs are as dry as himself.

The engines!—I hear them come rumbling;
   There's the Phœnix! the Globe! and the Sun!
What a row there will be, and a grumbling
   When the water don't start for a run!
See! there they come racing and tearing,
   All the street with loud voices is fill'd;
Oh! it's only the firemen a-swearing
   At a man they've run over and killed!

How sweetly the sparks fly away now,
   And twinkle like stars in the sky;
It's a wonder the engines don't play now,
   But I never saw water so shy!
Why there isn't enough for a snipe,
   And the fire it is fiercer, alas!
Oh! instead of the New River pipe,
   They have gone—that they have—to the gas!

Only look at the poor little P—'s
   On the roof—is there anything sadder?
My dears, keep fast hold, if you please,
   And they won't be an hour with the ladder!
But if any one's hot in their feet,
   And in very great haste to be saved,
Here's a nice easy bit in the street
   That M'Adam has lately unpaved!

There is some one—I see a dark shape
    At that window, the hottest of all,—
My good woman, why don't you escape?
    Never think of your bonnet and shawl;
If your dress isn't perfect, what is it
    For once in a way to your hurt?
When your husband is paying a visit
    There, at Number Fourteen, in his shirt!

Only see how she throws out her *chaney!*
    Her basins, and teapots, and all
The most brittle of *her* goods—or any,
    And they all break in breaking their fall:
Such things are not surely the best
    From a two-story window to throw—
She might save a good iron-bound chest,
    For there's plenty of people below!

Oh dear! what a beautiful flash!
    How it shone thro' the window and door;
We shall soon hear a scream and a crash,
    When the woman falls thro' the floor!
There! there! what a volley of flame,
    And then suddenly all is obscured!—
Well—I'm glad in my heart that I came;—
    But I hope the poor man is insured.

Thomas Hood: Collected Poems.

Moral Reflections on the Cross of St. Paul's

1820

THE man that pays his pence, and goes
    Up to thy lofty cross, St. Paul,
Looks over London's naked nose,
    Women and men:
    The world is all beneath his ken,
He sits above the *Ball*.
He seems on Mount Olympus' top,
Among the Gods, by Jupiter! and lets drop
    His eyes from the empyreal clouds
    On mortal crowds.

Seen from these skies,
How small those emmets in our eyes!
    Some carry little sticks—and one
His eggs—to warm them in the sun:
    Dear! what a hustle,
    And bustle!
And there's my aunt.   I know her by her waist,
    So long and thin
    And so pinch'd in
Just in the pismire taste.

Oh! what are men?—beings so small,
    That, should I fall
Upon their little heads, I must

Crush them by hundreds into dust !
And what is life ? and all its ages—
    There's seven stages !
Turnham Green ! Chelsea ! Putney ! Fulham !
    Brentford ! and Kew !
    And Tooting, too !
And oh ! what very little nags to pull 'em.
    Yet each would seem a horse indeed,
If here at Paul's tip-top we'd got 'em ;
    Although, like Cinderella's breed,
They're mice at bottom.
    Then let me not despise a horse
    Though he looks small from Paul's high cross !
Since he would be,—as near the sky,
    —Fourteen hands high.

What is the world with London in its lap ?
    Mogg's Map.
The Thames, that ebbs, and flows in its broad channel ?
    A *tidy* kennel.
The bridges stretching from its banks ?
    Stone planks.

Oh me ! hence could I read an admonition
    To mad Ambition !
But that he would not listen to my call,
Though I should stand upon the cross and *ball !*
            Thomas Hood : Collected Poems.

Unknown Romances

1847

OFT have I wandered when the first faint light
   Of morning shone upon the steeple vanes
Of sleeping London, through the silent night,
   Musing on memories of joys and pains ;—
And looking down long vistas of dim lanes
   And shadowy streets, one after other spread
In endless coil, have thought what hopes now dead
   Once bloomed in every house ; what tearful rains
Women have wept for husband, sire, or son,
   What love and sorrow ran their course in each,
And what great silent tragedies were done ;—
   And wished the dumb and secret walls had speech,
That they might whisper to me, one by one,
   The sad true lessons that their walls might teach.

Close and forgetful witnesses, they hide,
   In nuptial chamber, attic, or saloon,
Many a legend sad of desolate bride
   And mournful mother, blighted all too soon ;
Of strong men's agony, despair, and pride,
   And mental glory darkened ere its noon.
But let the legends perish in their place,
   For well I know where'er these walls have seen
Humanity's upturned and heavenly face,
   That there has virtue, there has courage been—
That ev'n 'mid passions foul, and vices base,
   Some ray of goodness interposed between.
Ye voiceless houses, ever as I gaze
   This moral flashes from your walls serene.

Charles Mackay : Town Lyrics.

The Balloon

To Mr. Graham, the Aeronaut

1825

DEAR Graham, whilst the busy crowd,
    The vain, the wealthy, and the proud,
  Their meaner flights pursue,
Let us cast off the foolish ties
That bind us to the earth, and rise
  And take a bird's-eye view!

A few more whiffs of my cigar
And then, in Fancy's airy car,
  Have with thee for the skies:
How oft this fragrant smoke upcurl'd
Hath borne me from this little world,
  And all that in it lies!

Away!—away!—the bubble fills—
Farewell to earth and all its hills!—
  We seem to cut the wind!—
So high we mount, so swift we go,
The chimney-tops are far below,
  The Eagle's left behind!

Ah me! my brain begins to swim!—
The world is growing rather dim;
  The steeples and the trees—
My wife is getting very small!
I cannot see my babe at all!—
  The Dollond, if you please!—

Do Graham, let me have a quiz,
Lord ! what a Lilliput it is,
    That little world of Mogg's !—
Are those the London Docks ?—that channel
The mighty Thames ?—a proper kennel
    For that small Isle of Dogs !

What is that seeming tea-urn there !
That fairy dome, St. Paul's !—I swear,
    Wren must have been a wren !—
And that small stripe ?—it cannot be
The City Road !—Good lack ! to see
    The little ways of men !

Little, indeed !—my eyeballs ache
To find a turnpike. I must take
    Their tolls upon my trust !—
And where is mortal labour gone ?
Look, Graham, for a little stone
    Mac Adamized to dust !

Look at the horses !—less than flies !—
Oh, what a waste it was of sighs
    To wish to be a Mayor !
What is the honour ?—none at all,
One's honour must be very small
    For such a civic chair !

And there's Guildhall !—'tis far aloof—
Methinks, I fancy thro' the roof
    Its little guardian Gogs,
Like penny dolls—a tiny show !—
Well,—I must say they're ruled below
    By very little logs !

Oh ! Graham, how the upper air
Alters the standards of compare ;
   One of our silken flags
Would cover London all about—
Nay, then—let's even empty out
   Another brace of bags !

Now for a glass of bright champagne
Above the clouds !—Come, let us drain
   A bumper as we go !
But hold !—for God's sake do not cant
The cork away—unless you want
   To brain your friends below.

Think ! what a mob of little men
Are crawling just within our ken
   Like mites upon a cheese !
Pshaw !—how the foolish sight rebukes
Ambitious thoughts !—can there be *Dukes*
   Of *Glo'ster* such as these !

Oh ! what is glory ?—what is fame ?
Hark to the little mob's acclaim,
   'Tis nothing but a hum !
A few near gnats would trump as loud
As all the shouting of a crowd
   That has so far to come !

Well—they are wise that choose the near,
A few small buzzards in the ear,
   To organs ages hence !—
Ah me, how distance touches all ;
It makes the true look rather small,
   But murders poor pretence.

Thomas Hood : Collected Poems.

Of Solitude

1663

HAIL, old Patrician Trees so great and good!
   Hail, ye Plebeian Underwood!
Where the poetic birds rejoice,
And for their quiet nests and plenteous food
Pay with their grateful voice.

Hail, the poor Muse's richest manor-seat!
Ye country houses and retreat,
Which all the happy gods so love,
That for you oft they quit their bright and great
Metropolis above.

.   .   .   .   .

Here let me, careless and unthoughtful lying,
Hear the soft winds above me flying,
With all their wanton boughs, dispute,
And the more tuneful birds to both replying,
Nor be myself too mute.

A silver stream shall roll his waters near,
Gilt with the sunbeams here and there,
On whose enamell'd bank I'll walk,
And see how prettily they smile, and hear
How prettily they talk.

.   .   .

Oh, Solitude! first state of humankind!
Which blest remain'd till Man did find
Ev'n his own helper's company:

As soon as two, alas ! together join'd,
The Serpent made up three.

.   .   .   .   .

Thou the faint beams of Reason's scatter'd light
Dost, like a burning glass, unite,
Dost multiply the feeble heat,
And fortify the strength, till thou dost bright
And noble fires beget.

Whilst this hard truth I teach, methinks I see
The monster LONDON laugh at me ;
I should at thee, too, foolish City !
If it were fit to laugh at misery ;
But thy estate I pity.

Let but thy wicked men from out thee go,
And all the fools that crowd thee so,
Ev'n thou, who dost thy millions boast,
A village less than Islington wilt grow,
A solitude almost.

Abraham Cowley : Verses upon
Several Occasions.

London Renounced

1738

THOUGH grief and fondness in my breast rebel
    When injur'd Thales bids the town farewell,
Yet still my calmer thoughts his choice commend,
I praise the hermit, but regret the friend,
Resolv'd at length from vice and London far,
To breathe in distant fields a purer air,

And fix'd in Cambria's solitary shore,
Give to St. David one true Britain more.
  For who wou'd leave, unbrib'd, Hibernia's land,
Or change the rocks of Scotland for the Strand?
There none are swept by sudden fate away,
But all whom hunger spares, with age decay:
Here malice, rapine, accident, conspire,
And now a rabble rages, now a fire;
Their ambush here relentless ruffians lay,
And here the fell attorney prowls for prey;
Here falling houses thunder on your head,
And here a female atheist talks you dead.
  While Thales waits the wherry that contains
Of dissipated wealth the small remains,
On Thames's banks, in silent thought we stood,
Where Greenwich smiles upon the silver flood;
Struck with the feat that gave Eliza birth,
We kneel, and kiss the consecrated earth;
In pleasing dreams the blissful age renew,
And call Britannia's glories back to view;
Behold her cross triumphant on the main,
The guard of commerce, and the dread of Spain,
Ere masquerades debauch'd, excise oppress'd,
Or English honour grew a standing jest.
  A transient calm the happy scenes bestow,
And for a moment lull the sense of woe.
At length awaking, with contemptuous frown,
Indignant Thales eyes the neighb'ring town.
  Since worth, he cries, in these degen'rate days
Wants ev'n the cheap reward of empty praise;
In those curs'd walls, devote to vice and gain,
Since unrewarded science toils in vain;
Since hope but soothes to double my distress,

And ev'ry moment leaves my little less;
While yet my steady steps no staff sustains,
And life still vig'rous revels in my veins;
Grant me, kind Heaven, to find some happier place,
Where honesty and sense are no disgrace;
Some pleasing bank where verdant osiers play,
Some peaceful vale with nature's paintings gay;
Where once the harass'd Briton found repose,
And safe in poverty defi'd his foes:
Some secret cell, ye pow'rs indulgent, give,
Let —— live here, for —— has learn'd to live.
Here let those reign, whom pensions can incite
To vote a patriot black, a courtier white;
Explain their country's dear-bought rights away,
And plead for pirates in the face of day;
With slavish tenets taint our poison'd youth,
And lend a lie the confidence of truth.

Could'st thou resign the park and play content,
For the fair banks of Severn or of Trent;
There might'st thou find some elegant retreat,
Some hireling senator's deserted seat;
And stretch thy prospects o'er the smiling land,
For less than rent the dungeons of the Strand;
There prune thy walks, support thy drooping flow'rs,
Direct thy rivulets, and twine thy bow'rs;
And, while thy grounds a cheap repast afford,
Despise the dainties of a venal lord:
There ev'ry bush with Nature's music rings,
There ev'ry breeze bears health upon its wings;
On all thy hours security shall smile,
And bless thine evening walk and morning toil.

Prepare for death if here at night you roam,
And sign your will before you sup from home.
Some fiery fop, with new commission vain,
Who sleeps on brambles till he kills his man;
Some frolic drunkard, reeling from a feast,
Provokes a broil, and stabs you for a jest.
Yet ev'n these heroes, mischievously gay,
Lords of the street, and terrors of the way,
Flush'd as they are with folly, youth, and wine,
Their prudent insults to the poor confine;
Afar they mark the flambeau's bright approach,
And shun the shining train and golden coach.

In vain these dangers past, your doors you close,
And hope the balmy blessings of repose:
Cruel with guilt, and daring with despair,
The midnight murd'rer bursts the faithless bar;
Invades the sacred hour of silent rest,
And leaves unseen a dagger in your breast.

Scarce can our fields, such crowds at Tyburn die,
With hemp the Gallows and the Fleet supply.
Propose your schemes, ye senatorian band,
Whose ways and means support the sinking land,
Lest ropes be wanting in the tempting spring,
To rig another convoy for the King.

A single gaol in Alfred's golden reign
Could half the nation's criminals contain;
Fair Justice then, without constraint ador'd,
Held high the steady scale, but sheath'd the sword;
No spies were paid, no special juries known,
Blest age! but ah! how diff'rent from our own!

Much could I add,—but see the boat at hand,
The tide retiring calls me from the land:
Farewell!—When youth, and health, and fortune spent,

Thou fli'st for refuge to the wilds of Kent;
And, tir'd like me with follies and with crimes,
In angry numbers warn'st succeeding times,
Then shall thy friend, nor thou refuse his aid,
Still foe to vice, forsake his Cambrian shade;
In virtue's cause once more exert his rage,
Thy satire point, and animate thy page.

Samuel Johnson : London.

A Loafer

1894

I HANG about the streets all day,
   At night I hang about;
I sleep a little when I may,
   But rise betimes the morning's scout;
For through the year I always hear
   Afar, aloft, a ghostly shout.

My clothes are worn to threads and loops;
   My skin shows here and there;
About my face like seaweed droops
   My tangled beard, my tangled hair;
From cavernous and shaggy brows
   My stony eyes untroubled stare.

I move from eastern wretchedness
   Through Fleet Street and the Strand;
And as the pleasant people press
   I touch them softly with my hand,
Perhaps to know that still I go
   Alive about a living land.

For, far in front the clouds are riven ;
   I hear the ghostly cry,
As if a still voice fell from heaven
   To where sea-whelmed the drowned folk lie
In sepulchres no tempest stirs,
   And only eyeless things pass by.

In Piccadilly spirits pass :
   Oh, eyes and cheeks that glow !
Oh, strength and comeliness !   Alas,
   The lustrous health is earth I know
From shrinking eyes that recognise
   No brother in my rags and woe.

I know no handicraft, no art,
   But I have conquered fate ;
For I have chosen the better part,
   And neither hope, nor fear, nor hate.
With placid breath on pain and death,
   My certain alms, alone I wait.

And daily, nightly comes the call,
   The pale unechoing note,
The faint 'Aha !' sent from the wall
   Of heaven, but from no ruddy throat
Of human breed or seraph's seed,
   A phantom voice that cries by rote.

John Davidson : Ballads and Songs.

The Song-Bird

19th Century

THERE was a young lady of Beverley,
    Whose friends said she sang very cleverly;
        "She'll win great renown
        In great London town,"
Said the good people of Beverley.

But in London this lady of Beverley
Found all her best notes fell but heavily;
        And when this she did find,
        She said, "Never mind,
They still think me a song-bird at Beverley."
          Nursery Rhymes: Old and New.

Sunday in London

1812

THE seventh day this; the jubilee of man.
    London! right well thou know'st the day of prayer:
Then thy spruce citizen, wash'd artizan,
And smug apprentice gulp their weekly air:
Thy coach of hackney, whisky, one-horse chair,
And humblest gig through sundry suburbs whirl;
To Hampstead, Brentford, Harrow, make repair;
Till the tired jade the wheel forgets to hurl,
Provoking envious gibe from each pedestrian churl.

Some o'er thy Thamis row the ribbon'd fair,
Others along the safer turnpike fly;

Some Richmond-hill ascend, some scud to Ware,
And many to the steep of Highgate hie.
Ask ye, Bœotian shades ! the reason why?
'Tis to the worship of the solemn Horn,
Grasp'd in the holy hand of Mystery,
In whose dread name both men and maids are sworn,
And consecrate the oath with draught, and dance till morn.

Lord Byron : Childe Harold.

A Calm

1894

A PLOT of grass reposing in
  The shadow of a lime,
A thoughtful cat, a puppy's tin,
  And half a whiff of thyme !
Suburban belfries that repeat
  Their wholesome invitation,
A Sabbath murmur in the street,
  A sense of the creation !
A heart at once subdu'd and free,
  A wise and idle calm ;
And London, like the breathless sea,
  Or like a breathéd psalm !

Anon.

Islington

1827

THY fields, fair Islington ! begin to bear
  Unwelcome buildings, and unseemly piles ;
The streets are spreading, and the Lord knows where

Improvement's hand will spare the neighb'ring stiles,
   The rural blandishments of Maiden Lane
   Are every day becoming less and less,
While kilns and lime roads force us to complain
   Of nuisances time only can suppress.
   A few more years, and Copenhagen House
   Shall cease to charm the tailor and the snob;
And where attornies' clerks in smoke carouse,
   Regardless wholly of to-morrow's job,
   Some Claremont Row, or Prospect Place shall rise,
   Or terrace, p'rhaps misnomer'd Paradise!

J. G.: Hone's Table Book.

Highgate

1827

ALREADY, Highgate! to thy skirts they bear
   Bricks, mortar, timber, in no small degree,
And thy once pure, exhilarating air
   Is growing pregnant with impurity!
The would-be merchant has his "country box,"
   A few short measures from the dusty road,
Where friends on Sunday talk about the stocks,
   Or praise the beauties of his "neat abode":
One deems the wall-flow'r garden, in the front,
   Unrivall'd for each aromatic bed;
Another fancies that his old sow's grunt
   "Is so much like the country," and, instead
Of living longer down in Crooked Lane,
   Resolves at once to "ruralize" again!

J. G.: Hone's Table Book.

To Hampstead

1815

THE baffled spell that bound me is undone,
  And I have breathed once more beneath thy sky,
Lovely-brow'd Hampstead; and my looks have run
O'er and about thee: and had scarce drawn nigh,
When I beheld, in momentary sun,
One of thy hills gleam bright and bosomy,
Just like that orb of orbs, a human one,
Let forth by chance upon a lover's eye.

Forgive me then, that not till now I spoke;
For all the comforts, miss'd in close distress,
With airy nod come up from every part,
O'er smiling speech: and so I gazed, and took
A long, deep draught of silent freshfulness,
Ample, and gushing round my feeble heart.

Leigh Hunt: Sonnets to Hampstead.

The Same

1815

A STEEPLE issuing from a leafy rise,
  With farmy fields in front and sloping green,
Dear Hampstead, is thy southern face serene,
Silently smiling on approaching eyes,
Within, thine ever-shifting looks surprise,
Streets, hills and dells, trees overhead now seen,

Now down below, with smoking roofs between—
A village, revelling in varieties.
Then northward what a range—with heath and pond !
Nature's own ground ; woods that let mansions through,
And cottaged vales with billowy fields beyond,
And clump of darkening pines, and prospects blue,
And that clear path through all, where daily meet
Cool cheeks, and brilliant eyes, and morn-elastic feet !

Leigh Hunt : Sonnets to Hampstead.

Sunday at Hampstead

1863

THIS is the Heath of Hampstead,
  There is the dome of Saint Paul's ;
Beneath, on the serried house-tops,
A chequered lustre falls :

And the mighty city of London,
Under the clouds and the light,
Seems a low wet beach, half shingle,
With a few sharp rocks upright.

Here will we sit, my darling,
And dream an hour away :
The donkeys are hurried and worried,
But we are not donkeys to-day :

Through all the weary week, dear,
We toil in the murk down there,

Tied to a desk and a counter,
A patient, stupid pair!

But on Sunday we slip our tether,
And away from the smoke and the smirch;
Too grateful to God for His Sabbath
To shut its hours in a church;

Away to the green, green country,
Under the open sky;
Where the earth's sweet breath is incense
And the lark sings psalms on high!

.   .   .   .

Would you grieve very much, my darling,
If all yon low wet shore
Were drowned by a mighty flood-tide,
And we never toiled there more?

Wicked?   There is no sin, dear,
In an idle dreamer's head;
He turns the world topsy-turvy
To prove that his soul's not dead.

I am sinking, sinking, sinking;
It is hard to sit upright!
Your lap is the softest pillow!
Good-night, my Love, good-night!

*James Thomson (Author of " The City of Dreadful Night"):
Collected Poems.*

A Day at Hampton Court

1889

IT is our custom, once in every year,
  Mine and two others', when the chestnut trees
Are white at Bushey, Ascot being near,
To drive to Hampton Court, and there, at ease
In that most fair of English palaces,
Spend a long summer's day.   What better cheer
Than the old "Greyhound's," seek it where you please?
And where a royal garden statelier?
The morning goes in tennis, a four set,
With George the marker.   'Tis a game for gods,
Full of return and volley at the net,
And laughter and mirth-making episodes
Not wholly classic.   But the afternoon
Finds us punt-fishing idly with our rods,
Nodding and half in dreams, till all too soon
Darkness and dinner drive us back to town.
                              Wilfrid Scawen Blunt.

Toward Green Plains

1795

THE Lord of Light shakes off his drowsyhed.
  Fresh from his couch up springs the lusty sun,
  And girds himself his mighty race to run;
Meantime, by truant love of rambling led,
I turn my back on thy detested walls,

Proud City, and thy sons I leave behind,
A selfish, sordid, money-getting kind,
Who shut their ears when holy Freedom calls.
I pass not thee so lightly, humble spire,
That mindest me of many a pleasure gone,
Of merriest days, of love and Islington,
Kindling anew the flames of past desire;
And I shall muse on thee, slow journeying on,
To the green plains of pleasant Hertfordshire.

Charles Lamb : Collected Poems.

Enough

1828

Needless it were to say how willingly
I bade the huge Metropolis farewell,
It's din, and dust and dirt, and smoke and smut,
'Thames' water, paviour's ground, and London sky :
Weary of hurried days and restless nights,
Watchmen, whose office is to murder sleep
When sleep might else have weighed one's eyelids down. . . .
Escaping from all this, the very whirl
Of mail-coach wheels bound outward from Lad-lane,
Was peace and quietness.   Three hundred miles
Of homeward way seemed to the body rest,
And to the mind repose.

Thomas Southey : Epistle to Allan Cunningham.

GO where we may, rest where we will,
     Eternal London haunts us still.

Thomas Moore : Rhymes on the Road.

LONDON RIVER

ABOVE all ryuers, thy Ryuer hath renowne,
    Whose beryall stremys, pleasant and preclare,
Under thy lusty wallys renneth down,
    Where many a swanne doth swymme with wingis fare ;
    Where many a barge doth saile, and row with are ;
Where many a ship doth rest with toppe-royall.
    O ! towne of townes, patrone and not compare :
London, thou art the Flour of Cities all.

DUNBAR.

GLIDE gently, thus for ever glide,
    O Thames ! that other bards may see
As lovely visions by thy side
As now, fair river ! come to me.
O glide, fair stream, for ever so,
Thy quiet soul on all bestowing,
Till all our minds for ever flow
As thy deep waters now are flowing.

William Wordsworth : Remembrance of Collins.

The Genius of the Thames

1810

EVEN now, methinks, in solemn guise,
    By yonder willowy islet gray,
I see thee, sedge-crowned Genius ! rise,
    And point the glories of thy way.
    Tall reeds around thy temples play ;
Thy hair the liquid crystal gems ;
    To thee I pour the votive lay,
Oh Genius of the silver Thames !

Along thy course no pine-clad steep,
  No alpine summits, proudly tower;
No woods, impenetrably deep,
  O'er thy pure mirror darkly lower;
  The orange-grove, the myrtle bower,
The vine, in rich luxuriance spread;
  The charms Italian meadows shower;
The sweets Arabian valleys shed;
The roaring cataract, wild and white;
The lotos-flower, of azure light;
The fields, where ceaseless summer smiles;
The bloom, that decks the Ægëan isles;
The hills, that touch the empyreal plain,
Olympian Jove's sublime domain;
To other streams all these resign:
Still none, oh Thames! shall vie with thine.

.   .   .   .   .

Far other charms than these possess,
Oh Thames! thy verdant margin bless:
Where peace, with freedom hand-in-hand,
Walks forth along the sparkling strand,
And cheerful toil, and glowing health,
Proclaim a patriot nation's wealth.
The blood-stained scourge no tyrants wield;
No groaning slaves invert the field;
But willing labour's careful train
Crown all thy banks with waving grain,
With beauty decks thy sylvan shades,
With livelier green invests thy glades,
And grace, and bloom, and plenty, pours
On thy sweet meads and willowy shores.

The plain, where herds unnumbered rove,
The laurelled path, the beechen grove,
The lonely oak's expansive pride,
The spire, through distant trees descried,
The cot, with woodbine wreathed around,
The field, with waving corn embrowned,
The fall, that turns the frequent mill,
The seat, that crowns the woodland hill,
The sculptured arch, the regal dome,
The fisher's willow-mantled home,
The classic temple, flower-entwined,
In quick succession charm the mind,
Till, where thy widening current glides
To mingle with the turbid tides,
Thy spacious breast displays unfurled
The ensigns of the assembled world.

.   .   .   .

And still before thy gentle gales,
The laden bark of Commerce sails ;
And down thy flood, in youthful pride,
Those mighty vessels sternly glide,
Destined, amid the tempest's rattle,
To hurl the thunder-bolt of battle,
To guard, in danger's hottest hour,
Britannia's old prescriptive power,
And through winds, floods, and fire, maintain
Her native empire of the main.

Thomas Love Peacock : The Genius
of the Thames.

Thames and Isis

1590

THEN was there heard a most celestiall sound
  Of dainty musicke, which did next ensew
Before the spouse: that was Arion crownd,
Who, playing on his harpe, unto him drew
The eares and hearts of all that goodly crew;
That even yet the dolphin, which him bore
Through the Ægean seas from pirates' vew,
Stood still by him astonisht at his lore,
And all the raging seas for ioy forgot to rore.

So went he playing on the watery plaine:
Soon after whom the lovely bridegroome came,
The noble Thamis, with all his goodly traine;
But him before there went, as best became,
His auncient parents, namely th' auncient Thame;
But much more aged was his wife than he,
The Ouze, whom men doe Isis rightly name;
Full weake and crooked creature seemed shee,
And almost blind through eld, that scarce her way could
    see.

Therefore on either side she was sustained
Of two smal grooms, which by their names were hight
The Churne and Charwell, two small streames, which
    pained
Themselves her footing to direct aright,
Which fayled oft through faint and feeble plight:
But Thame was stronger, and of better stay,

Yet seem'd full aged by his outward sight,
With head all hoary, and his beard all gray,
Deawed with silver drops that trickled downe alway,

And eke he somewhat seem'd to stoupe afore
With bowed backe, by reason of the lode
And auncient heavy burden which he bore
Of that faire City, wherein make abode
So many learned impes, that shoote abrode,
And with their braunches spred all Britany,
No lesse then do her elder sister's broode.
Joy to you both, ye double noursery
Of arts! but, Oxford, thine doth Thame most glorify.

But he their sonne full fresh and iolly was,
All decked in a robe of watchet hew,
On which the waves, glittering like christall glas,
So cunningly enwoven were, that few
Could weenen whether they were false or trew:
And on his head like to a coronet
He wore, that seemed strange to common vew,
In which were many towres and castels set,
That it encompast round as with a golden fret.

Like as the mother of the gods, they say,
In her great iron charet wonts to ride,
When to Love's pallace she doth take her way,
Old Cybele, aray'd with pompous pride,
Wearing a diademe embattild wide
With hundred turrets, like a turribant:
With such an one was Thamis beautifide;
That was to weet the famous TROYNOVANT,
In which her kingdomes throne is chiefly resiant.

And round about him many a pretty page
Attended duely, ready to obay;
All little rivers which owe vassallage
To him, as to their lord, and tribute pay:
The chaulky Kenet; and the Thetis gray;
The morish Cole; and the soft-sliding Breane;
The wanton Lee, that oft doth loose his way;
And the still Darent, in whose waters cleane
Ten thousand fishes play and decke his pleasant streame.

Edmund Spenser: The Faërie Queen.

Cooper's Hill

1643

MY eye, descending from the Hill, surveys
    Where Thames among the wanton valleys strays.
Thames! the most lov'd of all the Ocean's sons,
By his old sire, to his embraces runs,
Hasting to pay his tribute to the sea,
Like mortal life to meet eternity;
Though with those streams he no resemblance hold,
Whose foam is amber, and their gravel gold;
His genuine and less guilty wealth t'explore,
Search not his bottom, but survey his shore,
O'er which he kindly spreads his spacious wing,
And hatches plenty for th' ensuing spring;
Nor then destroys it with too fond a stay,
Like mothers which their infants overlay;
Nor with a sudden and impetuous wave,
Like profuse kings, resumes the wealth he gave.
No unexpected inundations spoil

The mower's hopes, nor mock the ploughman's toil;
But godlike his unweary'd bounty flows;
First loves to do, then loves the good he does.
Nor are his blessings to his banks confin'd,
But free and common as the sea or wind,
When he, to boast or to disperse his stores,
Full of the tribute of his grateful shores,
Visits the world, and in his flying tow'rs
Brings home to us, and makes both Indies ours;
Finds wealth where 'tis, bestows it where it wants,
Cities in deserts, woods in cities, plants.
So that to us no thing, no place, is strange,
While his fair bosom is the World's Exchange,
O could I flow like thee! and make thy stream
My great example, as it is my theme;
Though deep yet clear, though gentle yet not dull;
Strong without rage, without o'erflowing full.

Sir John Denham: Cooper's Hill.

Father Thames

1713

AT length, great Anna said, "Let discord cease!"
     She said, the world obeyed, and all was peace!
  In that blest moment, from his oozy bed
Old Father Thames advanced his rev'rend head;
His tresses dropp'd with dews, and o'er the stream
His shining horns diffused a golden gleam;
Graved on his urn appear'd the moon, that guides
His swelling waters, and alternate tides;
The figured streams in waves of silver roll'd,
And on her banks Augusta rose in gold.

Around his throne the sea-born brothers stood,
Who swell with tributary urns his flood :
First the famed authors of his ancient name,
The winding Isis and the fruitful Thame ;
The Kennet swift, for silver eels renown'd ;
The Loddon slow, with verdant alders crown'd ;
Cole, whose dark streams his flowery islands lave ;
And chalky Wey, that rolls a milky wave ;
The blue, transparent Vandalis appears ;
The gulfy Lea his sedgy tresses rears ;
And sullen Mole, that hides his diving flood ;
And silent Darent, stain'd with Danish blood.

   High in the midst, upon his urn reclined,
His sea-green mantle waving with the wind,
The god appear'd ; he turned his azure eyes
Where Windsor-domes and pompous turrets rise ;
And the hush'd waves glide softly to the shore :—
   " Hail, sacred Peace ! hail, long-expected-days,
That Thames's glory to the stars shall raise !
Though Tiber's streams immortal Rome behold,
Though foaming Hermus swells with tides of gold,
From heaven itself though seven-fold Nilus flows,
And harvests on a hundred realms bestows ;—
These now no more shall be the Muse's themes,
Lost in my fame, as in the sea their streams.
Let Volga's banks with iron squadrons shine,
And groves of lances glitter on the Rhine ;
Let barb'rous Ganges arm a servile train :
Be mine the blessings of a peaceful reign.
No more my sons shall dye with British blood
Red Iber's sands, or Ister's foaming flood :
Safe on my shore each unmolested swain
Shall tend the flocks, or reap the bearded grain ;

The shady empire shall retain no trace
Of war or blood, but in the sylvan chase;
The trumpet sleep while cheerful horns are blown,
And arms employ'd on birds and beasts alone.
Behold! th' ascending villas on my side
Project long shadows o'er the crystal tide;
Behold! Augusta's glitt'ring spires increase,
And temples rise, the beauteous works of peace.
I see, I see, where two fair cities bend
Their ample bow, a new Whitehall ascend!
There mighty nations shall inquire their doom,
The world's great oracle in times to come;
Three kings shall sue, and suppliant states be seen
Once more to bend before a British queen.

Alexander Pope : Windsor Forest.

The Thames

From Richmond Hill

1727

SAY, shall we wind
Along the streams? or walk the smiling mead?
Or court the forest glades? or wander wild
Among the waving harvests? or ascend,
While radiant Summer opens all its pride,
Thy hill, delightful Shene? Here let us sweep
The boundless landscape: now the raptur'd eye,
Exulting, swift to huge Augusta send,
Now to the Sister Hills that skirt her plain,
To lofty Harrow now, and now to where
Majestic Windsor lifts his princely brow.

In lovely contrast to this glorious view,
Calmly magnificent; then will we turn
To where the silver Thames first rural grows.
There let the feasted eye unwearied stray:
Luxurious, there, rove through the pendent woods
That nodding hang o'er Harrington's retreat;
And, stooping thence to Ham's embow'ring walks,
Beneath whose shades, in spotless peace retir'd,
With her, the pleasing partner of his heart,
The worthy Queensberry yet laments his Gay,
And polish'd Cornbury wooes the willing Muse.
Slow let us trace the matchless vale of Thames;
Fair winding up to where the Muses haunt
In Twit'nam's bowers, and for their Pope implore
The healing god, to royal Hampton's pile,
To Clermont's terraced height, and Esher's groves,
Where in the sweetest solitude, embrac'd
By the soft windings of the silent Mole,
From courts and senates Pelham finds repose.
Enchanting vale! beyond whate'er the Muse
Has of Achaia or Hesperia sung!
O vale of bliss!   O softly swelling hills!
On which the power of cultivation lies,
And joys to see the wonders of his toil.

Heavens! what a goodly prospect spreads around,
Of hills, and dales, and woods, and lawns, and spires,
And glittering towns, and gilded streams, till all
The stretching landscape into smoke decays!
Happy Britannia! where the Queen of Arts,
Inspiring vigour, Liberty abroad
Walks, unconfin'd, even to thy farthest cots,
And scatters plenty with unsparing hand.

James Thomson: Summer.

Windsor to London

1612

BUT now this mighty flood, upon his voyage prest,
 (That found how with his strength, his beauties still
  increas'd,
From where brave Windsor stood on tip-toe to behold
The fair and goodly Thames, so far as e'er he could,
With kingly houses crown'd, of more than earthly pride,
Upon his either banks, as he along doth glide),
With wonderful delight doth his long course pursue,
Where Oatlands, Hampton Court, and Richmond he doth
  view.
Then Westminster the next great Thames doth entertain,
That vaunts her palace large, and her most sumptuous fane :
The land's tribunal seat that challengeth for her's,
The crowning of our Kings, their famous sepulchres.
Then goes he on along by that more beauteous strand,
Expressing both the wealth and bravery of the land.
(So many sumptuous bowers, within so little space,
The all-beholding Sun scarce sees in all his race.)
And on by London leads, which like a crescent lies,
Whose windows seem to mock the star-befreckled skies ;
Besides her rising spires, so thick themselves that show,
As do the bristling reeds within his banks that grow.
There sees his crowded wharfs, and people-pest'red shores,
His bosom overspread with shoals of lab'ring oars ;
With that most costly Bridge that doth him most renown,
By which he clearly puts all other rivers down.
      Michael Drayton : Polyolbion.

Two Asylums

1792

GO, with old Thames, view Chelsea's glorious pile,
　　And ask the shattered hero, whence his smile?
Go, view the splendid domes of Greenwich—go;
And own what raptures from reflection flow.
Hail, noblest structures imag'd in the wave!
A nation's grateful tribute to the brave.
Hail, blest retreats from war and shipwreck, hail!
That oft arrest the wondering stranger's sail.
Long have ye heard the narratives of age,
The battle's havoc, and the tempest's rage;
Long have ye known Reflection's genial ray
Gild the calm close of Valour's various day.

Samuel Rogers : The Pleasures of Memory.

A Riddle of the Thames

1894

AT windows that from Westminster
　　Look southward to the Lollard's Tower,
She sat, my lovely friend.   A blur
　　Of gilded mist,—('twas morn's first hour,)—
Made vague the world : and in the gleam
Shivered the half-awakened stream.

Through tinted vapour looming large,
    Ambiguous shapes obscurely rode.
She gazed where many a laden barge
    Like some dim-moving saurian showed.
And 'midst them, lo! two swans appeared,
And proudly up the river steered.

Two stately swans! What did they there?
    Whence came they? Whither would they go?
Think of them,—things so faultless fair,—
    'Mid the black shipping down below!
On through the rose and gold they passed,
And melted in the morn at last.

Ah, can it be, that they had come
    Where Thames in sullied glory flows,
Fugitive rebels, tired of some
    Secluded lake's ornate repose,
Eager to taste the life that pours
Its muddier wave 'twixt mightier shores?

We ne'er shall know: our wonderment
    No barren certitude shall mar.
They left behind them, as they went,
    A dream than knowledge ampler far;
And from our world they sailed away
Into some visionary day.

          William Watson: Odes and Other Poems.

On the Report of a Wooden Bridge
to be built at Westminster

1737

BY Rufus' hall, where Thames polluted flows,
　　Provok'd, the Genius of the river rose,
And thus exclaim'd : " Have I, ye British swains,
Have I for ages lav'd your fertile plains ?
Giv'n herds, and flocks, and villages increase,
And fed a richer than a golden fleece ?
Have I, ye merchants, with each swelling tide,
Poured Afric's treasure in, and India's pride ?
Lent you the fruit of every nation's toil ?
Made every climate yours, and every soil ?
Yet pilfer'd from the poor, by gaming base,
Yet must a wooden bridge my waves disgrace ?
Tell not to foreign streams the shameful tale,
And be it publish'd in no Gallic vale,"
He said :—and plunged into his crystal dome,
While o'er his head the circling waters foam.

James Thomson : Collected Poems.

Composed upon Westminster Bridge
September 3, 1802

EARTH has not anything to show more fair :
　　Dull would he be of soul who could pass by
A sight so touching in its majesty :
This City now doth, like a garment, wear

The beauty of the morning ; silent, bare,
Ships, towers, domes, theatres, and temples lie
Open unto the fields, and to the sky ;
All bright and glittering in the smokeless air.

Never did sun more beautifully steep
In his first splendour, valley, rock, or hill ;
Ne'er saw I, never felt, a calm so deep !
The river glideth at his own sweet will :
Dear God ! the very houses seem asleep ;
And all that mighty heart is lying still !

William Wordsworth : Miscellaneous Sonnets.

Westminster

1892

ST. Margaret's bells,
    Quiring their innocent, old-world canticles,
Sing in the storied air
All rosy-and-golden, as with memories
Of woods at evensong, and sands and seas
Disconsolate for that the night is nigh.
O, the low, lingering lights ! The large last gleam
(Hark ! how those brazen choristers cry and call !)
Touching these solemn ancientries, and there,
The silent River ranging tide-mark high
And the callow, grey-faced Hospital,
With the strange glimmer and glamour of a dream !
The Sabbath peace is in the slumbrous trees,
And from the wistful, the fast-widowing sky

(Hark! how those plangent comforters call and cry!)
Falls as in August plots late roseleaves fall.
The sober Sabbath stir—
Leisurely voices, desultory feet!—
Comes from the dry, dust-coloured street,
Where in their summer frocks the girls go by,
And sweethearts lean and loiter and confer,
Just as they did an hundred years ago,
Just as an hundred years to come they will:—
When you and I, Dear Love, lie lost and low,
And sweet-throats none our welkin shall fulfil,
Nor any sunset fade serene and slow;
But, being dead, we shall not grieve to die.

William Ernest Henley: London Voluntaries

Westminster Abbey

1765

OFT let me range the gloomy aisles alone,
   Sad luxury! to vulgar minds unknown,
Along the walls where speaking marbles show
What worthies form the hallow'd mould below;
Proud names, who once the reins of empire held;
In arms who triumph'd; or in arts excell'd;
Chiefs, grac'd with scars, and prodigal of blood;
Stern patriots, who for sacred freedom stood;
Just men, by whom impartial laws were given;
And saints who taught, and led, the way to Heaven!

*Thomas Tickell: Dedication of Addison's Works
to the Earl of Warwick.*

Lines on the Tombs in Westminster

1640

MORTALITY, behold and fear !
   What a change of flesh is here !
Think how many royal bones
Sleep within these heaps of stones ;
Here they lie, had realms and lands,
Who now want strength to stir their hands ;
Where from their pulpits seal'd with dust
They preach, "In greatness is no trust."
Here's an acre sown indeed
With the richest, royallest seed
That the earth did e'er suck in,
Since the first man died for sin :
Here the bones of birth have cried,
"Though gods they were, as men they died !"
Here are sands, ignoble things,
Dropt from the ruin'd sides of kings :
Here's a world of pomp and state
Buried in dust, once dead by fate.

Francis Beaumont : Miscellaneous Poems.

The Temple of Reconciliation

1808

HERE where the end of earthly things
    Lays heroes, patriots, bards, and kings;
Where stiff the hand, and still the tongue,
Of those who fought, and spoke, and sung;
Here, where the fretted aisles prolong
The distant notes of holy song,
As if some angel spoke again,
" All peace on earth, good-will to men";
If ever from an English heart,
Oh, *here* let prejudice depart!

*Sir Walter Scott: Introduction to Canto 1
of " Marmion."*

The Burial of Addison

1765

CAN I forget the dismal night that gave
    My soul's best part for ever to the grave!
How silent did his old companions tread,
By midnight lamps, the mansions of the dead,
Through breathing statues, then unheeded things,
Through rows of warriors, and through walks of kings!
What awe did the slow solemn knell inspire;
The pealing organ, and the pausing choir;
The duties by the lawn-rob'd prelate pay'd;
And the last words, that dust to dust convey'd!

While speechless o'er thy closing grave we bend,
Accept these tears, thou dear departed friend.
Oh, gone for ever! take this long adieu;
And sleep in peace, next thy lov'd Montague.

*Thomas Tickell: Dedication of Addison's Works
to the Earl of Warwick.*

The Coronation

1612

GOD save you, sir!   Where have you been broiling?
   3rd Gent.   Among the crowd i' the Abbey; where a
     finger
Could not be wedg'd in more; I am stifled
With the mere rankness of their joy.
   2nd Gent.   You saw the ceremony?
   3rd Gent.   That I did.
   1st Gent.   How was it?
   3rd Gent.   Well worth the seeing.
   2nd Gent.   Good sir, speak it to us.
   3rd Gent.   As well as I am able.   The rich stream
Of lords and ladies, having brought the Queen
To a prepar'd place in the choir, fell off
A distance from her; while her grace sat down
To rest a while, some half an hour or so,
In a rich chair of state, opposing freely
The beauty of her person to the people.
Believe me, sir, she is the goodliest woman
That ever lay by man: which when the people
Had the full view of, such a noise arose
As the shrouds make at sea in a stiff tempest,

As loud, and to as many tunes : hats, cloaks,
(Doublets, I think) flew up ; and had their faces
Been loose, this day they had been lost.   Such joy
I never saw before.   Great-bellied women,
That had not half a week to go, like rams
In the old time of war, would shake the press,
And make them reel before them.   No man living
Could say, "This is my wife," there ; all were woven
So strangely in one piece.
    2nd Gent.   But, pray, what follow'd ?
    3rd Gent.   At length her grace rose, and with modest paces
Came to the altar ; where she kneel'd, and saint-like
Cast her fair eyes to heaven, and pray'd devoutly.
Then rose again, and bow'd her to the people :
When by the Archbishop of Canterbury
She had all the royal makings of a queen ;
As holy oil, Edward Confessor's crown,
The rod, and bird of peace, and all such emblems
Laid nobly on her : which perform'd, the choir,
With all the choicest music of the kingdom,
Together sung *Te Deum.*   So she parted,
And with the same full state pac'd back again,
To York place, where the feast is held.

Shakespeare : Henry VIII.

Somerset House

1668

BEFORE my gate a street's broad channel goes,
    Which still with waves of crowding people flows,
And ev'ry day there passes by my side,
Up to its western reach, the London tide,

The springtides of the term : my front looks down
On all the pride and bus'ness of the Town.

.   .   .   .   .

My other fair and more majestic face
(Who can the fair to more advantage place ?)
For ever gazes on itself below,
In the best mirror that the world can show.

And here behold, in a long, bending row,
How two joint cities make one glorious bow ;
The midst, the noblest place, possess'd by me,
Best to be seen by all, and all o'ersee.
Which way soe'er I turn my joyful eye,
Here the great Court, there the rich Town, I spy ;
On either side dwells Safety and Delight,
Wealth on the left, and Pow'r upon the right.
T' assure yet my defence, on either hand,
Like mighty forts, in equal distance stand
Two of the best and stateliest piles which e'er
Man's lib'ral piety of old did rear.
Where the two princes of th' apostle's band,
My neighbours and my guards, watch and command.

.

And thou, fair River ! who still pay'st to me
Just homage in thy passage to the sea,
Take here this one instruction as thou go'st :
When thy mix'd waves shall visit every coast,
When round the world their voyage they shall make
And back to thee some secret channels take,
Ask them what nobler sight they e'er did meet,

Except thy mighty Master's sov'reign fleet,
Which now triumphant o'er the main does ride,
The terror of all lands, the ocean's pride !

Abraham Cowley : Miscellanies.

Dawn

1892

.   .   .

STILL, still the streets, between their carcanets
     Of linking gold, are avenues of sleep.
But see how gable ends and parapets
In gradual beauty and significance
Emerge !   And did you hear
That little twitter-and-cheep,
Breaking inordinately loud and clear
On this still, spectral, exquisite atmosphere ?
'Tis a first nest at matins !   And behold
A rakehell cat—how furtive and acold !
A spent witch homing from some infamous dance—
Obscene, quick-trotting, see her tip and fade
Through shadowy railings into a pit of shade !
And now ! a little wind and shy,
The smell of ships (that earnest of romance),
A sense of space and water, and thereby
A lamplit bridge ouching the troubled sky,
And look, O, look ! a tangle of silver gleams
And dusky lights, our River and all his dreams,
His dreams that never save in our deaths can die.
What miracle is happening in the air,
Charging the very texture of the gray

With something luminous and rare?
The night goes out like an ill-parcelled fire,
And, as one lights a candle, it is day.
The extinguisher, that perks it like a spire
On the little formal church, is not yet green
Across the water; but the house-tops nigher,
The corner-lines, the chimneys—look how clean,
How new, how naked!   See the batch of boats,
Here at the stairs, washed in the fresh-sprung beam!
And those are barges that were goblin floats,
Black, hag-steered, fraught with devilry and dream!
And in the piles the water frolics clear,
The ripples into loose rings wander and flee,
And we—we can behold that could but hear
The ancient River singing as he goes
New-mailed in morning to the ancient Sea.

.   .   .   .   .

William Ernest Henley: London Voluntaries.

A Spousall

1596

.   .   .   .

A T length they all to mery London came,
      To mery London, my most kindly Nurse,
That to me gave this Life's first native source
Though from another place I take my name,
An house of auncient fame:
There when they came, whereas those bricky towres
The which on Themmes brode aged backe doe ryde,
Where now the studious Lawyers have their bowers,

There whylome wont the Templer Knights to byde,
Till they decayd through pride :
Next whereunto there standes a stately place
Where oft I gained giftes and goodly grace
Of that great Lord, which therein wont to dwell,
Whose want too well now feeles my freendless case ;
But ah ! here fits not well
Olde woes, but joyes, to tell
Against the bridale daye, which is not long ;
   Sweete 'Themmes ! runne softly, till I end my Song.

Yet therein now doth lodge a noble Peer,
Great England's glory, and the World's wide wonder,
Whose dreadfull name late through all Spaine did thunder,
And Hercules' two pillors standing neere
Did make to quake and feare :
Faire branch of Honor, flower of Chevalrie !
That fillest England with thy triumphe's fame,
Joy have thou of thy noble victorie,
And endlesse happinesse of thine owne name
That promiseth the same ;
That through thy prowesse, and victorious armes
Thy country may be freed from forraine harmes ;
And great Elisa's glorious name may ring
Through all the world, fil'd with thy wide alarmes
Which some brave muse may sing
To ages following.
Upon the brydale day, which is not long :
   Sweete Themmes ! runne softly till I end my Song.

From those high towers this noble Lord issuing
Like Radiant Hesper, when his golden hayre
In th' Ocean billows he hath bathèd fayre,

Descended to the River's open vewing,
With a great traine ensuing.
Above the rest were goodly to bee seene
Two gentle Knights of lovely face and feature,
Beseeming well the bower of anie Queen,
With gifts of wit, and ornaments of nature,
Fit for so goodly stature,
That like the twins of Jove they seem'd in sight,
Which decke the bauldricke of the Heavens bright ;
They two, forth pacing to the River's side,
Received those two faire Brides, their loves delight ;
Which, at th' appointed tyde,
Each one did make his Bryde
Against their brydale day, which is not long :
    Sweete Themmes ! runne softly, till I end my Song.

           Edmund Spenser : Prothalamion.

Shakespeare

1640

SWEET Swan of Avon ! what a sight it were
    To see thee in our water yet appear,
And make those flights upon the banks of Thames,
That so did take Eliza, and our James !

        Ben Jonson : To the Memory of my Beloved
        Master, William Shakespeare.

Tears to Thamesis

1648

I SEND, I send here my supremest kiss
    To thee, my silver-footed Thamesis.
No more shall I reiterate thy Strand,
Whereon so many stately structures stand :
Nor in the summer's sweeter evenings go
To bathe in thee, as thousand others do ;
No more shall I along thy crystal glide
In barge with boughs and rushes beautifi'd,
With soft, smooth virgins for our chaste disport,
To Richmond, Kingston, and to Hampton Court.
Never again shall I with finny oar
Put from, or draw unto the faithful shore,
And landing here, or safely landing there,
Make way to my belovèd Westminster,
Or to the golden Cheapside, where the earth
Of Julia Herrick gave to me my birth.
May all clean nymphs and curious water-dames
With swan-like state float up and down thy streams :
No drought upon thy wanton waters fall
To make them lean and languishing at all.
No ruffling winds come hither to disease
Thy pure and silver-wristed Naiades !
Keep up your state, ye streams ; and as ye spring,
Never make sick your banks by surfeiting !
Grow young with tides, and though I see ye never
Receive this vow, so fare ye well for ever !

Robert Herrick : Hesperides.

The Great Frost

1684

THE various sports behold here in this piece,
    Which for six weeks were seen upon the ice ;
Upon the Thames the great variety
Of plays and booths is here brought to your eye.
Here coaches, as in Cheapside, run on wheels,
Here man (out-tipling of the fishes) reels :
Instead of waves that us'd to beat the shore,
Here bulls they bait, till loudly they do roar ;
Here boats do slide, where boats were wont to row,
Where ships did sail, the sailors do them tow ;
And passengers in boats the river crost,
For the same price as 'twas before the frost.
There is the printing booth of wondrous fame,
Because that each man there did print his name,
And sure, in former ages, ne'er was found,
A press to print, where men so oft were drown'd.
In blanket booths, that sit at no ground rent,
Much coin in beef and brandy there is spent.
The Dutchmen here in nimble cutting skates,
To please the crowd do show their tricks and feats ;
The rabble here in chariots run around,
Coffee, and tea, and mum doth here abound.
The tinkers here do march at sound of kettle,
And all men know that they are men of mettle :
Here roasted was an ox before the court,
Which to much folks afforded meat and sport ;
At nine-pins here they play, as in Moorfields,
This place the pastime us of foot-ball yields :

The common hunt here makes another show,
As he to hunt an hare is wont to go ;
But though no woods are here or hares so fleet,
Yet men do often foxes catch and meet ;
Into a hole here one by chance doth fall,
At which the watermen began to bawl,
What, will you rob our cellar of its drink ?
When he, alas ! poor man, no harm did think.
Here men well mounted do on horses ride
Here they do throw at cocks as at Shrovetide ;
A chariot here so cunningly was made,
That it did move itself without the aid
Of horse or rope, by virtue of a spring
That Vulcan did contrive, who wrought therein.
The rocks at nine-holes here do flock together
As they are wont to do in summer weather.
Three ha'porth for a penny, here they cry,
Of gingerbread, come, who will of it buy ?
This is the booth where men did money take,
For crape and ribbons that they there did make ;
But in six hours, this great and rary show
Of booths and pastimes all away did go.

Anon. : Old Ballad.

The Great Thaw

1684

THIS Winter was sharp, it did plainly appear,
    The like has not been for this many a year ;
The River of Thames was congeal'd to a rock,
And people in multitudes thither did flock ;

Thus many poor tradesmen were out of employ,
The truth I am certain there's none to deny.
    Then let us be thankful, and praise God therefor,
    For He in good time heard the cry of the Poor.

The Frost it was sharp, most bitter and cold,
It pierced all people the time it did hold ;
Great coal-merchants, they that had laid in their store,
Were void of all pity, and grinded the poor ;
And in their extremity it did appear,
They bought 'em in cheap, but they sold 'em out dear.
    Then let us be thankful . . .

Poor tradesmen, alas, that great charge must maintain,
I needs must confess they had cause to complain :
Their hearts were oppressed with sorrow and care ;
They walked up and down, but most bleak was the air,
And Charity that was as cold as the wind
By woful experience some hundreds did find.
    Then let us be thankful . . .

In this mighty River they there did invent
All kinds of vain pastime to reap their content ;
They acted all rudeness there with one accord,
And little regarded the hand of the Lord :
Many poor families suffered this time,
Whilst some drowned sorrow in glasses of wine.
    Then let us be thankful . . .

From Westminster Hall to the Temple each day
The River of Thames 'twas made a high-way ;
For foot-men and horsemen, and coaches beside,
And many brave gentlemen in them did ride.

But all this great triumph, we justly might fear,
Might make our sad judgment to fall most severe.
  Then let us be thankful . . .

Then during the Frost there they followed their blows,
In music, and gaming, and acting of shows;
On this mighty River they roasted an ox,
They bated the bull, and they hunted the fox:
For fear that our Lord He should angry be.
  Then let us be thankful . . .

But when they perceiv'd the great Frost it did break,
They were forc'd to pack up, and then Thames to forsake:
The wind and the tide they have broke it in sunder,
And now we will leave them to talk of the wonder.
Then let us rejoice still, and be of good cheer,
We hope we may have a most plentiful year.
  Then let us be thankful . . .

The Water-men now at all stairs they shall fly,
"Next Oars!" and "Next Sculler!" let this be their cry:
For now you may see they have changed their notes,
They pull'd down their tents, and they row in their boats.
'Twas the work of the Lord, we may well understand,
He made mighty rivers as firm as the land.
  Then let us be thankful, and praise God therefor,
  For He in good time heard the cry of the Poor.

       Anon.: Old Ballad.

Ballade of Cleopatra's Needle

1880

YE giant shades of Ra and Tum,
   Ye ghosts of gods Egyptian,
If murmurs of our planet come
To exiles in the precincts wan
Where, fetish or Olympian,
To help or harm no more ye list,
Look down, if look ye may, and scan
This monument in London mist!

Behold, the hieroglyphs are dumb
That once were read of him that ran
When seistron, cymbal, trump, and drum
Wild music of the Bull began;
When through the chanting priestly clan
Walk'd Ramses, and the high sun kiss'd
This stone, with blessing scored and ban—
This monument in London mist.

The stone endures though gods be numb;
Though human effort, plot, and plan
Be sifted, drifted, like the sum
Of sands in wastes Arabian.
What king may deem him more than man,
What priest says Faith can Time resist
While *this* endures to mark their span—
This monument in London mist?

ENVOY

Prince, the stone's shade on your divan
Falls; it is longer than ye wist:
It preaches, as Time's gnomon can,
This monument in London mist!

Andrew Lang: Ballades in Blue China.

Song: to Celia

1616

KISS me, sweet: the wary lover
  Can your favours keep, and cover,
When the common courting jay
All your bounties will betray.
Kiss again! no creature comes.
Kiss, and score up wealthy sums
On my lips, thus hardly sundered,
While you breathe.   First give a hundred,
Then a thousand, then another
Hundred, then unto the other
Add a thousand, and so more:
Till you equal with the store,
All the grass that Rumney yields,
Or the sands in Chelsea Fields,
Or the drops in silver Thames,
Or the stars, that gild his streams,
In the silent summer-nights,
When youths ply their stolen delights;

That the curious may not know
How to tell 'em as they flow,
And the envious, when they find
What their number is, be pined.

Ben Jonson : The Forest.

London Bridge

1657

WHEN Neptune from his billows London spi'd,
    Brought proudly thither by a high spring-tide ;
As through a floating wood he steer'd along,
And dancing castles cluster'd in a throng ;
When he beheld a mighty Bridge give law
Unto his surges, and their fury awe ;
When such a shelf of cataracts did roar,
As if the Thames with Nile had chang'd her shore ;
When he such massy walls, such tow'rs did eye,
Such posts, such irons upon his back to lie ;
When such vast arches he observ'd, that might
Nineteen Rialtos make for depth and height ;
When the cerulean god these things survey'd,
He shook his trident, and astonish'd said,
Let the whole Earth now all her wonders count,
This Bridge of wonders is the paramount.

Lines Prefixed to Howell's
Londinopolis.

Shooting the Bridge

1798

SO thy dark arches, London Bridge, bestride
  Indignant Thames, and part his angry tide ;
Where oft—returning from those green retreats,
Where fair Vauxhallia decks her sylvan seats ;—
Where each spruce nymph, from city compters free,
Sips the frothed syllabub, or fragrant tea ;
While with sliced ham, scraped beef, and burnt champagne,
Her 'prentice lover soothes his amorous pain ;
—There oft, in well-trimmed wherry, glide along
Smart beaux and giggling belles, a glittering throng ;
Smells the tarred rope—with undulation fine
Flaps the loose sail—the silken awnings shine ;
    "Shoot we the bridge !"—the venturous boatmen cry—
    "Shoot we the bridge !"—the exulting fare reply.
—Down the steep fall the headlong waters go,
Curls the white foam, the breakers roar below.
—The veering helm the dexterous steersman stops,
Shifts the thin oar, the fluttering canvas drops ;
Then with closed eyes, clenched hands, and quick-drawn
    breath,
Darts at the central arch, nor heeds the gulf beneath.
—Full 'gainst the pier the unsteady timbers knock ;
The loose planks starting own the impetuous shock ;
The shifted oar, dropped sail, and steadied helm,
With angry surge the closing waters whelm—
Laughs the glad Thames, and clasps each fair one's charms
That screams and scrambles in his oozy arms.

—Drenched each smart garb, and clogged each struggling
    limb,
Far o'er the stream the cockneys sink or swim :
While each badged boatman clinging to his oar,
Bounds o'er the buoyant wave, and climbs the applauding
    shore.

        George Canning : The Loves of the Triangles.

Farewell to Old London Bridge

1832

A DIEU ! thou old and honor'd way
    Across the rolling tide,
In strength and beauty thou hast stretch'd
    Thy form from side to side.

On thee the peaceful Pilgrim train
    Have met the blessing sight,
And laurell'd Kings and Conquerors
    Pass'd proudly from the fight !

The traitor and the true man too,
    The graceless and the good,
By turns have blacken'd in the sun
    Where thy proud portals stood ;

But Pilgrim's rest, and Warrior's sleep,
    And Martyrdom can ne'er
Again with evil eye behold
    Her sickening horrors there !

O'er thee the choral song of praise,
    The incense and the pray'r

From Superstition's altar rose,
    And fill'd the fragrant air;

On thee the dance was lightly trod,
    The banquet gaily spread,
By nimble feet by busy hands
    Now number'd with the dead.

The pomp of tourney and of tilt
    Thy battlements could boast,
And many a train of loveliness
    And many a warlike host—

In fairest show of pageantry
    They trod thy causeway o'er,
But none, or beautiful, or brave,
    Shall tread that causeway more.

Thy strength is fled—thy beauty lost—
    And each proportion true
Is fading fast—and soon will all
    Have ceas'd to greet the view:

And many a massy stone is sent,
    A tribute fair from thee,
To deck a bright and sunny bay
    In our unconquer'd sea;

And well I wean, of all the crowds
    Who now unfearing tread
That miracle of masonry,
    Which stretches in thy stead

Across the broad and busy stream,
    There doth not wander one
Who will not from his heart of heart
    Rejoice when thou art gone !

For thou dost make the flowing tide
    The grave of gentle youth :
And boyhood's heart of hopefulness,
    And beauty's eye of truth,

By thee—thou Moloch of the flood—
    Were doom'd on either shore,
To beat with wild ambition's throb
    And smile in love no more :—

Yet thou had charms in Fancy's eye ;
    And Memory's tablet fair,
The record of thy glories past
    Unfadingly shall bear ;

And on the scroll of ages trac'd
    Thy ev'ry grace shall stand,
Thou ancient waymark of the stream
    And wonder of the land !

J. P.: Carmen Ante Paestum.

A Merry Wherry-Ferry Voyage

1662

THE year which I do call as others do,
    Full 1600, adding twenty-two :
The month of July that's for ever fam'd,
Because 'twas so by Julius Caesar nam'd,

Just when six days, and to each day a night,
The dogged Dog-days had begun to bite,
On that day which doth blest remembrance bring,
The name of an Apostle, and our King,
On that remarkable good day, Saint James,
I undertook my voyage down the Thames.
So I with colours finely did repair
My boat's defaults, and made her fresh and fair.
Thus, being furnish'd with good wine and beer,
And bread and meat (to banish hunger's fear),
With sails, with anchor, cables, sculls, and oars,
With card and compass, to know seas and shores,
With lanthorne, candle, tinder-box, and match,
And with good courage, to work, ward, and watch,
Well mann'd, well ship'd, well victual'd, well appointed,
Well in good health, well timber'd and well jointed:
All wholly well, and yet not half fox'd well,
'Twixt Kent and Essex, we to Gravesend fell.
There I had welcome of my friendly host
(A Gravesend trencher and a Gravesend toast),
Good meat and lodging at an easy rate,
And rose betimes, although I lay down late.
Bright Lucifer, the messenger of day,
His burnisht twinkling splendour did display:
Rose cheek'd Aurora hid her blushing face,
She, spying Phœbus coming, gave him place,
Whilst Zephyrus and Auster mix'd together,
Breath'd gently, as fore-boding pleasant weather.
Old Neptune had his daughter Thames supplied
With ample measure of a flowing tide,
But Thames supposed it was but borrowed goods,
And with her ebbs paid Neptune back his floods.
Then at the time of this auspicious dawning,

I roused my men, who scrubbing, stretching, yawning,
Arose, left Gravesend, rowing down the stream,
And near to Lee, we to an anchor came.
Because the sands were bare, and water low,
We rested there, till it two hours did flow:
And then to travel went our galley foyst,
Our anchor quickly weigh'd, our sail up hoist,
Where thirty miles we passed, a mile from shore,
The water two foot deep, or little more.
Thus passed we on the brave East Saxon coast,
From three at morn, till two, at noon almost,
By Shoebury, Wakering, Foulness, Tillingham,
And then we into deeper water came.
There is a crooked bay runs winding far
To Maldon, Esterford, and Colchester,
Which, 'cause 'twas much about (to ease men's pain),
I left the land, and put into the main.

*John Taylor: A Very Merry Wherry-Ferry Voyage,
or York for My Money.*

Mr. Pope Welcomed to London

1720

L ONG hast thou, friend, been absent from thy soil,
    Like patient Ithacus at siege of Troy;
I have been witness of thy six years' toil,
    Thy daily labours and thy nights' annoy,
Lost to thy native land with great turmoil,
    On the wide sea, oft threatening to destroy:
Methinks with thee I've trod Sigaean ground,
And heard the shores of Hellespont resound.

Did I not see thee when thou first sett'st sail
To seek adventures fair in Homer's land?
Did I not see thy sinking spirits fail,
    And wish thy bark had never left the strand?
Ev'n in mid ocean often didst thou quail,
    And oft lift up thy holy eye and hand,
Praying the Virgin dear, and saintly choir,
Back to the port to bring thy bark entire.

Cheer up, my friend! thy dangers now are o'er;
    Methinks—nay, sure the rising coasts appear;
Hark! how the guns salute from either shore,
    As thy trim vessel cuts the Thames so fair:
Shouts answering shouts from Kent and Essex roar,
    And bells break loud through every gust of air:
Bonfires do blaze, and bones and cleavers ring,
As at the coming of some mighty king.

Now pass we Gravesend with a friendly wind,
    And Tilbury's white fort, and long Blackwall;
Greenwich, where dwells the friend of human kind,
    More visited than either park or hall,
Withers the good, and (with him ever join'd)
    Facetious Disney, greet thee first of all:
I see his chimney smoke, and hear him say,
    Duke! that's the room for Pope, and that for Gay.

Come in, my friends! here shall ye dine and lie,
    And here shall breakfast, and here dine again;
And sup and breakfast on (if ye comply),
    For I have still some dozens of champagne:
His voice still lessens as the ship sails by;
    He waves his hand to bring us back in vain;

For now I see, I see proud London's spires;
　　Greenwich is lost, and Deptford Dock retires.

Oh, what a concourse swarms on yonder quay!
　　The sky re-echoes with new shouts of joy;
By all this show, I ween, 'tis Lord Mayor's day;
　　I hear the voice of trumpet and hautboy,—
No, now I see them near—oh, these are they
　　Who come in crowds to welcome thee from Troy.
Hail to the bard, whom long as lost we mourn'd;
　　From siege, from battle, and from storm, return'd!

.　　　.　　　.　　　.　　　.

How loved, how honour'd thou!　Yet be not vain!
　　And sure thou art not, for I hear thee say—
"All this, my friends, I owe to Homer's strain,
　　On whose strong pinions I exalt my lay.
What from contending cities did he gain?
　　And what rewards his grateful country pay?
None, none were paid—why then all this for me?
　　These honours, Homer, had been just to thee."
　　　　　　　　　John Gay : Collected Poems.

The Port of London

1744

NOW silver Isis brightening flows along,
　　Echoing from Oxford shore each classic song;
Then weds with Tame; and these, O London, see
Swelling with naval pride, the pride of thee!
Wide, deep, unsullied Thames, meandering glides
And bears thy wealth on mild majestic tides.

Thy ships, with gilded palaces that vie,
In glittering pomp strike wondering China's eye;
And thence returning bear, in splendid state,
To Britain's merchants, India's eastern freight.
India, her treasures from her western shores,
Due at thy feet, a willing tribute pours;
Thy warring navies distant nations awe,
And bid the world obey thy righteous law.
Thus shine thy manly sons of liberal mind;
Thy Change deep-busied, yet as courts refin'd;
Councils, like senates, that enforce debate,
With fluent eloquence and reason's weight,
Whose patriot virtue, lawless power controls;
Their British emulating Roman souls.
Of these the worthiest still selected stand,
Still lead the senate, and still save the land:
Social, not selfish, here, O Learning, trace
Thy friends, the lovers of all human race!

Richard Savage : London and Bristol Delineated.

Hogarth's Tour

1732

'TWAS first of morn on Saturday,
The seven-and-twentieth day of May,
When Hogarth, Thornhill, Tothall, Scott,
And Forrest, who this journal wrote,
From Covent-Garden took departure,
To see the world by land and water.
Our march we with a song begin;
Our hearts were light, our breeches thin,

We meet with nothing of adventure
Till Billingsgate's Dark-house we enter,
Where we diverted were, while baiting,
With ribaldry, not worth relating
(Quite suited to the dirty place).
But what most pleas'd us was his Grace
Of Puddle Dock, a porter grim,
Whose portrait Hogarth, in a whim,
Presented him in caricature,
He pasted on the cellar door.
    But hark! the Watchman cries "Past one,"
'Tis time that we on board were gone.
Clean straw we find laid for our bed,
A tilt for shelter over head.
The boat is soon got under sail,
Wind near S.E. a mack'rel gale,
Attended by a heavy rain;
We try to sleep, but try in vain,
So sing a song, and then begin
To feast on biscuit, beef, and gin.
    At Purfleet find three men of war,
The Dursley galley, Gibraltar,
And Tartar pink, and of this last
The pilot begg'd of us a cast
To Gravesend, which he greatly wanted,
And readily by us was granted.
The grateful man, to make amends,
Told how the officers and friends
Of England were by Spaniards treated,
And shameful instances repeated.
    While he these insults was deploring,
Hogarth, like Premier, fell to snoring,
But waking cry'd, "I dream'd"—and then

Fell fast asleep, and snor'd again.
The morn clear'd up, and after five
At port of Gravesend we arrive.

.   .   .   .

We made a shift to land by six,
And up to Mrs. Bramble's go
(A house that we shall better know),
There get a barber for our wigs,
Wash hands and faces, stretch our legs,
Had toast and butter, and a pot
Of coffee (our third breakfast) got:
Then, paying what we had to pay,
For Rochester we took our way,
Viewing the new church as we went,
And th' unknown person's monument.
The beauteous prospects found us talk,
And shorten'd much our two hours' walk,
Though by the way we did not fail
To stop and take three pots of ale,
And this enabled us by ten
At Rochester to drink again.

.   .   .   .   .
.   .   .   .

Tobacco then, and wine provide,
Enough to serve us for this tide.
Get dinner, and our reckoning pay,
And next prepare for London hey;
So, hiring to ourselves a wherry,
We put off, all alive and merry.
    The tide was strong, fair was the wind,
Gravesend is soon left far behind,

Under the tilt on straw we lay,
Observing what a charming day,
There stretch'd at ease we smoke and drink
Londoners like, and now we think
Our cross adventures all are past,
And that at Gravesend was the last :
But cruel Fate to that says no ;
One yet shall Fortune find his foe.
　　While we (with various prospects cloy'd)
In clouds of smoke ourselves enjoy'd,
More diligent and curious, Scott
Into the forecastle had got,
And took his papers out, to draw
Some ships which right ahead he saw,
There sat he, on his work intent,
When, to increase our merriment,
So luckily we shipped a sea,
That he got sous'd, and only he.

　　　　·　　　　·　　　　·　　　　·

　　Nothing more happen'd worthy note :
At Billingsgate we change our boat,
And in another through bridge get,
By two, to Stairs of Somerset,
Welcome each other to the shore,
To Covent Garden walk once more,
And, as from Bedford Arms we started,
There wet our whistles ere we parted.
　　With pleasure I observe, none idle
Were in our travels, or employ'd ill.
Tothall, our treasurer, was just,
And worthily discharg'd his trust ;
(We all sign'd his accounts as fair ;)

Sam Scott and Hogarth, for their share,
The prospects of the sea and land did ;
As Thornhill of our tour the plan did ;
And Forrest wrote this true relation
Of our five days' peregrination.
This to attest our names we've wrote all,
Viz. Thornhill, Hogarth, Scott, and Tothall.

W. Gostling.

The Jolly Young Waterman

1774

AND did you not hear of a jolly young waterman,
Who at Blackfriars Bridge used to ply ?
He feather'd his oars with such skill and dexterity,
Winning each heart and delighting each eye.
He look'd so neat and row'd so steadily,
The maidens all flocked to his boat so readily ;
And he ey'd the young rogues with so charming an air,
That this waterman ne'er was in want of a fare.

What sights of fine folks he row'd in his wherry,
'Twas clean'd out so nice and so painted withal ;
He was always first oars when the fine city ladies
In a party to Ranelagh went, or Vauxhall.
And oftentimes would they be giggling and leering,
But 'twas all one to Tom, their jibing and jeering ;
For loving or liking he little did care,
For this waterman ne'er was in want of a fare.

And yet but to see how strangely things happen,
  As he row'd along thinking of nothing at all,
He was plied by a damsel so lovely and charming,
  That she smiled and so straightway in love did he fall.
And would this young damsel but banish his sorrow,
He'd wed her to-night, before to-morrow ;
And how should this waterman ever know care,
When he's married and never in want of a fare ?

      Charles Dibdin : The Waterman, or the
          First of August.

Poll of Wapping

1810

YOUR London girls, with all their airs,
  Must strike to Poll of Wapping Stairs,
No tighter lass is going,
From Iron Gate to Limehouse Hole
You'll never meet a kinder soul :
  Not while the Thames is flowing.

And sing Pull away, pull away, Pull ! I say,
Not while the Thames is flowing !

Her father, he's a hearty dog,
Poll makes his flip, and serves his grog,
  And never stints his measure ;
She minds full well the house affairs,
She seldom drinks, and never swears ;
  And isn't that a pleasure ?

And sing Pull away, pull away, Pull ! I say,
Not while the Thames is flowing !
And when we wed, the happy time,
The bells of Wapping all shall chime ;
And, ere we go to Davy,
The girls like her shall work and sing,
The boys like me shall serve the King,
On board Old England's Navy !

And sing Pull away, pull away, Pull ! I say,
Not while the Thames is flowing !

Charles Dibdin : Songs.

Wapping Old Stairs

1790

YOUR Molly has never been false, she declares,
    Since last time we parted at Wapping Old Stairs,
When I swore that I still would continue the same,
And gave you the 'bacco box mark'd with your name ;
When I pass'd a whole fortnight between decks with you,
Did I e'er give a kiss, Tom, to one of the crew ?
To be useful and kind, with my Thomas I stay'd,
For his trousers I wash'd, and his grog, too, I made.

Though you threaten'd, last Sunday, to walk in the Mall
With Susan from Deptford, and likewise with Sal,
In silence I stood your unkindness to hear,
And only upbraided my Tom with a tear :

Why should Sal, or should Susan, than me be more priz'd?
For the heart that is true, Tom, should ne'er be despis'd;
Then be constant and kind, nor your Molly forsake,
Still your trousers I'll wash, and your grog, too, I'll make.

"Arley": The British Album.

A Whitebait Dinner

1812

ALL day we sat, until the sun went down—
   'Twas summer, and the Dog-star scorched the town—
At fam'd Blackwall, O Thames! upon thy shore,
Where Lovegrove's tables groan beneath their store;
We feasted full on every famous dish,
Dress'd many ways, of sea and river fish—
Perch, mullet, eels, and salmon, all were there,
And whitebait, daintiest of our fishy fare;
Then meat of many kinds, and venison last,
Quails, fruit, and ices, crowned the rich repast.
Thy fields, Champagne, supplied us with our wine,
Madeira's Island, and the rocks of Rhine.
The sun was set, and twilight veiled the land:
Then all stood up,—all who had strength to stand,
And pouring down, of Maraschino, fit
Libations to the gods of wine and wit,
In steam-wing'd chariots, and on iron roads,
Sought the great City and our own abodes.

Thomas Love Peacock: Collected Poems.

The Boy at the Nore

1836

I SAY, little Boy at the Nore,
  Do you come from the small Isle of Man?
Why, your history a mystery must be,—
  Come tell us as much as you can,
      Little Boy at the Nore!

You live, it seems, wholly on water,
  Which your Gambier calls living in clover;
But how comes it, if that is the case,
  You're eternally half-seas over,—
      Little Boy at the Nore?

While you ride, while you dance, while you float,
  Never mind your imperfect orthography;
But give us as well as you can,
  Your watery autobiography,
      Little Boy at the Nore!

BOY AT THE NORE (*loquitur*).

I'm the tight little Boy at the Nore,
  In a sort of sea negus I dwells;
Half and half 'twixt salt-water and Port,
  I'm reckoned the first of the swells,—
      I'm the Boy at the Nore!

I lives with my toes to the flounders,
  And watches through long days and nights;
Yet, cruelly eager, men look
  To catch the first glimpse of my lights,—
      I'm the Boy at the Nore.

I never gets cold in the head,
 So my life on salt-water is sweet;
I think I owes much of my health
 To being well used to wet feet—
     As the Boy at the Nore.

There's one thing, I'm never in debt;
 Nay!—I liquidates more than I oughter;
So the man to beat Cits as goes by,
 In keeping the head above water,
     Is the Boy at the Nore.

I've seen a good deal of distress,
 Lots of Breakers in Ocean's Gazette;
They should do as I do,—rise o'er all;
 Ay, a good floating capital get,
     Like the Boy at the Nore!

I'm a'ter the sailor's own heart,
 And cheers him, in deep water rolling;
And the friend of all friends to Jack Junk,
 Ben Backstay, Tom Pipes, and Tom Bowling,
     Is the Boy at the Nore!

Could I e'er but grow up, I'd be off
 For a week to make love to my wheedles;
If the tight little Boy at the Nore
 Could but catch a nice girl at the Needles,
     We'd have *two* at the Nore!

They thinks little of sizes on water,
 On big waves the tiny one skulks,—

While the river has Men of War on it,—
  Yes, the Thames is oppressed with Great Hulks,
      And the Boy's at the Nore !

But I've done,—for the water is heaving
  Round my body as though it would sink it !
And I've been so long pitching and tossing,
  That sea-sick—you'd hardly now think it—
      Is the Boy at the Nore !
          Thomas Hood : Collected Poems.

Father of Cities

1897

FATHER of cities, on whose bosom vast
  A thousand golden argosies have lain,
  Wilt thou yet flow dishonoured to the main
With all thy mighty palaces down cast ?
Broken as Tyre's of old thy myriad mast ?
    Night's diadems on gleaming arch and fane
    That crown thee as a monarch, sunk and vain ?
Scrolled on a barren wilderness thy past ?

If so, proud river ! still thy boast may be
That thou dost bear to the forgetful sea
    Such spoil as never yet oblivion
    Hath sepulchred within her furrow wan ;
And that hath perished with thy fame and thee
    The brightest aureole from glory gone.
          Margaret Armour : Thames Sonnets.

LONDON CITY

Thy famous Maire, by pryncely governaunce,
  With swerd of justice the ruleth prudently.
No Lord of Paris, Venyce, or Floraunce
  In dygnitie or honoure goeth to hym nye.
  He is exampler, loodë-star, and guye,
Principall patrone and roose orygynalle,
  Above all Maires as maister moost worthy ;
London, thou art the Flour of Cities all.
                              Dunbar.

CLERK of the Bow bell with the yellow locks,
    For thy late ringing thy head shall have knocks.

Children of Cheap, hold you all still,
For you shall have the Bow bell rung at your will.

Old City Rhyme.

London Praised and Cursed

1682

LONDON, thou great Emporium of our isle,
    O, thou too bounteous, thou too fruitful Nile !
How shall I praise or curse to thy desert ?
Or separate thy sound from thy corrupted part ?
I call'd thee Nile ; the parallel will stand :
Thy tides of wealth o'erflow the fatten'd land ;
Yet monsters from thy large increase we find
Engender'd on the slime thou leav'st behind.
Sedition has not wholly seiz'd on thee ;
Thy nobler parts are from infection free.
Of Israel's tribes thou hast a numerous band ;
But still the Canaanite is in the land ;

Thy military chiefs are brave and true ;
Nor are thy disenchanted burghers few.
The head is loyal which thy heart commands ;
But what's a head with two such gouty hands ?
The wise and wealthy love the surest way ;
And are content to thrive and to obey.
But wisdom is to sloth too great a slave ;
None are so busy as the fool and knave.
Those let me curse ; what vengeance will they urge,
Whose ordures neither plague nor fire can purge ;
Nor sharp experience can to duty bring,
Nor angry Heaven, nor a forgiving king !

John Dryden : The Medal.

A London Prentice

About 1387

A PRENTIS whylom dwelled in our citee,
    And of a craft of vitaillers was he ;
Gaillard he was, as goldfinch in the shawe,
Broun as a berie, a propre short felawe,
With lokkës blake, y-kempt ful fetisly.
Dauncen he could so wel and jolily,
That he was cleped Perkin Revelour.
He was as ful of love and paramour
As is the hivë ful of honey swete ;
Wel was the wenchë with him mightë mete.
At every brydale woulde he singe and hoppe,
He lovéd bet the taverne than the shoppe.
For whan ther any ryding was in Chepe,
Out of the shoppë thider wolde he lepe,

Til that he haddë al the sighte y-seyn,
And dauncéd wel, he wolde nat come ageyn ;
And gadered him a meinee of his sort
To hoppe and singe, and maken swich disport.
And ther they setten steven for to mete
To pleyen at the dys in swich a strete.
For in the tounë was ther no prentys
That fairer coudë caste a paire of dys
Than Perkin coude, and there-to he was free
Of his dispense, in place of privetee.
That fond his maister wel in his chaffare ;
For often tyme he fond his box ful bare.

For soothly a prentis, a revelour,
That haunteth dys, riot, or paramour,
His maister shal it in his shoppe abye,
Al have he no part of the minstralcye ;
For thefte and riot, they ben convertible,
Al conne he pleye on giterne or ribible.
Revel and trouthe, as in a low degree,
They ben ful wrothe al day, as men may see.

This ioly prentis with his maister abood,
Til he were ny out of his prentishood,
Al were he snibbéd bothe erly and late,
And somtyme lad with revel to Newgate ;
But atté laste his maister him bethoghte,
Up-on a day, whan he his paper soghte,
Of a proverbë that seith this same word,
" Wel bet is roten appel out of hord
Than that it rotie al the remënaunt."
So fareth it by a riotous servaunt ;
It is wel lasse harm to lete him pace,
Than he shende alle the servaunts in the place.
Therefore his maister yaf him aquitance,

And bad him go with sorwe and with meschance;
And thus this ioly prentis hadde his leve.
Now lat him riote al the night or leve.

Geoffrey Chaucer: Canterbury Tales.

To Ring the Bells of London Town

18th Century

Gay go up and gay go down,
To ring the bells of London Town.

Oranges and lemons,
Say the bells of St. Clement's.

Bull's eyes and targets
Say the bells of St. Marg'ret's.

Brickbats and tiles,
Say the bells of St. Giles'.

Halfpence and farthings,
Say the bells of St. Martin's.

Pancakes and fritters,
Say the bells of St. Peter's.

Two sticks and an apple,
Say the bells of Whitechapel.

Pokers and tongs,
Say the bells of St. John's.

Kettles and pans,
Say the bells of St. Ann's.

Old father Baldpate,
Say the slow bells of Aldgate.

You owe me ten shillings,
Say the bells of St. Helen's.

When will you pay me?
Say the bells of Old Bailey.

When I grow rich,
Say the bells of Shoreditch.

Pray when will that be,
Say the bells of Stepney.

I do not know,
Says the great bell of Bow.

Gay go up and gay go down,
To ring the bells of London Town.

Nursery Rhyme.

Sir Richard Whittington's Advancement

16th Century

HERE must I tell the praise
    Of worthy Whittington,
Known to be in his days
    Thrice lord-mayor of London.

But of poor parentage
    Born was he, as we hear,
And in his tender age
    Bred up in Lancashire.

Poorly to London then
    Came up this simple lad;
Where, with a merchant-man,
    Soon he a dwelling had;

And in a kitchen plac'd
    A scullion for to be;
Where a long time he pass'd
    In labour drudgingly.

His daily service was
    Turning at the fire;
And to scour pots of brass,
    For a poor scullion's hire:

Meat and drink all his pay,
    Of coin he had no store;
Therefore to run away
    In secret thought he bore.

So from the merchant-man
 Whittington secretly
Towards his country ran,
 To purchase liberty.

But as he went along
 In a fair summer's morn,
London's bells sweetly rung
 Whittington's back return ;

Evermore sounding so—
 " Turn again, Whittington ;
For thou, in time, shall grow
 Lord-mayor of London."

Whereupon, back again
 Whittington came with speed,
A servant to remain
 As the Lord had decreed.

Still blessed be the bells,
 This was his daily song ;
This my good fortune tells,
 Most sweetly have they rung.

If God so favour me,
 I will not prove unkind ;
London my love shall see,
 And my large bounties find.

But, see his happy chance !
 This scullion had a cat,
Which did his state advance,
 And by it wealth he gat.

His master ventur'd forth,
  To a land far unknown,
With merchandize of worth
  As is in stories shown:

Whittington had no more
  But his poor cat as then,
Which to the ship he bore
  Like a brave, valiant man.

Vent'ring the same, quoth he,
  I may get store of gold,
And mayor of London be,
  As the bells have me told.

Whittington's merchandize,
  Carried to a land
Troubled with rats and mice
  As they did understand;

The king of the country there,
  As he at dinner sat,
Daily remain'd in fear
  Of many mouse and rat.

Meat that on trenchers lay,
  No way they could keep safe;
But by rats bore away,
  Fearing no wand or staff;

Whereupon, soon they brought
  Whittington's nimble cat;
Which by the king was bought,
  Heaps of gold given for that.

DICK WHITTINGTON

Home again came these men,
    With their ship laden so;
Whittington's wealth began
    By this cat thus to grow:

Scullion's life he forsook,
    To be a merchant good,
And soon began to look
    How well his credit stood.

After that, he was chose
    Sheriff of the City here,
And then full quickly rose
    Higher, as did appear:

For, to the City's praise,
    Sir Richard Whittington
Came to be in his days
    Thrice mayor of London.

More his fame to advance,
    Thousands he lent the king,
To maintain war in France,
    Glory from thence to bring.

And after, at a feast
    Which he the king did make,
He burnt the bonds all in jest,
    And would no money take.

Ten thousand pounds he gave
    To his prince willingly;
And would no penny have
    For this kind courtesy.

As God thus made him great,
   So he would daily see
Poor people fed with meat,
   To shew his charity;

Prisoners poor cherish'd were,
   Widows sweet comfort found;
Good deeds, both far and near
   Of him do still resound.

Whittington's college is
   One of his charities;
Record reporteth this
   To lasting memories.

Newgate he builded fair,
   For prisoners to lie in;
Christ-church he did repair
   Christian love for to win.

Many more such like deeds
   Were done by Whittington;
Which joy and comfort breeds,
   To such as look thereon.
                              Old Ballad.

Pretty Bessee and the London Merchant

About 1550

ITT was a blind beggar, had long lost his sight,
   He had a faire daughter of bewty most bright:
And many a gallant brave suiter had shee,
For none was soe comelye as prettye Bessee.

And though shee was of favor most faire,
Yett seeing shee was but a poor beggar's heyre
Of ancyent housekeepers despised was shee
Whose sonnes came as suiters to prettye Bessee.

Wherefore in great sorrow faire Bessy did say,
Good father and mother, let me goe away
To seeke out my fortune, whatever it bee.
This suite then they granted to prettye Bessee.

Then Bessy, that was of bewtye soe bright,
All cladd in gray russett, and late in the night
From father and mother alone parted shee;
Who sighed and sobbed for prettye Bessee.

Shee went till shee came to Stratford-le-Bow;
Then knew shee not whither, nor which way to goe;
With teares she lamented her hard destinie,
So sadd and soe heavy was prettye Bessee.

Shee kept on her journey untill it was day,
And went unto Rumford along the hye way;
Where at the Queenes Armes entertained was shee :
So faire and wel favoured was prettye Bessee.

Shee had not been there a month to an end,
But master and mistress and all was her friend :
And every brave gallant, that once did her see
Was streight-way enamourd of prettye Bessee.

Great gifts they did send her of silver and gold,
And in their songs daylye her love was extold ;
Her bewtye was blazed in every degree ;
Soe fayre and soe comlye was prettye Bessee.

The young men of Rumford in her had their joy,
Shee shewed herself courteous and modestlye coye;
And at her commandment still wold they bee;
Soe fayre and soe comlye was prettye Bessee.

Foure suitors att once unto her did goe;
They craved her favor, but still she sayd noe;
I wold not wish gentles to marry with mee.
Yett ever they honored prettye Bessee.

The first of them was a gallant young knight,
And he came unto her disguisde in the night,
The second a gentleman of good degree,
Who wooed and sued for prettye Bessee.

A merchant of London, whose wealth was not small,
He was the third suiter, and proper withall;
Her master's own sonne the fourth man must bee,
Who swore he would dye for prettye Bessee.

And, if thou wilt marry with mee, quoth the knight,
Ile make thee a ladye with joy and delight;
My hart's so inthralled by thy bewtie,
That soone I shall dye for prettye Bessee.

The gentleman sayd, Come marry with mee,
As fine as a ladye my Bessy shal bee:
My life is distressed: O heare me, quoth hee;
And grant me thy love, my prettye Bessee.

Let me bee thy husband, the merchant cold say,
Thou shalt live in London both gallant and gay;
My shippes shall bring home rych jewells for thee,
And I will for ever love prettye Bessee.

Then Bessy shee sighed, and thus shee did say,
My father and mother I meane to obey;
First gett there good will, and be faithfull to mee,
And you shall enjoye your prettye Bessee.

To every one this answer shee made,
Wherefore unto her they joyfullye sayd,
This thing to fulfill wee all doe agree;
But where dwells thy father, my prettye Bessee?

My father, shee said, is soone to be seene;
The seely blind beggar of Bednall-greene,
That daylye sits begging for charitie,
He is the good father of prettye Bessee.

His markes and his tokens are knowen very well;
He alwayes is led with a dogg and a bell;
A seely olde man, God knoweth, is hee,
Yett hee is the father of prettye Bessee.

Nay then, quoth the merchant, thou art not for mee:
Nor, quoth the innholder, my wiffe thou shalt bee:
I lothe, sayd the gentle, a beggar's degree,
And therefore, adewe, my prettye Bessee!

Why then, quoth the knight, hap better or worse,
I waighe not true love by the waight of the purse,
And bewtye is bewtye in every degree;
Then welcome unto me, my prettye Bessee.

With thee to thy father forthwith I will goe.
Nay soft, quoth his kinsmen, it must not be soe;
A poor beggar's daughter noe ladye shall bee,
Then take thy adew of prettye Bessee.

But soone after this, by breake of the day
The knight had from Rumford stole Bessy away.
The younge men of Rumford, as thicke might bee,
Rode after to feitch againe prettye Bessee.

As swifte as the winde to ryde they were seene,
Untill they came neare unto Bednall-greene ;
And as the knight lighted most courteouslie
They all fought against him for prettye Bessee.

But rescew came speedilye over the plaine,
Or else the young knight for his love had been slaine.
This fray being ended, then straitway he see
His kinsmen come rayling at prettye Bessee.

Then spake the blind beggar, Although I bee poore,
Yett rayle not against my child at my own doore ;
Though shee be not decked in velvett and pearle,
Yett will I drop angells with you for my girle.

And then, if my gold may better her birthe,
And equall the gold that you lay on the earth,
Then neyther rayle nor grudge you to see
The blind beggar's daughter a lady to bee.

But first you shall promise, and have itt well knowne,
The gold that you drop shall all be your owne.
With that they replyed, Contented bee wee.
Then here's quoth the beggar for prettye Bessee.

With that an angell he cast on the ground,
And dropped in angels full three thousand pound ;
And oftentimes itt was proved most plaine,
For the gentlemen's one the beggar droppt twayne.

Soe that the place, wherein they did sitt,
With gold it was covered every whitt.
The gentlemen then having dropt all their store,
Sayd, Now, beggar, hold, for wee have noe more.

Thou hast fulfilled thy promise aright.
Then marry, quoth he, my girle to this knight;
And heere, added hee, I will now throwe you downe
A hundred pounds more to buy her a gowne.

The gentlemen all, that this treasure had seene,
Admired the beggar of Bednall-greene :
And all those, that were her suiters before,
Their fleshe for very anger they tore.

Thus was faire Besse matched to the knight,
And then made a ladye in others despite ;
A fairer ladye there never was seene,
Than the blind beggar's daughter of Bednall-greene.

But of their sumptuous marriage and feast,
What brave lords and knights thither were prest,
The second fitt shall set forth to your sight
With marveilous pleasure and wished delight.
Percy's Reliques of Ancient English Poetry.

London's Seven Images

1668

THOUGH most of the images be pulled down,
        And none be thought remain in town,
I am sure there be in London yet
Seven images in such and such a place ;

And few or none I think will hit,
Yet every day they show their face,
And thousands see them every year,
But few I think can tell me where,
Where Jesu Christ aloft doth stand :
Law and Learning on either hand,
Discipline in the Devil's neck,
And hard by her are three direct,
There Justice, Fortitude, and Temperance stand,
Where find ye the like in all this land ?

Inscription in the Porch of the Old Guildhall.

London's Welcome to Henry V.

1415

THE Mayr of London was redy bown,
    With alle the craftes of that Citee,
Alle clothyd in red through out the town,
A semely sight it was to se :
To the Blak heth thanne rod he,
And spredde the way on every syde :
XX^{ti} M^l men myght well se,
Our comely Kyng for to abyde.
    Wot ye right well that thus it was,
    Gloria tibi Trinitas.

The Kyng from Eltham sone he cam,
Hys presenors with hym dede brynge,
And to the Blak heth ful sone he cam,
He saw London withoughte lesynge ;

Heil, ryall London, seyde oure Kyng,
Crist the kepe evere from care ;
And thanne gaf it his blessyng,
And praied to Crist that it well fare.
    Wot ye right well that thus it was,
    Gloria tibi Trinitas.

The Mair hym mette with moche honour,
With all the aldermen without lesyng ;
Heil, seyde the mair, the conquerour,
The grace of God with the doth spryng ;
Heil duk, heil prynce, heil comely Kyng,
Most worthiest Lord under Crist ryall,
Heil rulere of Remes withoute lettyng,
Heil flour of knyghts now over all.
    Wot ye right well that thus it was,
    Gloria tibi Trinitas.

Here is come youre Citee all,
Yow to worchepe and to magnyfye,
To welcome yow, bothe gret and small,
With yow everemore to lyve and dye.
Grauntmercy, Sires, our Kyng gan say ;
And toward London he gan ride ;
This was upon seynt Clementys day,
They wolcomed hym on every syde.
    Wot ye right well that thus it was,
    Gloria tibi Trinitas.

The lordes of Fraunce, thei gan say then,
Ingelond is nought as we wen,
It farith be these Englisshmen,
As it doth be a swarm of ben ;

Ingland is like an hive withinne,
There fleeres makith us full well to wryng,
Tho ben there arrowes sharpe and kene,
Through oure harneys they do us styng.
    Wot ye right well that thus it was,
    Gloria tibi Trinitas.

To London Brigge thanne rood oure Kyng,
The processions there they mette hym ryght,
" Ave Rex Anglor," their gan syng,
" Flos mundi," thei seyde, Goddys knyght,
To London Brigge whan he com ryght,
Upon the gate ther stode on hy,
A gyaunt that was full grym of syght,
To teche the Frensshmen curtesye.
    Wot ye right well that thus it was,
    Gloria tibi Trinitas.

And at the drawe brigge, that is faste by,
Two toures there were upright;
An antelope and a lyon stondyng hym by,
Above them seynt George oure lady knyght,
Besyde hym many an angell bright,
" Benedictus " thei gan synge,
" Qui venit in nomine domin," goddes knyght,
" Gracia Dei " with yow doth sprynge.
    Wot ye right well that thus it was,
    Gloria tibi Trinitas.

Into London thanne rood oure Kyng,
Full goodly there thei gonnen hym grete;
Through out the town thanne gonne they syng,
For joy and merthe y yow behete;

Men and women for joye they alle,
Of his comyn thei weren so fayn,
That the Condyd bothe grete and smalle,
Ran wyn ich on as y herde sayn.
    Wot ye right well that thus it was,
    Gloria tibi Trinitas.

The tour of Cornhill that is so shene,
I may well say now as y knowe,
It was full of Patriarkes alle be dene,
" Cantate " thei songe upon a rowe ;
There bryddes thei gon down throwe,
An hundred there flewe aboughte oure kyng,
" Laus ejus " bothe hyghe and lowe
" In ecclesia sanctorum," thei dyd syng.
    Wot ye right well that thus it was,
    Gloria tibi Trinitas.

Unto the Chepe thanne rood oure Kyng ;
To the Condyt whanne he com tho,
The XII apostelys thei gon syng,
" Benedict, anima domino."
XII kynges there were on a rowe,
They kneyld doun be on asent,
And obles aboughte oure Kyng gan throwe
And wolcomyd hym with good entent.
    Wot ye right well that thus it was,
    Gloria tibi Trinitas.

The Cros in Chepe verrament,
It was gret joy it for to beholde ;
It was araied full reverent,
With a castell right as God wolde,

R

With baners brighte beten with gold.
And angelys senssyd hym that tyde ;
With besaunts riche many a fold,
They strowed oure Kyng on every syde.
   Wot ye right well that thus it was,
   Gloria tibi Trinitas.

Virgynes out of the castell gon glyde,
For joy of hym they were daunsyng,
They kneyld a doun alle in that tyde,
" Nowell," " Nowell," alle thei gon syng.
Unto Poules thanne rood oure Kyng,
XIII bysshopes hym mette there right,
The grete bellys thanne did they ryng,
Upon his feet full faire he light.
   Wot ye right well that thus it was,
   Gloria tibi Trinitas.

And to the heighe auter he went right,
" Te Deum " for joye thanne thei gon syng ;
And there he offred to God almyght :
And thanne to Westminster he wente withoute dwellyng.
In XV wekes forsothe, he wroughte al this,
Conquered Harfleu and Agincourt ;
Crist brynge there soules all to blys,
That in that day were mort.
   Wot ye right well that thus it was,
   Gloria tibi Trinitas.

Crist that is oure Hevene Kyng,
His body and soule save and se ;
Now all Ingelond may say and syng,
" Blyssyd mote be the Trinite,"

This jornay have ye herd now alle be done,
The date of Crist I wot it was,
A thousand foure hundred and fyftene.
Wot ye right well that thus it was,
Gloria tibi Trinitas.

John Lydgate: Minor Poems.

After Agincourt

1599

BEHOLD, the English beach
  Pales in the flood with men, with wives, and boys,
Whose shouts and claps out-voice the deep-mouth'd sea,
Which, like a mighty whiffler 'fore the king,
Seems to prepare his way: so let him land ;
And solemnly see him set on to London.
So swift a pace hath thought, that even now
You may imagine him upon Blackheath ;
Where that his lords desire him to have borne
His bruisèd helmet, and his bended sword,
Before him through the city : he forbids it,
Being free from vainness and self-glorious pride ;
Giving full trophy, signal, and ostent,
Quite from himself to God.   But now behold,
In the quick forge and working-house of thought,
How London doth pour out her citizens !
The mayor and all his brethren, in best sort,—
Like to the senators of th' antique Rome,
With the plebeians swarming at their heels,—
Go forth, and fetch their conquering Cæsar in.

William Shakespeare: Henry V.

Lines Spoken at the Opening of the New River

1613

LONG have we labour'd, long desir'd and pray'd,
        For this great work's perfection : And by the aid
Of Heaven, and good men's wishes, 'tis at length
Happily conquer'd by cost, art, and strength,
And after five years' dear expense in days,
Travail, and pains, beside the infinite ways
Of envy, malice, false suggestions,
Able to daunt the spirits of mighty ones
In wealth and courage.   This, a work so rare,
Only by one man's industry, cost, and care,
Is brought to blest effect, so much withstood ;
His only aim, the City's general good.
And where (before) many unjust complaints,
Enviously seated, caused oft restraints,
Stops, and great crosses, to our master's charge
And the work's hindrance : Favour now at large
Spreads itself open to him, and commends
To admiration both his pains and ends :
The king's most gracious love.   Perfection draws
Favour from princes, and from all applause.
Then worthy magistrates, to whose content,
(Next to the state) all this great care was bent,
And for the public good (which grace requires)
Your loves and furtherance chiefly he desires,
To cherish these proceedings, which may give
Courage to some that may hereafter live,

To practise deeds of goodness and of fame,
And gladly light their actions by his name.

Clerk of the work, reach me the book to show,
How many arts from such a labour flow.
First, here's the overseer, this tri'd man,
An ancient soldier, and an artisan.
The clerk, next him, mathematician,
The master of the timber-work takes place
Next after these; the measurer, in like case,
Bricklayer, and engineer; and after those,
The borer and the pavior.   Then it shows
The labourers; next keeper of Amwell-head,
The walkers last: so all their names are read.
Yet these but parcels of six hundred more,
That (at one time) have been employ'd before.
Yet these in sight, and all the rest will say,
That all the week they had their ready pay.
Now for the fruits then: Flow forth, precious Spring,
So long and dearly sought for, and now bring
Comfort to all that love thee; loudly sing,
And with thy crystal murmurs strook together,
Bid all thy true well-wishers welcome hither.

City Poet: Stow's Survey of London.

King James I. at St. Paul's

1619

GOD bless our noble king,
     Was there ever such a thing!
In March, when the weather waxed cold,

He went from Whitehall
To the church of St. Paul,
Which oft-time hath been bought and sold.

When he came to Temple Bar,
Which you know it is not far,
The streets were rail'd on every side;
There were many gay babies,
And fair brave painted ladies,
"God bless our noble king!" they all cried.

The Mayor of the town
Came in a velvet gown,
And with him never catchpole or varlet,
But jobbernolls there were plenty,
Aldermen almost twenty,
And most of them were clad all in scarlet.

The Mayor laid down his mace,
And cry'd, "God save Your Grace,
And keep our king from all evil!"
With all my heart, I then wist
The good mace had been in my fist,
To ha' pawn'd it for supper at the *Devil*.

The master Recorder,
In very seemly order
Made unto the king such a speech,
In such mild and loving sort,
As most men do report,
It made their hearts to fall into their breech.

It would have done your hearts good
To ha' seen how the company stood,
With their flags and their banners so gay ;
Their wives they were not there,
Might a man not safely swear
There was many a cuckold made that day ?

Archie came in gold
Most glorious to behold,
Which made the people fall into a laughter ;
Some men that stood by,
When the fool they did spy
Expected many lords to follow after.

When they miss'd the king's cloak,
It sore amaz'd the folk,
To see him in his doublet and his hose ;
His horse had, before and behind,
Two feathers to keep off the wind,
Which was as good as you may well suppose.

But when he came to Paul's
God bless all Christian souls !
Open flew the great west door,
And in the king did enter,
Was he not bold to venture,
That never was in Paul's in life before.

The priests in their copes,
Like to so many popes,
Sung all to rejoicing of the people ;
And as they all sung,
The bells they should have rung,
But i' faith there was but one in the steeple.

God bless our noble king,
In winter and in spring,
The prince and the lady so gay !
God bless our lords and many more,
The bishops, earls, and judges,
Would ever rejoice to see this day.

Old Ballad.

The Great Fire

1666

AS when some dire usurper Heaven provides
    To scourge his country with a lawless sway,
His birth perhaps some petty village hides
And sets his cradle out of fortune's way :

Till fully ripe, his swelling fate breaks out,
    And hurries him to mighty mischiefs on :
His prince, surprised at first, no ill could doubt,
    And wants the power to meet it when 'tis known.

Such was the rise of this prodigious Fire
    Which, in mean buildings first obscurely bred,
From thence did soon to open streets aspire,
    And straight to palaces and temples spread.

The diligence of trades and noiseful gain,
    And luxury, more late, asleep were laid :
All was the Night's, and in her silent reign,
    No sound the rest of nature did invade.

In this deep quiet, from what source unknown,
    These seeds of fire their fatal birth disclose ;
And, first, few scattering sparks about were blown,
    Big with the flames that to our ruin rose.

There in some close-pent room it crept along,
    And, smouldering as it went, in silence fed ;
Till th' infant monster, with devouring strong,
    Walked boldly upright with exalted head.

THE ALARM

At length the crackling noise and dreadful blaze
    Called up some waking lover to the sight ;
And long it was ere he the rest could raise,
    Whose heavy eyelids yet were full of night.

The next to danger, hot pursued by fate,
    Half-clothed, half-naked, hastily retire ;
And frighted mothers strike their breasts, too late,
    For helpless infants left amidst the fire.

Their cries soon waken all the dwellers near ;
    Now murmuring noises rise in every street ;
The more remote run stumbling with their fear,
    And in the dark men justle as they meet.

So weary bees in little cells repose ;
    But if night-robbers lift the well-stored hive,
A humming through their waxen city grows,
    And out upon each other's wings they drive.

Now streets grow thronged and busy as by day :
    Some run for buckets to the hallowed quire ;
Some cut the pipes, and some the engines play,
    And some, more bold, mount ladders to the fire.

In vain : for from the east a Belgian wind
    His hostile breath through the dry rafters sent ;
The flames impelled soon left their foes behind,
    And forward, with a wanton fury, went.

A key of fire ran all along the shore,
    And lightened all the river with a blaze ;
The wakened tides began again to roar,
    And wondering fish in shining waters gaze.

Old Father Thames raised up his reverend head,
    But feared the fate of Simois would return ;
Deep in his ooze he sought his sedgy bed,
    And shrunk his waters back into his urn.

DAY AND THE KING

Now day appears, and with the day the King,
    Whose early care had robbed him of his rest ;
Far off the cracks of falling houses ring,
    And shrieks of subjects pierce his tender breast.

Near as he draws, thick harbingers of smoke,
    With gloomy pillars, cover all the place,
Whose little intervals of night are broke
    By sparks that drive against his sacred face.

More than his guards his sorrows made him known,
    And pious tears which down his cheeks did shower;
The wretched in their grief forgot their own;
    So much the pity of a king has power!

He wept the flames of what he loved so well,
    And what so well had merited his love;
For never prince in grace did more excel,
    Or royal city more in duty strove.

Nor with an idle care did he behold;
    (Subjects may grieve, but monarchs must redress;)
He cheers the fearful, and commends the bold,
    And makes despairers hope for good success.

Himself directs what first is to be done,
    And orders all the succours which they bring:
The helpful and the good about him run,
    And form an army worthy such a king.

He sees the dire contagion spread so fast,
    That, where it seizes, all relief is vain,
And therefore must unwillingly lay waste
    That country which would else the foe maintain.

The powder blows up all before the fire:
    Th' amazed flames stand gathered on a heap,
And from the precipice's brink retire,
    Afraid to venture on so large a leap.

    .   .   .   .   .

No help avails; for, hydra-like, the fire
    Lifts up his hundred heads to aim his way,
And scarce the wealthy can one-half retire,
    Before he rushes in to share the prey.

The rich grow suppliant, and the poor grow proud ;
  Those offer mighty gain, and those ask more :
So void of pity is th' ignoble crowd,
  When others' ruin may increase their store !

. . .

Night in the Fields

Night came, but without darkness or repose,
  A dismal picture of the general doom ;
Where souls distracted when the trumpet blows,
  And half unready, with their bodies come.

Those who have homes, when home they do repair,
  To a last lodging call their wandering friends ;
Their short uneasy sleeps are broke with care,
  To look how near their own destruction tends.

Those who have none sit round where once it was,
  And with full eyes each wonted room require ;
Haunting the yet warm ashes of the place,
  As murdered men walk where they did expire.

Some stir up coals and watch the vestal fire,
  Others in vain from sight of ruin run ;
And while through burning labyrinths they retire,
  With loathing eyes repeat what they would shun.

The most in fields, like herded beasts, lie down,
  To dews obnoxious, on the grassy floor ;
And while their babes in sleep their sorrows drown,
  Sad parents watch the remnants of their store.

While by the motion of the flames they guess
    What streets are burning now, and what are near,
An infant, waking, to the paps would press,
    And meets, instead of milk, a falling tear.

.   .

A NEW LONDON

Methinks already, from this chymic flame,
    I see a City of more precious mould,
Rich as the town which gives the Indies name,
    With silver paved, and all divine with gold.

Already, labouring with a mighty fate,
    She shakes the rubbish from her mounting brow,
And seems to have renewed her charter's date,
    Which Heaven will to the death of time allow.

More great than human now, and more august,
    Now deified, she from her fires does rise ;
Her widening streets on new foundations trust,
    And, opening, into larger parts she flies.

Before, she like some shepherdess did show,
    Who sat to bathe her by a river's side :
Not answering to her fame, but rude and low,
    Nor taught the beauteous arts of modern pride.

Now, like a maiden queen, she will behold,
    From her high turrets, hourly suitors come :
The East with incense, and the West with gold,
    Will stand like suppliants to receive her doom.

The silver Thames, her own domestic flood,
   Shall bear her vessels like a sweeping train ;
And often wind, as of his mistress proud,
   With longing eyes to meet her face again.

The wealthy Tagus, and the wealthier Rhine,
   The glory of their towns no more shall boast,
And Seine, that would with Belgian rivers join,
   Shall find her lustre stained, and traffic lost.

The venturous merchant, who designed more far,
   And touches on our hospitable shore,
Charmed with the splendour of this northern star
   Shall here unlade him, and depart no more.

Our powerful navy shall no longer meet,
   The wealth of France or Holland to invade ;
The beauty of this town, without a fleet,
   From all the world shall vindicate her trade.

And while this famed Emporium we prepare,
   The British Ocean shall such triumphs boast
That those who now disdain our trade to share,
   Shall rob, like pirates, on our wealthy coast.

Already we have conquered half the war,
   And the less dangerous part is left behind ;
Our trouble now is but to make them dare,
   And not so great to vanquish as to find.

Thus to the Eastern wealth through storms we go,
   But now, the Cape once doubled, fear no more ,
A constant trade-wind will securely blow,
   And gently lay us on the spicy shore.

                 John Dryden : Annus Mirabilis.

A Song for the Lord Mayor's Table

1674

LET all the Nine Muses lay by their abuses,
    Their ralling and drolling on tricks of the Strand,
To pen us a ditty in praise of the City,
    Their treasure, and pleasure, their pow'r and command.
Their feast, and guest, so temptingly drest,
    Their kitchens all kingdoms replenish ;
In bountiful bowls they do succour their souls,
    With claret, Canary, and Rhenish :
Their lives and wives in plenitude thrives,
    They want neither meat nor money ;
The Promised Land's in a Londoner's hand,
    They wallow in milk and honey.

For laws, and good orders, Lord Mayor and Recorders,
    And Sheriff, with Councils, keep all in decorum ;
The simple in safety from cruel and crafty,
    When crimes of the times are presented before 'em.
No town as this in Christendom is
    So quiet by day and night ;
No ruffian or drab dares pilfer or stab,
    And hurry away by flight ;
Should danger come, at beat of drum
    (It is in such strong condition),
An army 'twould raise in a very few days,
    With money and ammunition.

For science, and reading, true wit, and good breeding,
    No city's exceeding in bountiful fautors ;

No town under heaven doth give, or has given,
   Such portions to sons, or such dowries to daughters.
Their name and fame doth through all the world flame,
   For courage and gallant lives :
No nation that grows are more curst to their foes,
   Or kinder unto their wives :
For bed and board, this place doth afford
   A quiet repose for strangers ;
The Lord Mayor and Shrieves take such order with thieves,
   Men sleep without fear of dangers.

For gownsmen and swordsmen, this place did afford men,
   That were of great policy, power, and renown ;
A Mayor of this City, stout, valiant, and witty,
   Subdu'd a whole army by stabbing of one ;
A traitor, that ten thousand men gat
   Together in warlike swarms ;
And for this brave feat, his red dagger is set
   In part of the City arms.
Should I declare the worthies that are,
   And did to this place belong,
'Twould puzzle my wit : and I think it more fit
   For a chronicle than a song.

One meanly descended, and weakly attended,
   By Fortune befriended, in this city plac'd,
From pence unto crowns, from crowns unto pounds,
   Up to hundreds of thousands hath risen at last.
In chain of gold, and treasure untold,
   In scarlet, on horseback to boot ;
(To th' joy of his mother) when his elder brother
   It may be, has gone on foot.

Such is the fate of temporal state,
    For Providence thinks it fit,
Since the eldest begat must enjoy the estate,
    The youngest shall have the wit.

Plague, famine, fire, sword, as our stories record,
    Did unto this city severely fix,
And flaming September will make us remember
    One thousand six hundred sixty-six,
When house, and hall, and churches did fall
    (A punishment due for our sin),
No town so quick burn'd, into ashes was turn'd
    And sooner was built again.
Such is the fate of London's estate,
    Sometimes sh' has a sorrowful sup
Of misery's bowl; but to quicken her soul,
    For mercy doth hold her up.

Our ruins did show, five or six years ago,
    Like an object of woe to all eyes that came nigh us:
Yet now 'tis as gay as a garden in May,
    Guildhall and th' Exchange are in *Statu quo prius.*
Our feasts in halls, each company calls,
    To treat 'em as welcome men:
The Muses, all nine, do begin to drink wine;
    Apollo doth shine again.
True union and peace make plenty increase,
    And every trade to spring;
The city so wall'd, may be properly call'd
    The chamber of Charles, our king.

Our princes have been (as on record is seen),
    Good authors and fautors of love to this place;

By many good charters, to strengthen our quarters,
  With divers indulgences, favour, and grace,
Their love so much to London is such,
  They do, as occasion calls,
Their freedom partake, for society sake,—
  Kings have been made free of halls !
If city and court together consort,
  This nation can never be undone :
Then let the hall ring with God prosper the King !
  And bless the Lord Mayor of London.
                    Thomas Jordan : The Goldsmiths' Jubilee.

The Worshipful Drapers

1679

SELECTED citizens i' th' morning all,
    At sev'n o'clock, do meet at *Drapers-Hall*,
The masters, wardens, and assistants, join
For the first rank, in their gowns fac'd with foin ;
The second order do, in merry moods,
March in gowns fac'd with budge and livery hoods ;
In gowns and scarlet hoods thirdly appears
A youthful number of foins bachelors.
Forty budge bachelors the triumph crowns,
Gravely attir'd in scarlet hoods and gowns.
Gentlemen-ushers which white staves do hold
Sixty ; in velvet coats and chains of gold.
Next, thirty more in plush and buff there are,
That several colours wave, and banners bear,
The serjeant trumpet thirty-six more brings,
Twenty the Duke of York's, sixteen the King's,

The serjeant wears two scarfs, whose colours be,
One the Lord Mayor's, t'other's the Company.
The king's drum-major follow'd by four more
Of the king's drums and fifes, make London roar.

Then thus attir'd, with gown, fur, hood, and scarf,
March all through King's-street down to Three-
   Crane-wharf;
Where the Lord Mayor and th' Aldermen discharge
A few gentlemen waiters, and take barge
At the west end o' th' wharf; and at the east
The court assistant, livery, and the best
Gentlemen-ushers: such as stay on shore
Are ushers, foins, and the budge bachelor:
Who for a time repose themselves and men,
Until his lordship shall return again:
Who now with several companies make haste
To Westminster, but in the way is plac'd
A pleasure-boat that hath great guns aboard,
And with two broadsides doth salute my Lord.
They row in triumph all along by th' Strand,
But when my Lord and Companies do land
At the new Palace-stairs, orderly all
Do make a lane to pass him to the hall,
Where having took an oath that he will be
Loyal and faithful to His Majesty,
His government, his crown and dignity,
With other ceremonials said and done,
In order to his confirmation;
Sealing of writs in courts, and such-like things,
As show his power abstracted from the King's,
He takes his leave o' th' lords and barons, then

With his retinue he retreats again
To th' water-side, and (having given at large
To the poor of Westminster) doth re-embarge,
And scud along the river 'till he comes
To Blackfriars-stairs, where guns and thund'ring drums
Proclaim his landing; when he's set ashore,
He is saluted by three volleys more.

Thomas Jordan: London in Luster.

The Mercers' Company's Song

1686

ADVANCE the Virgin, lead the van,
    Of all that are in London free
The Mercer is the foremost man
    That founded a society.
Chorus.—Of all the trades that London grace
    We are the first in time and place.

When Nature in perfection was,
    And virgin beauty in her prime,
The Mercer gave the nymph a gloss,
    And made e'en beauty more sublime.
Chorus.—In this above our brethren blest,
    The Virgin's since our coat and crest.

Let others boast of lions bold,
    The camel, leopard, and the bear,
That tigers fierce their arms uphold,
    And ravenous wolves their scutcheons rear,
Chorus.—To our Virgin innocence
    Is both supporter and defence.

Then let a loyal peal go round,
   There's none dare claim priority ;
To Caesar's health each glass be crown'd
   Whose predecessors made us free.
Chorus.—Of all the trades that London grace,
   Ours first in dignity and place.
            City Poet : London Yearly Jubilee.

The Merchant Taylors' Glory : or Four Famous Feasts of England

1692

ENGLAND is a kingdom,
   Of all the world admired ;
More stateliness in pleasures
   Can no way be desired :
The court is full of bravery,
   The city stor'd with wealth,
The law preserveth unity,
   The country keepeth health.

Yet no like pomp and glory
   Our chronicles record,
As four great feasts of England
   Do orderly afford.
All others be but dinners called,
   Or banquets of good sort ;
And none but four be named feasts
   Which here I will report.

St. George, our English champion,
    In most delightful sort,
Is celebrated, year by year,
    In England's royal court.
The King, with all his noble train,
    In good and rich array,
Still glorifies the festival
    Of great St. George's day.

The honoured Mayor of London
    The second feast ordains,
By which the worthy citizen
    Much commendation gains :
For lords and judges of the land,
    And knights of good request,
To Guildhall come to countenance
    Lord Mayor of London's feast.

Also the serjeants of the law,
    Another feast affords,
With grace and honour glorified
    By England's noble lords.
And this we call the Serjeants' feast,
    A third in name and place ;
But yet there is a fourth, likewise,
    Deserves a gallant grace.

The Merchant Taylors' Company,
    The fellowship of fame,
To London's lasting dignity,
    Lives honour'd with the same.
A gift King Henry the Seventh gave,
    Kept once in three years still ;

Where gold and gowns be to poor men
  Given by King Henry's will.

Full many a good fat buck he sent,
  The fairest and the best,
The King's large forests can afford,
  To grace this worthy feast.
A feast that makes the number just,
  And last account of four ;
Therefore let England thus record,
  Of feasts there be no more.

Then let all London companies,
  So highly in renown ;
Give Merchant Taylors name and fame
  To wear the laurel crown :
For seven of England's royal kings
  Thereof have all been free,
And with their loves and favours grac'd
  This worthy Company.

King Richard, once the Second nam'd,
  Unhappy in his fall,
Of all his race of royal kings,
  Was freeman first of all.
Bolinbroke, fourth Henry next,
  By order him succeeds,
To glorify his brotherhood,
  By many princely deeds.

Fifth Henry, which so valiantly
  Deserved fame in France,
Became free of this Company,
  Fair London to advance.

Sixth Henry, the next in reign,
　　Though luckless in his days,
Of Merchant Taylors freeman was,
　　To their eternal praise.

Fourth Edward, that most worthy king,
　　Beloved of great and small,
Also performed a freeman's love
　　In this renowned hall.
Third Richard, which by cruelty,
　　Brought England many woes,
Unto this worthy company
　　No little favour shows.

But richest favours yet at last,
　　Proceeded from a King,
Whose kingdom round about the world
　　In princes' ears do ring.
King Henry, whom we call the Seventh,
　　Made them the greatest grac'd,
Because in Merchant Taylors' hall
　　His picture now stands plac'd.

Their charter was his princely gift,
　　Maintained to this day;
He added *Merchant* to the name
　　Of Taylors, as some say.
So Merchant Taylors they be call'd,
　　His royal love was so,
No London Company the like
　　Estate of kings can show.

From time to time, we thus behold,
　The Merchant Taylors' glory,
Of whose renown, the Muses' pen
　May make a lasting story.
This love of kings begat such love
　Of our now royal Prince,
For greater love than this to them
　Was ne'er before nor since,

It pleased so his princely mind,
　In meek kind courtesy,
To be a friendly Freeman made
　Of this brave company.
O London, then in heart rejoice,
　And Merchant Taylors sing
Forth praises of this gentle Prince,
　The son of our good King.

To tell the welcome to the world
　He then in London had,
Might fill us full of pleasant joys,
　And make our hearts full glad.
His triumphs were perform'd and done,
　Long lasting will remain,
And chronicles report aright,
　The order of it plain.

City Poet.

Hyde Park Camp

1665

HELP now (Minerva) stand a soldier's friend,
    Direct my muse that I may not offend.
The absent to inform is all my aim
A worthy work can never purchase blame.

In July, sixteen hundred sixty and five
(O happy is the man that's now alive),
When God's Destroying Angel sore did smite us,
'Cause he from sin by no means could invite us;
When lovely London was in mourning clad,
And not a countenance appear'd but sad;
When the contagion all about was spread;
And people in the streets did fall down dead;
When moneyed fugitives away did flee,
And took their heels in hope to be scot-free;
Just then we march'd away, the more's the pity,
And took our farewell of the Doleful City.
With heavy hearts unto Hyde Park we came,
To choose a place whereat we might remain:
Our ground we view'd, then straight to work we fall,
And build up houses without any wall,
We pitch'd our tents on ridges, and in furrows,
And there encampt, fearing the Almighty arrows,
But O alas! What did all this avail;
Our men (ere long) began to droop and quail.
Our lodgings cold, and some not us'd thereto,
Fell sick and died, and made no more ado.
At length the Plague amongst us 'gan to spread
When every morning some were found stark dead.

Down to another field the sick were ta'en ;
But few went down, that e'er came up again.
For want of comfort, many I observ'd
Perish'd and died, which might have been preserv'd.
But that which most of all did grieve my soul,
To see poor Christians dragg'd into a hole :
Tie match about them, as they had been logs
And draw them into holes, far worse than dogs.

. . . . .

Methinks I hear some say, " Friend, prithee hark,
Where got you drink and victuals in the park ? "
Aye, there's the query ; we shall soon decide it,
Why, we had men, call'd sutlers, provided :
Subtle they were, before they drove this trade,
But by this means, they all were subtler made.
No wind, or weather, ere could make them flinch,
Yet they would have the soldiers at a pinch.
For my part, I know little of their way,
But what I heard my fellow-soldiers say ;
One said, their meat and pottage was too fat ;
Yes, quoth another, we got none of that :
Besides, quoth he, they have a cunning sleight,
In selling out their meat by pinching weight ;
To make us pay sixpence a pound for beef,
To a poor soldier, is no little grief.
Their bread is small, their cheese is mark'd by th' inch,
And to speak truth, they're all upon the pinch,
As for their liquor, drink it but at leisure,
And you shall ne'er be drunk with over measure.
Alas, Hyde Park, these are with thee sad days,
Thy coaches are all turn'd to brewers' drays ;
Instead of girls with oranges and lemons,
The bakers' boys they brought in loaves by dozens ;

And by that means they kept us pretty sober,
Until the latter end of wet October.
They promis'd we should march, and then we leapt,
But all their promises were brok' (or kept),
They made us all, for want of winter quarters,
Ready to hang ourselves in our own garters.

At last the dove came with the olive branch,
And told for certain that we should advance
Out of the field; O then we leapt for joy,
And cry'd with one accord, *Vive le Roy*.

Upon Gunpowder Treason Day (at night),
We burnt our bed-straw, to make bonfire light;
And went to bed, that night, so merry hearted
For joy, we and our lodgings should be parted:
Next morning we were up by break of day,
To be in readiness to march away.
We bid adieu to Hyde Park's fruitful soil,
And left the country to divide the spoil.
With flying colours we the City enter,
And then into our quarters boldly venture.
Our landladies said " Welcome " (as was meet)
But for our landlords, some look'd sour, some sweet,
So soon as we were got into warm bed,
We look'd as men new metamorphosed.
But now I think 'tis best to let them sleep,
Whilst I out of the chamber softly creep,
To let you know that now my task is done,
Would I had known as much when I begun.
A sadder time, I freely dare engage
Was never known before in any age.
God bless King Charles, and send him long to reign
And grant we never may know the like again.

Anon. : Old Broadside.

Lord Mayor's Show

1832

IF ye would delighted be,
   Little Cockneys come to me ;
I will tell you all I know
Of the City's shining show ;
I will tell you how the great
Rode to Westminster in state,
Partly in their gilded coaches
Which no vulgar form approaches ;
Partly in their barges strong
Row'd by Nelson's Nobs along ;
I will tell how people stare
At the Sheriffs and Lord Mayor :
Not because they're better then
In themselves than other men,
But because they're finer drest,
And more gaudy than the rest !
I will tell how great and small
Go to breakfast at Guildhall ;
Where as loyal souls they take,
For the constitution's sake,
Of roast beef a pound and quarter,
Ere they venture on the water !

Hark, the bells are pealing loudly,
While the flags are waving proudly :
Horn and trumpet, drum and fife,
By the strong, in deadly strife,

Each to drown the other, sounded,
Make confusion more confounded !
Lo ! in coats of flaming red,
Staff in hand, and plume on head,
O'er the stones on chargers, rattle
Marshals who were ne'er in battle !
See when decked in armour gay,
Dubb'd for only half a day,
Ride like tailors on a board
Knights that never drew a sword :
While with step that seldom tires
Trudge, exalted to Esquires,
People who had ne'er till then
Been so much as gentlemen.

Now aside the curtain draw
From the sages of the law,
And behold the legal sport
In the great Exchequer Court !
Then the new Lord Mayor is shown,
And his smiles around are thrown,
Though by custom not a word
From his longing lips is heard ;
But for phrase of sounding sense,
In the mines of eloquence,
The Recorder deeply digs,
While the Barons nod their wigs ;
And the Chief, with speech polite,
Bows the party from his sight !
Then they hasten one and all
To the banquet at Guildhall !
There the Lady Mayoress walks,
Dines and dances, smiles and talks,

Showing well the City's beauties
How with grace to do their duties.
There the turtle rich they see,
Calipash and Calipee.
And when they have eat enough,
Of the greasy gouty stuff,
Then his Lordship standing up
Pledges in the loving cup,
Ev'ry Prelate, Prince, and Peer
Who may happen to be near!
Then begins the puff inventing
Giving healths and complimenting,
While they have the power to think
Men will speechify and drink;
And when that is all gone by
They will drink and speechify.
To the ballroom now retire
Lest the joys too soon expire;
There some light and laughing spark,
Doctor's son, or lawyer's clerk,
Seeks his pleasures to enhance,
Sweating through a country dance,
Swings his tail with matchless skill
Gliding through a gay quadrille;
And the scene (with aching head)
Ends by reeling home to bed!

Little Cockneys would you know
All the moral of this Show—
'Tis that daily diligence,
Time, and truth, and common sense,
Oft will raise an honest man
More than birth or fortune can :—

'Tis that men in life's gay dream
Are not always what they seem :-
'Tis that pomp and outward glare,
Won by toil, and sought with care,
Are but for a season bright ;
Soon they vanish from the sight :—
'Tis—but I no further press on
Here's sufficient for one lesson.
Now to think of what you know,
Little Cockneys you may go !

J. P. : Carmen Ante Paestum.

A Good Lord Mayor

1832

A GOOD Lord Mayor is one who does not need
The office gold his family to feed ;
But rather gives from out his private store,
For honour's sake, as much again or more.

A good Lord Mayor is one who will not strain,
Like some of old, to save, and gripe, and gain ;
And all forgetful of his festive state,
Let the cat kitten in the kitchen grate !

A good Lord Mayor is one who will not send
For many a guest to serve some private end ;
And when they do his bidding, whisper loud,
Scar'd at the number, " Bless me ! what a crowd ! "

A good Lord Mayor is one who will not play
At cards all night and in the morning pray;
But constant strive, in all his deeds to be
A bright example of consistency!

A good Lord Mayor is one who will maintain
The City's rights; nor, some low praise to gain,
Let sleep the power which o'er the Thames it sways,
And wink at fishing in unlawful ways.

A good Lord Mayor is one who will not say
Men must not worship in the open way;
Nor bid the warning voice for all be dumb
To church who will not, or who cannot, come!

A good Lord Mayor is one who will essay
The law's strong arm upon the bad to lay:
Nor bear that culprits should in crimes run on,
And do five hundred, while confin'd for one!

A good Lord Mayor is one who will not mix
His office duties with his politics;
Nor, idly anxious for the mob's applause,
Neglect the just dispensing of the laws!

A good Lord Mayor is one who will not smile
Alike upon the valued and the vile;
Nor seek around his social hearth to draw
The Son of Belial and the man of straw!

A good Lord Mayor, just like a clock that goes
From week to week, nor variation knows,
To all who ask to tell will ne'er refuse,
Nor through his office either gain or lose!

T

A good Lord Mayor—but I must end my song,
Lest it should prove too costly or too long:
To cap the climax thus, I am not sorry,
A good Lord Mayor—will be Sir Peter Laurie!

J. P.: Carmen Ante Paestum.

The Curtain Theatre in Shoreditch

1599

O FOR a Muse of fire, that would ascend
    The brightest heaven of invention!
A kingdom for a stage, princes to act,
And monarchs to behold the swelling scene!
Then should the warlike Harry, like himself,
Assume the port of Mars; and, at his heels,
Leash'd in like hounds, should famine, sword, and fire,
Crouch for employment.   But pardon, gentles all,
The flat unraised spirit that hath dar'd,
On this unworthy scaffold, to bring forth
So great an object: Can this cockpit hold
The vasty fields of France? or may we cram
With this *Wooden O* the very casques
That did affright the air at Agincourt?
O, pardon! since a crooked figure may
Attest in little space, a million;
And let us, ciphers to this great accompt,
On your imaginary forces work:
Suppose, within the girdle of these walls
Are now confin'd two mighty monarchies,
Whose high upreared and abutting fronts

The perilous, narrow ocean parts asunder.
Piece out our imperfections with your thoughts;
Into a thousand parts divide one man,
And make imaginary puissance;
Think, when we talk of horses, that you see them
Printing their proud hoofs i' the receiving earth:
For 'tis your thoughts that now must deck our kings,
Carry them here and there; jumping o'er times:
Turning the accomplishment of many years
Into an hour-glass.

Shakespeare: King Henry V.

Bartholomew Fair

1762

WHILE gentlefolks strut in their silver and satins,
    We poor folks are tramping in straw hat and pattens;
Yet as merrily old English ballads can sing-o,
As they at their opperores outlandish ling-o;
Calling out bravo, anckoro, and caro
Tho 'f I will sing nothing but Bartlemew fair-o.

Here was, first of all, crowds against other crowds driving,
Like wind and tide meeting, each contrary striving;
Shrill fiddling, sharp fighting, and shouting and shrieking,
Fifes, trumpets, drums, bagpipes, and barrow girls squeaking,
Come my rare round and sound, here's choice of fine ware-o,
Though all was not sound sold at Bartlemew fair-o.

There was drolls, hornpipe dancing, and showing of postures,
With frying black-puddings; and op'ning of oysters;
With salt-boxes solos, and gallery folks squalling,
The taphouse guests roaring, and mouthpieces bawling,
Pimps, pawnbrokers, strollers, fat landladies, sailors,
Bawds, bailiffs, jilts, jockeys, thieves, tumblers, and tailors.

Here's Punch's whole play of the Gun-powder Plot, sir,
With beasts all alive, and pease-porridge all hot, sir;
Fine sausages fry'd, and the black on the wire,
The whole court of France, and nice pig at the fire.
Here's the up and downs; who'll take a seat in the chair-o?
Tho' there's more up and downs than at Bartlemew fair-o.

Here's Whittington's cat, and the tall dromedary,
The chaise without horses, and queen of Hungary:
Here's the merry-go-rounds, come who rides, come who
        rides, sir?
Wine, beer, ale, and cakes, fire-eating besides, sir;
The fam'd learned dog that can tell all his letters,
And some men, as scholars, are not much his betters.

The world's a wide fair, where we ramble 'mong gay things;
Our parsons, like children, are tempted by play-things;
By sound and by show, by track and by trumpery,
The fal-lals of fashion and Frenchify'd frumpery.
What is life but a droll, rather wretched than rare-o?
And thus ends the ballad of Bartlemew fair-o.

*George Alexander Stevens : A Description
of Bartholomew Fair in London.*

The Ballad of Sally in our Alley

1713

O F all the girls that are so smart
    There's none like pretty Sally,
She is the darling of my heart,
    And she lives in our alley.
There is no lady in the land
    Is half so sweet as Sally,
She is the darling of my heart,
    And she lives in our alley.

Her father he makes cabbage-nets,
    And through the streets does cry 'em ;
Her mother she sells laces long,
    To such as please to buy 'em ;
But sure such folks could ne'er beget
    So sweet a girl as Sally !
She is the darling of my heart,
    And she lives in our alley.

When she is by I leave my work
    (I love her so sincerely),
My master comes like any Turk,
    And bangs me most severely,
But, let him bang his belly full,
    I'll bear it all for Sally ;
She is the darling of my heart,
    And she lives in our alley.

Of all the days that's in the week,
    I dearly love but one day,

And that's the day that comes betwixt
 A Saturday and Monday ;
For then I'm drest, all in my best,
 To walk abroad with Sally ;
She is the darling of my heart,
 And she lives in our alley.

My master carries me to church,
 And often am I blamed,
Because I leave him in the lurch,
 As soon as text is named :
I leave the church in sermon time
 And slink away to Sally ;
She is the darling of my heart,
 And she lives in our alley.

When Christmas comes about again,
 O then I shall have money ;
I'll hoard it up, and box and all
 I'll give it to my Honey :
And, would it were ten thousand pounds ;
 I'd give it all to Sally :
She is the darling of my heart,
 And she lives in our alley.

My master and the neighbours all,
 Make game of me and Sally ;
And (but for her) I'd better be
 A slave and row a galley :
But when my seven long years are out,
 O then I'll marry Sally !
O then we'll wed and then we'll bed,
 But not in our alley.
      Henry Carey : Poems.

The Bailiff's Daughter of Islington

1672

THERE was a youth, and a well-belov'd youth,
      And he was a Squire's son ;
And he loved the bailiff's daughter dear
      That lived in Islington.

Yet she was coy, and would not believe
      That he did love her so,
No, nor at any time would she
      Any countenance to him show.

But when his friends did understand
      His fond and foolish mind,
They sent him up to London
      An apprentice for to bind.

And when he had been seven long years,
      And never his love did see :
Many a tear have I shed for her sake,
      When she little thought of me.

Then all the maids of Islington
      Went forth to sport and play,
All but the bailiff's daughter dear ;
      She secretly stole away.

She pulled off her gown of green
      And put on ragged attire,
And to fair London she would go,
      Her true love to enquire.

And as she went along the high road,
  The weather being hot and dry,
She sat her down upon a green bank,
  And her true love came riding by.

She started up with a colour so red,
  Catching hold of his bridle-rein;
One penny, one penny, kind sir, she said,
  Will ease me of much pain.

Before I give you one penny, sweet-heart,
  Pray tell me where you were born:
At Islington, kind sir, said she,
  Where I have had many a scorn.

I prythee, sweet-heart, tell to me,
  O tell me whether you know
The bailiff's daughter of Islington?
  She is dead, sir, long ago.

If she be dead, then take my horse,
  My saddle and bridle also;
For I will unto some far country,
  Where no man shall me know.

O stay, O stay, thou goodly youth,
  She standeth by thy side;
She is here alive, she is not dead,
  And ready to be thy bride.

O farewell grief, and welcome joy,
  Ten thousand times therefore,
For now I have found mine own true love,
  Whom I thought I should never see more.

Old Ballad.

A City Shower

1710

CAREFUL observers may foretell the hour
    (By sure prognostics) when to dread a shower.
While rain depends, the pensive cat gives o'er
Her frolics, and pursues her tail no more.
Returning home at night, you'll find the sink
Strike your offended sense with double stink.
If you be wise, then go not far to dine;
You'll spend in coach-hire more than save in wine.
A coming shower your shooting corns presage,
Old aches will throb, your hollow tooth will rage.
Sauntering in coffee-house is Dulman seen;
He damns the climate, and complains of spleen.

    Meanwhile the south, rising with dabbled wings,
A sable cloud athwart the welkin flings,
That swill'd more liquor than it could contain,
And, like a drunkard, gives it up again.
Brisk Susan whips her linen from the rope,
While the first drizzling shower is borne aslope.
Such is that sprinkling which some careless quean
Flirts on you from her mop, but not so clean;
You fly, invoke the gods; then, turning, stop
To rail; she, singing, still whirls on her mop.
Not yet the dust that shunn'd th' unequal strife,
But, aided by the wind, fought still for life;
And, wafted with its foe by violent gust,
'Twas doubtful which was rain, and which was dust.
Ah! where must needy poet seek for aid,
When dust and rain at once his coat invade?

Sole coat! where dust, cemented by the rain,
Erects the nap, and leaves a cloudy stain!
    Now in contiguous drops the flood comes down,
Threatening with deluge this devoted Town.
To shops in crowds the draggled females fly,
Pretend to cheapen goods, but nothing buy.
The Templar spruce, while every spout's abroach,
Stays till 'tis fair, yet seems to call a coach.
The tuck'd-up sempstress walks with hasty strides,
While streams run down her oil'd umbrella's sides.
Here various kinds, by various fortunes led,
Commence acquaintance underneath a shed.
Triumphant Tories and desponding Whigs
Forget their feuds, and join to save their wigs.
Box'd in a chair, the beau impatient sits,
While spouts run clattering o'er the roof by fits,
And ever and anon with frightful din
The leather sounds; he trembles from within.
So when Troy chairmen bore the Wooden Steed,
Pregnant with Greeks impatient to be freed
(Those bully Greeks, who, as the moderns do,
Instead of paying chairmen, ran them through),
Laocoön struck the outside with his spear,
And each imprison'd hero quak'd for fear.
    Now from all parts the swelling kennels flow,
And bear their trophies with them as they go:
Filths of all hues and odours seem to tell
What street they sail'd from by their sight and smell.
They, as each torrent drives, with rapid force,
From Smithfield or St. 'Pulchres shape their course,
And in huge confluence join'd at Snowhill ridge,
Fall from the conduit prone to Holborn bridge.

Jonathan Swift: Collected Poems.

A City Calendar

1716

EXPERIENC'D men, inur'd to City ways,
    Need not the calendar to count their days.
When through the town with slow and solemn air
Led by the nostril, walks the muzzled bear ;
Behind him moves majestically dull,
The pride of Hockley-hole, the surly bull ;
Learn hence the periods of the week to name,
Mondays and Thursdays are the days of game.

When fishy stalls with double store are laid ;
The golden-belly'd carp, the broad-finned maid,
Red-speckled trouts, the salmon's silver jowl,
The jointed lobster, and unscaly sole,
And luscious 'scallops to allure the tastes
Of rigid zealots to delicious fasts ;
Wednesdays and Fridays you'll observe from hence,
Days, when our sires were doom'd to abstinence.

When dirty waters from balconies drop,
And dext'rous damsels twirl the sprinkling mop,
And cleanse the spatter'd sash, and scrub the stairs ;
Know Saturday's conclusive morn appears.

Successive cries the season's change declare,
And mark the monthly progress of the year.
Hark, how the street with treble voices ring,
To sell the bounteous product of the Spring !
Sweet-smelling flow'rs, and elder's early bud,
With nettle's tender shoots, to cleanse the blood :

And when June's thunder cools the sultry skies,
Ev'n Sundays are profan'd by mack'rel cries.

Walnuts the fruit'rer's hand, in Autumn, stain,
Blue plums and juicy pears augment his gain ;
Next oranges the longing boys entice,
To trust their copper fortunes to the dice.

When rosemary and bays, the poet's crown,
Are bawl'd in frequent cries through all the town,
Then judge the festival of Christmas near,
Christmas, the joyous period of the year.
Now with bright holly all your temples strow,
With laurel green and sacred mistletoe.
Now, heav'n-born Charity, thy blessings shed !
Bid meagre Want uprear her sickly head ;
Bid shiv'ring limbs be warm ; let Plenty's bowl
In humble roofs make glad the needy soul.
See, see, the heaven-born maid her blessings shed ;
Lo ! meagre Want uprears her sickly head ;
Cloth'd are the naked, and the needy glad,
While selfish Avarice alone is sad.

John Gay : Trivia.

Marketing

1716

SHALL the large mutton smoke upon your boards ?
 Such, Newgate's copious market best affords.
Would'st thou with mighty beef augment thy meal ?
Seek Leaden-hall ; St. James's send thee veal ;

Thames-street gives cheese; Covent Garden fruits;
Moor-fields old books; and Monmouth-street old suits.
Hence may'st thou well supply the wants of life,
Support thy family, and clothe thy wife.

Volumes on shelter'd stall expanded lie,
And various science lures the learned eye;
And bending shelves, with pond'rous scholiasts groan,
And deep divines to modern shops unknown;
Here, like the bee, that on industrious wing
Collects the various odours of the Spring,
Walkers, at leisure, learning's flow'rs may spoil
Nor watch the wasting of the midnight oil,
May morals snatch from Plutarch's tatter'd page,
A mildew'd Bacon, or Stagyra's sage.
Here fauntering 'prentices o'er Otway weep,
O'er Congreve smile, or over D—— sleep!
Pleas'd sempstresses the Lock's fam'd Rape unfold,
And Squirts read Garth, till apozems grow cold.

John Gay: Trivia.

Cakes and Ale

1676

A T' Islington
      A fair they hold,
Where cakes and ale
      Are to be sold.
At Highgate, and
      At Holloway
The like is kept
      Here every day,

> At Totnam Court
> And Kentish Town,
> And all those places
> Up and down.
>
> *Poor Robin's Almanack.*

Summer's Return

1642

NOW damsel young, that dwells in Cheap,
    For very joy begins to leap,
Her elbow small she oft does rub ;
Tickled with hope of syllabub !
For mother (who does gold maintain
On thumb, and keys in silver chain)
In snow-white clout, wrapt nook of pie,
Fat capon's wing, and rabbit's thigh,
And said to hackney coachman " Go,
Take shillings six ; say ay, or no,"—
" Whither says he ? " Quoth she, " Thy team
Shall drive to place where groweth cream."
But husband gray now comes to stall,
For prentice notch'd he straight does call,

.   .   .

Ho, ho ! to Islington ; enough ;
Fetch Job my son, and our dog Ruffe ;
For there in pond through mire and muck,
We'll cry, hey duck, there Ruffe, hey duck !
    Sir William Davenant : The Long Vacation.

London in July

1893

WHAT ails my senses thus to cheat?
  What is it ails the place,
That all the people in the street
  Should wear one woman's face?

The London trees are dusty-brown
  Beneath the summer sky;
My love, she dwells in London town,
  Nor leaves it in July.

O various and intricate maze,
  Wide waste of square and street;
Where, missing through unnumbered days,
  We twain at last may meet!

And who cries out on crowd and mart?
  Who prates of stream and sea?
The summer in the city's heart—
  That is enough for me.
Amy Levy: A London Plane Tree and other Poems.

The Little Dancers

1895

LONELY, save for a few faint stars, the sky
  Dreams; and lonely, below, the little street
Into its gloom retires, secluded and shy.
Scarcely the dumb roar enters this soft retreat;

And all is dark, save where come flooding rays
From a tavern window : there, to the brisk measure
Of an organ that down in an alley merrily plays,
Two children, all alone and no one by,
Holding their tattered frocks, through an airy maze
Of motion, lightly threaded with nimble feet,
Dance sedately : face to face they gaze,
Their eyes shining, grave with a perfect pleasure.

Laurence Binyon : London Visions (First Series.)

White Conduit House

1760

WITH "Sunday's come" mirth brightens ev'ry face,
  And paints the rose upon the housemaid's cheek,
Harriet, or Mol, more ruddy.   Now the heart
Of prentice resident in ample street,
Or alley kennel-wash'd, Cheapside, Cornhill,
Or Cranborne, thee for calcuments renown'd
With joy distends.   His meal meridian o'er
With switch in hand, he to White Conduit House
Hies merry-hearted.   Human beings here
In couples multitudinous assemble,
Forming the drollest groups, that ever trod
Fair Islingtonian plains.   Male after male,
Dog after dog succeeding—husbands—wives—
Fathers and mothers—brothers—sisters—friends—
And pretty little boys and girls.   Around,
Across, along, the gardens shrubby maze,
They walk, they sit, they stand.   What crowds press on
Eager to mount the stairs, eager to catch

First vacant bench or chair in long-room plac'd.
Here prig with prig holds conference polite,
And indiscriminate the gaudy beau
And sloven mix.   Here he, who all the week
Took bearded mortals by the nose, or sat
Weaving dead hairs, and whistling wretched strain,
And eke the sturdy youth, whose trade it is
Stout oxen to contund, with gold-bound hat
And silken stocking, strut.   The red-arm'd belle
Here shews her tasty gown, proud to be thought
The butterfly of fashion : and forsooth
Her haughty mistress deigns for once to tread
The same unhallow'd floor—'Tis hurry all
And rattling cups and saucers.   Waiter here,
And waiter there, and waiter here and there,
At once is called—Joe—Joe—Joe—Joe—Joe
Joe on the right—and Joe upon the left,
For every vocal pipe re-echoes Joe—
Alas Poor Joe !   Like Francis in the play
He stands confounded, anxious how to please
The many-headed throng.   But shou'd I paint
The language, humours, custom of the place,
Together with all curt'sies, lowly bows,
And compliments extern, 'twould swell my page
Beyond its limits due.   Suffice it then
For my prophetic Muse to say, " So long
As fashion rides upon the wing of time,
While tea and cream and butter'd rolls can please,
While rival beaux, and jealous belles exist,
So long, White Conduit House, shall be thy fame."

W. Woty : Gentleman's Magazine.

U

On the University Carrier, who Sickened in the Time of his Vacancy, being Forbid to go to London by Reason of the Plague

1631

HERE lies old Hobson; Death hath broke his girt,
    And here, alas, hath laid him in the dirt,
Or else, the ways being foul, twenty to one,
He's here stuck in a slough, and overthrown.
'Twas such a shifter, that if truth be known,
Death was half glad when he had got him down;
For he had any time this ten years full
Dodged with him, betwixt Cambridge and the Bull.
And surely Death could never have prevail'd
Had not his weekly course of carriage fail'd;
But lately finding him so long at home,
And thinking now his journey's end was come,
And that he had ta'en up his latest inn,
In the kind office of a chamberlain,
Shew'd him his room where he must lodge that night,
Pull'd off his boots, and took away the light:
If any ask for him, it shall be said,
Hobson has supp'd, and's newly gone to bed.

John Milton: Minor Poems.

The Cit's Country-Box
1757

THE wealthy Cit, grown old in trade,
   Now wishes for the rural shade,
And buckles to his one-horse chair
Old *Dobbin*, or the founder'd mare;
While wedg'd in closely by his side,
Sits Madam, his unwieldy bride,
With *Jacky* on a stool before 'em,
And out they jog in due decorum.
Scarce past the turnpike half a mile,
How all the country seems to smile!
And as they slowly jog together,
The Cit commends the road and weather;
While Madam doats upon the trees,
And longs for ev'ry house she sees,
Admires its views, its situation,
And thus she opens her oration.
   " What signify thy loads of wealth,
Without that richest jewel health?
Excuse the fondness of a wife,
Who doats upon your precious life!
Such ceaseless toil, such constant care,
Is more than human strength can bear.
One may observe it in your face—
Indeed, my dear, you break apace:
And nothing can your health repair,
But exercise and country air.
Sir Traffic has a house, you know,
About a mile from Chency-row;
He's a *good* man, indeed 'tis true,
But not so *warm*, my dear, as you:

And folks are always apt to sneer—
One would not be out-done, my dear!"
   Sir 'Traffic's name so well apply'd,
Awak'd his brother merchant's pride;
And Thrifty, who had all his life
Paid utmost deference to his wife,
Confess'd her arguments had reason,
And by th' approaching summer season,
Draws a few hundreds from the stocks,
And purchases his country-box.
   Some three or four miles out of town,
An hour's ride will bring you down,
He fixes on his choice abode,
Not half a furlong from the road:
And so convenient does it lay,
The stages pass it ev'ry day:
And then so snug, so mighty pretty,
To have a house so near the City!
Take but your places at the Boar
You're set down at the very door.
   Well then, suppose them fix'd at last,
White-washing, painting, scrubbing past,
Hugging themselves in ease and clover,
With all the fuss of moving over;
Lo a new heap of whims are bred,
And wanton in my lady's head!
   "Well to be sure, it must be own'd,
It is a charming spot of ground;
So sweet a distance for a ride,
And all about so *countrified!*
'Twould come but to a trifling price
To make it quite a paradise;
I cannot bear those nasty rails,

Those ugly broken mouldy pales :
Suppose, my dear, instead of these,
We build a railing all Chinese.
Although one hates to be expos'd,
'Tis dismal to be thus enclos'd ;
One hardly any object sees—
I wish you'd fell those odious trees,
Objects continual passing by
Were something to amuse the eye.
But to be pent within the walls—
One might as well be at St. Paul's.
Our house beholders would adore,
Was there a level lawn before,
Nothing its view to incommode,
But quite laid open to the road ;
While ev'ry trav'ler in amaze,
Should on our little mansion gaze,
And pointing to the choice retreat,
Cry, 'That's Sir Thrifty's country seat."
   No doubt her arguments prevail,
For Madam's taste can never fail.
Blest age ! when all men may procure
The title of a connoisseur ;
When noble and ignoble herd
Are governed by a single word ;
Though, like the royal German dames,
It bears a hundred Christian names ;
As genius, fancy, judgment, *goût*,
Whim, caprice, *je ne scai quoi, virtù ;*
Which appellations all describe
TASTE, and the modern tasteful tribe.
   Now bricklayers, carpenters, and joiners,
With Chinese artists and designers,

Produce their scheme of alteration,
To work this wond'rous reformation.
The useful dome, which secret stood,
Enbosom'd in the yew-tree wood,
The trav'ler with amazement sees
A temple, Gothic or Chinese,
With many a bell and tawdry rag on,
And crested with a sprawling dragon;
A wooden arch is bent astride
A ditch of water, four foot wide,
With angles, curves, and zig-zag lines,
From Halfpenny's exact designs.
In front a level lawn is seen,
Without a shrub upon the green,
Where taste would want its first great law,
But for the skulking, sly *ha-ha*,
By whose miraculous assistance,
You gain a prospect two-fields' distance.
And now from Hyde Park Corner come
The gods of Athens and of Rome :
Here squabby Cupids take their places,
With Venus, and the clumsy Graces :
Apollo there, with aim so clever,
Stretches his leaden bow for ever;
And there, without the pow'r to fly,
Stands fix'd a tip-toe Mercury.
    The villa thus completely grac'd,
All own that Thrifty has a taste;
And Madam's female friends and cousins,
With common-council-men by dozens,
Flock every Sunday to the seat,
To stare about them, and to eat.

Robert Lloyd: The Connoisseur.

The Poet Baffled

1772

IN that broad spot, where two great roads divide,
    And invalids stop doubtful where to ride;
Whether the salutary air to breathe
On Highgate's steepy hill, or Hampstead's heath;
Where Mother Red-cap shows her high-crown'd hat,
Upon a stile a past'ral poet sat.

    Him not Apollo nor the Muses nine
Inspir'd with love of verse, but hopes to dine:
He labour'd not for that vain meed renown,
But fill'd the stated sheet for half-a-crown;
And, all regardless what the critics said,
The churlish bookseller was all his dread.
For him he pens the unharmonious strain,
For him he racks his unprolific brain,
For him he reads on Privy-garden wall,
For him turns o'er the books on ev'ry stall,
For him the pillag'd line he makes his own,
From authors long forgot, or never known,
For him he braves the parching sun and wind,
To store with images his vacant mind,
For him he now strays o'er the dusty green,
To make a past'ral for the Magazine.

.   .   .   .   .

In vain, alas, shall City bards resort,
For past'ral images, to Tottenham-court;
Fat droves of sheep, consign'd from Lincoln fens,
That swearing drovers beat to Smithfield pens,
Give faint ideas of Arcadian plains,
With bleating lambkins, and with piping swains.

I've heard of Pope, of Phillips, and of Gay,
They wrote not past'rals in the King's highway:
On Thames' smooth banks, they fram'd the rural song,
And wander'd free, the tufted groves among ;
Cull'd every flow'r the fragrant mead affords,
And wrote in solitude, and din'd with lords.
Alas for me ! what prospects can I find
To raise poetic ardour in my mind ?
Where'er around, I cast my wand'ring eyes,
Long burning rows of fetid bricks arise,
And nauseous dunghills swell in mould'ring heaps,
Whilst the fat sow beneath their covert sleeps.
I spy no verdant glade, no gushing rill,
No fountain bubbling from the rocky hill,
But stagnant pools adorn our dusty plains,
Where half-starv'd cows wash down their meal of grains.
No traces here of sweet simplicity,
No lowing herd winds gently o'er the lea,
No tuneful nymph, with cheerful roundelay,
Attends, to milk her kine, at close of day,
But droves of oxen through yon clouds appear,
With noisy dogs and butchers in their rear,
To give poetic fancy small relief,
And tempt the hungry bard with thoughts of beef.
From helps like these, how very small my hopes !
My past'rals, sure, will never equal Pope's.
Since then no images adorn the plain,
But what are found as well in Gray's-Inn Lane,
Since dust and noise inspire no thought serene,
And three-horse stages little mend the scene,
I'll stray no more to seek the vagrant Muse,
But ev'n go write at home, and save my shoes.

Charles Jenner: Town Eclogues.

The Spread of London

1813

SAINT George's Fields are fields no more,
  The trowel supersedes the plough ;
Huge inundated swamps of yore
  Are changed to civic villas now.

The builder's plank, the mason's hod,
  Wide, and more wide extending still,
Usurp the violated sod,
  From Lambeth Marsh to Balaam Hill.

Pert poplars, yew trees, water tubs,
  No more at Clapham meet the eye,
But velvet lawns, acacian shrubs,
  With perfume greet the passer-by.

Thy carpets, Persia, deck our floors,
  Chintz curtains shade the polish'd pane,
Verandas guard the darken'd doors,
  Where dunning Phoebus knocks in vain.

Not thus acquir'd was Gresham's hoard,
  Who founded London's mart of trade ;
Not such thy life, Grimalkin's lord,
  Who Bow's recalling peal obey'd.

In Mark or Mincing Lane confin'd,
  In cheerful toil they pass'd the hours ;
'Twas theirs to leave their wealth behind,
  To lavish, while we live, is ours.

> They gave no treats to thankless kings,
>   Many their gains, their wants were few;
> They built no house with spacious wings,
>   To give their riches pinions too.
>
> Yet sometimes leaving in the lurch
>   Sons, to luxurious folly prone,
> Their funds rebuilt the parish church—
>   Oh! pious waste, to us unknown.
>
> We from our circle never roam,
>   Nor ape our sires' eccentric sins;
> Our charity begins at home,
>   And mostly ends where it begins.
>   *Horace and James Smith: Horace in London.*

Rural Felicity

1839

WELL, the country's a pleasant place, sure enough, for
    people that's country born,
And useful, no doubt, in a natural way, for growing our
    grass and corn.
It was kindly meant of my cousin Giles, to write and invite
    me down,
Tho' as yet all I've seen of a pastoral life only makes one
    more partial to Town.

At first I thought I was really come down into all sorts of
    rural bliss;

For Porkington Place, with its cows and its pigs, and its
    poultry, looks not much amiss ;
There's something about a dairy farm, with its different
    kinds of live stock,
That puts one in mind of Paradise, and Adam and his
    innocent flock ;
But somehow the good old Elysium fields have not been
    well handed down,
And as yet I have found no fields to prefer to dear
    Leicester Fields up in town.

      .   .   .   .   .

And after all, an't there new-laid eggs to be had upon
    Holborn Hill ?
And dairy-fed pork in Broad St. Giles's, and fresh butter
    wherever you will ?
And a covered cart that brings cottage bread quite rustical-
    like and brown ?
So one isn't so very uncountrified in the very heart of the
    town.

      .   .   .   .

Howsomever my mind's made up, and although I'm sure
    cousin Giles will be vext,
I mean to book me an inside place up to town upon Satur-
    day next,
And if nothing happens, soon after ten, I shall be at the old
    Bell and Crown,
And perhaps I may come to the country again, when
    London is all burnt down.

Thomas Hood: Collected Poems.

The Diverting History of John Gilpin

1782

JOHN GILPIN was a citizen
  Of credit and renown,
A trainband captain eke was he
  Of famous London town.

John Gilpin's spouse said to her dear,
  "Though wedded we have been
These twice ten tedious years, yet we
  No holiday have seen.

To-morrow is our wedding day,
  And we will then repair
Unto the Bell at Edmonton,
  All in a chaise and pair.

My sister, and my sister's child,
  Myself, and children three,
Will fill the chaise; so you must ride
  On horseback after we."

He soon replied,—"I do admire
  Of womankind but one,
And you are she, my dearest dear,
  Therefore it shall be done.

I am a linendraper bold,
  As all the world doth know,
And my good friend the calender
  Will lend his horse to go."

Quoth Mrs. Gilpin,—" That's well said ;
    And for that wine is dear,
We will be furnished with our own,
    Which is both bright and clear."

John Gilpin kissed his loving wife ;
    O'erjoyed was he to find,
That, though on pleasure she was bent,
    She had a frugal mind.

The morning came, the chaise was brought,
    But yet was not allowed
To drive up to the door, lest all
    Should say that she was proud.

So three doors off the chaise was stayed,
    Where they did all get in ;
Six precious souls, and all agog
    To dash through thick and thin.

Smack went the whip, round went the wheels,
    Were never folk so glad,
The stones did rattle underneath,
    As if Cheapside were mad.

John Gilpin at his horse's side
    Seized fast the flowing mane,
And up he got, in haste to ride,
    But soon came down again ;

For saddletree scarce reached had he,
    His journey to begin,
When, turning round his head, he saw
    Three customers come in.

So down he came; for loss of time,
    Although it grieved him sore,
Yet loss of pence, full well he knew,
    Would trouble him much more.

'Twas long before the customers
    Were suited to their mind,
When Betty screaming came down stairs,—
    "The wine is left behind!"

"Good lack!" quoth he, "yet bring it me,
    My leathern belt likewise,
In which I bear my trusty sword
    When I do exercise."

Now Mistress Gilpin (careful soul!)
    Had two stone bottles found,
To hold the liquor that she loved,
    And keep it safe and sound.

Each bottle had a curling ear,
    Through which the belt he drew,
And hung a bottle on each side,
    To make his balance true.

Then over all, that he might be
    Equipped from top to toe,
His long red cloak, well brushed and neat,
    He manfully did throw.

Now see him mounted once again
    Upon his nimble steed,
Full slowly pacing o'er the stones,
    With caution and good heed.

But finding soon a smoother road
    Beneath his well-shod feet,
The snorting beast began to trot,
    Which galled him in his seat.

So "Fair and softly," John he cried,
    But John he cried in vain :
That trot became a gallop soon,
    In spite of curb and rein.

So stooping down, as needs he must,
    Who cannot sit upright,
He grasped the mane with both his hands,
    And eke with all his might.

His horse, who never in that sort
    Had handled been before,
What thing upon his back had got
    Did wonder more and more.

Away went Gilpin, neck or nought ;
    Away went hat and wig ;
He little dreamt, when he set out,
    Of running such a rig.

The wind did blow, the cloak did fly,
    Like streamer long and gay,
Till, loop and button failing both,
    At last it flew away.

Then might all people well discern
    The bottles he had slung ;
A bottle swinging at each side,
    As hath been said or sung.

The dogs did bark, the children screamed,
　　Up flew the windows all;
And every soul cried out, "Well done!"
　　As loud as he could bawl.

Away went Gilpin—who but he?
　　His fame soon spread around;
"He carries weight!" "He rides a race!"
　　"'Tis for a thousand pound!"

And still, as fast as he drew near,
　　'Twas wonderful to view,
How in a trice the turnpike men
　　Their gates wide open threw.

And now, as he went bowing down
　　His reeking head full low,
The bottles twain behind his back
　　Were shattered at a blow.

Down ran the wine into the road,
　　Most piteous to be seen,
Which made his horse's flanks to smoke
　　As they had basted been.

But still he seemed to carry weight,
　　With leathern girdle braced;
For all might see the bottle necks
　　Still dangling at his waist.

Thus all through merry Islington
　　These gambols he did play,
Until he came unto the Wash
　　Of Edmonton so gay;

And there he threw the Wash about,
　On both sides of the way,
Just like unto a trundling mop,
　Or a wild goose at play.

At Edmonton, his loving wife
　From the balcony spied
Her tender husband, wondering much
　To see how he did ride.

"Stop, stop, John Gilpin!—Here's the house!"
　They all at once did cry;
"The dinner waits, and we are tired:"—
　Said Gilpin—"So am I!"

But yet his horse was not a whit
　Inclined to tarry there;
For why?—his owner had a house
　Full ten miles off, at Ware.

So like an arrow swift he flew,
　Shot by an archer strong;
So did he fly—which brings me to
　The middle of my song.

Away went Gilpin, out of breath,
　And sore against his will,
Till, at his friend the calender's,
　His horse at last stood still.

The calender, amazed to see
　His neighbour in such trim,
Laid down his pipe, flew to the gate,
　And thus accosted him:—

"What news? what news? your tidings tell;
    Tell me you must and shall—
Say why bareheaded you are come,
    Or why you come at all?"

Now Gilpin had a pleasant wit,
    And loved a timely joke;
And thus unto the calender,
    In merry guise, he spoke:—

"I came because your horse would come;
    And, if I well forbode,
My hat and wig will soon be here,—
    They are upon the road."

The calender, right glad to find
    His friend in merry pin,
Returned him not a single word,
    But to the house went in;

Whence straight he came with hat and wig;
    A wig that flowed behind,
A hat not much the worse for wear,
    Each comely in its kind.

He held them up, and in his turn,
    Thus showed his ready wit:
"My head is twice as big as yours,
    They therefore needs must fit.

But let me scrape the dirt away
    That hangs upon your face;
And stop and eat, for well you may
    Be in a hungry case."

Said John,—"It is my wedding day,
    And all the world would stare,
If wife should dine at Edmonton,
    And I should dine at Ware."

So turning to his horse, he said,
    "I am in haste to dine ;
'Twas for your pleasure you came here,
    You shall go back for mine."

Ah ! luckless speech, and bootless boast,
    For which he paid full dear :
For while he spake, a braying ass
    Did sing most loud and clear ;

Whereat his horse did snort, as he
    Had heard a lion roar,
And galloped off with all his might,
    As he had done before.

Away went Gilpin, and away
    Went Gilpin's hat and wig :
He lost them sooner than at first,
    For why ?—they were too big.

Now Mistress Gilpin, when she saw
    Her husband posting down
Into the country far away,
    She pulled out half-a-crown ;

And thus unto the youth she said,
    That drove them to the Bell, ·
" This shall be yours, when you bring back
    My husband safe and well."

The youth did ride, and soon did meet
  John coming back amain ;
Whom in a trice he tried to stop
  By catching at his rein ;

But not performing what he meant,
  And gladly would have done,
The frighted steed he frighted more,
  And made him faster run.

Away went Gilpin, and away
  Went postboy at his heels,
The postboy's horse right glad to miss
  The lumbering of the wheels.

Six gentlemen upon the road,
  Thus seeing Gilpin fly,
With postboy scampering in the rear,
  They raised a hue and cry :—

"Stop thief ! stop thief !—a highwayman !"
  Not one of them was mute ;
And all and each that passed that way
  Did join in the pursuit.

And now the turnpike-gates again
  Flew open in short space ;
The toll-men thinking as before,
  That Gilpin rode a race.

And so he did, and won it too,
  For he got first to town ;
Nor stopped till where he had got up
  He did again get down.

Now let us sing, long live the King,
And Gilpin, long live he ;
And when he next doth ride abroad,
May I be there to see !

William Cowper.

Bow Bells

1869

AT the brink of a murmuring brook
A contemplative Cockney reclined ;
And his face wore a sad sort of look,
As if care were at work on his mind.
He sigh'd now and then as we sigh
When the heart with soft sentiment swells ;
And a tear came and moisten'd each eye
As he mournfully thought of Bow Bells.

I am monarch of all I survey !
(Thus he vented his feelings in words)—
But my kingdom, it grieves me to say,
Is inhabited chiefly by birds.
In this brook that flows lazily by
I believe that *one* tittlebat dwells,
For I saw something jump at a fly
As I lay here and long'd for Bow Bells.

Yonder cattle are grazing—it's clear
From the bob of their heads up and down ;—
But I cannot love cattle down here
As I should if I met them in town.

Poets say that each pastoral breeze
  Bears a melody laden with spells;
But I don't find the music in these
  That I find in the tone of Bow Bells.

I am partial to trees, as a rule;
  And the rose is a beautiful flower.
(Yes, I once read a ballad at school
  Of a rose that was wash'd in a shower.)
But, although I may doat on the rose,
  I can scarcely believe that it smells
Quite so sweet in the bed where it grows
  As when sold within sound of Bow Bells.

No; I've tried it in vain once or twice,
  And I've thoroughly made up my mind
That the country is all very nice—
  But I'd much rather mix with my kind.
Yes; to-day—if I meet with a train—
  I will fly from these hills and these dells;
And to-night I will sleep once again
  (Happy thought!) within sound of Bow Bells.

Henry S. Leigh: Carols of Cockayne.

In an Old City Church

1879

ONE dull, foggy day in December,
  When biting and bleak was the air,
I once lost my way, I remember,
And paused in a quaint City square.

Though lacking all splendour or gladness,
The flavour of good long ago
Clung close to the place in its sadness,
And grave-yard half covered with snow ;
While the black, puny branches, all leafless and bare,
Seemed to add to the gloom of this dull City square !

The railings were rusty and rimy,
The church looked so mouldy and grim ;
The houses seemed haunted and grimy,
The windows were gruesome and dim.
The iron gate scrooped on its hinges,
The clock struck a querulous chime,
As though it were feeling some twinges
'Twas almost forgotten by Time.
But I opened the door, and the picture was fair,
In the fine ancient church, in this sad City square !

A fair little lass, holly-laden—
With eyes of cerulean blue—
Is helping a sweet dark-eyed maiden
Twine ivy with laurel and yew ;
How busy the deft taper fingers !
What taste and what art they display !
How lovingly each of them lingers,
Adjusting a leaf or a spray !—
I close the door softly, I've no business there,
And drift out in the fog of the grim City square.

J. Ashby-Sterry : The Lazy Minstrel.

The Reverie of Poor Susan

1800

AT the corner of Wood Street, when daylight appears,
    Hangs a thrush that sings loud, it has sung for three
    years :
Poor Susan has pass'd by the spot, and has heard
In the silence of morning the song of the bird.

'Tis a note of enchantment ; what ails her ? She sees
A mountain ascending, a vision of trees ;
Bright volumes of vapour through Lothbury glide,
And a river flows on through the vale of Cheapside.

Green pastures she views in the midst of the dale
Down which she so often has tripp'd with her pail ;
And a single small cottage, a nest like a dove's,
The one only dwelling on earth that she loves.

She looks, and her heart is in heaven ; but they fade
The mist and the river, the hill and the shade ;
The stream will not flow, and the hill will not rise,
And the colours have all pass'd away from her eyes !
William Wordsworth : Lyrical Ballads.

In City Streets

1898

YONDER in the heather there's a bed for sleeping,
  Drink for one athirst, ripe blackberries to eat ;
Yonder in the sun the merry hares go leaping,
  And the pool is clear for travel-wearied feet !

Sorely throb my feet, a-tramping London highways
  (Ah, the springy moss upon a northern moor !)
Through the endless streets, the gloomy squares and byways,
  Homeless in the City, poor among the poor !

London streets are gold—ah, give me leaves a-glinting
  'Midst grey dykes and hedges in the autumn sun !
London water's wine, poured out for all unstinting—
  God ! for the little brooks that tumble as they run !

O my heart is fain to hear the soft wind blowing,
  Soughing through the fir-tops up on northern fells !
O my eye's an-ache to see the brown burns flowing
  Through the peaty soil and tinkling heather-bells !

Ada Smith : Le Quartier Latin.

Vision

1898

BETWEEN New Cross and London Bridge,
 I peered from a third-class "Smoker,"
Over the grimy waste of roofs,
 Into the yellow ochre.

When lo ! from the midst of the chimney pots
 Up rose a brave three-master,
With brand new canvas on every spar
 As fair as alabaster.

And, gazing on that gallant sight,
 In a moment's space, or sooner,
The smoke gave place to a southern breeze,
 The train to a bounding schooner.

Again the vessel stood to sea,
 Majestic, snowy-breasted ;
Again great ships rode nobly by,
 On purple waves foam-crested.

Again we passed mysterious coasts,
 Again soft nights enwound us ;
Again the rising sun revealed
 Strange fishing craft around us.

The spray was salt, the air was glad—
 When—bump !—we reached the station !
What did I care though the fog was there,
 With *this* for compensation !

E. V. Lucas : The Spectator.

The Child in the City

1894

A CITY child, half girl, half elf,
   With tattered boots and gipsy hair,
Hops quaintly, babbling to herself,
   Along the great Cathedral stair.

To catch her inattentive ear
   The half of London roars in vain;
Nor with a glance does she revere
   The power of Paul's impending fane.

She hops and skips in sober sort,
   And to herself serenely smiles,
As though her soul were in her sport,
   Her feet were following fairies' wiles.

So on some tide-beleaguered beach
   We in our childish days have played,
Unmindful of the blue sea's reach,
   And by its murmurs undismayed.

So, though no more with childhood's name,
   Yet babes in ignorance and faith,
Men play life's all-absorbing game,
   Nor heed the imminence of death.

Wilson Benington.

An Evening Song

1869

FADES into twilight the last golden gleam
    Thrown by the sunset on upland and stream ;
Glints o'er the Serpentine—tips Notting Hill—
Dies on the summit of proud Pentonville.

Day brought us trouble, but Night brings us peace ;
Morning brought sorrow, but Eve bids it cease.
Gaslight and Gaiety, beam for a while ;
Pleasure and Paraffin, lend us a smile.

Temples of Mammon are voiceless again—
Lonely policemen inherit Mark Lane—
Silent is Lothbury—quiet Cornhill—
Babel of Commerce, thine echoes are still.

Far to the South—where the wanderer strays
Lost among graveyards and riverward ways,
Hardly a footfall and hardly a breath
Comes to dispute Laurence—Pountney with Death.

Westward the stream of Humanity glides ;—
'Busses are proud of their dozen insides,
Put up thy shutters, grim Care, for to-day—
Mirth and the lamplighter hurry this way.

Out on the glimmer weak Hesperus yields !
Gas for the cities and stars for the fields.
Daisies and buttercups, do as ye list ;
I and my friends are for music and whist.

           Henry S. Leigh : Carols of Cockayne.

The Bell-Man

1648

FROM noise of scare-fires rest ye free
From murders, Benedicite;
From all mischances that may fright
Your pleasing slumbers in the night
Mercy secure ye all, and keep
The goblin from ye, while ye sleep.
—Past one a clock, and almost two,—
My masters all, Good day to you.

Robert Herrick : Hesperides.

Fire

1873

" FIRE!
Away there to the east—
Towards the Surrey ridge,—
I see a puff of dunnish smoke
Over the Southwark bridge ";
A single curl of murky mist
That scales the summer air :—
And the watchman wound his listless way
Slow down the turret stair.

.   .   .

London ! that deck'st thyself with wave-won wealth,
Sea-spoils, fanes, palaces,
And temples high ;
Well said the turbaned traveller of the East
" Behold—and die ! "

Behold these streets; survey these monster marts,—
The lordly Changes of our merchant kings;
Consider the great Thames, and all its breast
Brave with white wings;

Wharves, stately with warehouses,
Docks, with a world's treasure-chest in bail,
What hand shall touch ye?
What rash foe assail?

"*Fire!—to the eastward—Fire!!*"

A hurrying tramp of feet:
A sickly haze that wraps the town
Like a leaden winding sheet:
A smothering smoke is in the air—
A crackling sound—a cry—
And yonder, up over the furnace-pot
That smokes like the smoke of the cities of Lot
There's something fierce and hissing and hot
That licks the very sky.
Fire! fire! ghostly fire!—
It broadens overhead,—
Red glow the roofs in lurid light
The heav'ns are glowing-red;

From east to west—from west to east—
Blood-red the turbid Thames—
"Fire!—fire!—The engines!—Fire!—
Or half the town's in flames—
Fire"
. . . A raging, quivering gulf . . .
A wild stream blazing by . . .
Black ruin . . . fearful flaming heaps
White faces to the sky . . .

"The engines, Ho ! back for your lives !"
The swarthy helmets gleam :
Flash fast, broad wheel !—
Hold, wood and steel !—
Whilst the shout rings up, and the wild bells peal,
And the flying hoofs strike flame.
Stand from the causeway—horse and man—
Back, while there's time for aid ;
Back gilded coach—back lordly steed—
A hundred lives hang on their speed
And fear and fate and daring deed—
Room for the Fire Brigade !

H. Cholmondeley Pennell : Modern Babylon.

Midnight

1822

UNFATHOMABLE Night ! how dost thou sweep
    Over the flooded earth, and darkly hide
  The mighty City under thy full tide ;
Making a silent palace for old Sleep
Like his own temple under the hushed deep,
    Where all the busy day he doth abide,
    And forth at the late dark, outspreadeth wide
His dusky wings, whence the cold waters sweep !
How peacefully the living millions lie !
    Lulled unto death beneath his poppy spells,
There is no breath—no living stir—no cry—
No tread of foot—no song—no music—call—
    Only the sound of melancholy bells—
The voice of Time—survivor of them all !

Thomas Hood : Collected Poems.

OUR revels now are ended: these our actors,
    As I foretold you, were all spirits, and
Are melted into air, into thin air:
And like the baseless fabrick of this vision,
The cloud-capp'd towers, the gorgeous palaces,
The solemn temples, the great globe itself,
Yea, all that it inherit, shall dissolve;
And like this insubstantial pageant faded,
Leave not a rack behind.

Shakespeare : The Tempest.

NOTES

NOTES

LONDON TOWN

Page 3.—LONDON; THAT GREAT SEA. Shelley saw the dark and mixed sides of London life. The stanzas entitled "Hell" in *Peter Bell the Third* are evidence of this :

> Hell is a city much like London—
> A populous and a smoky city ;
> There are all sorts of people undone,
> And there is little or no fun done ;
> Small justice shown, and still less pity.

Some cheerless concessions are made in one of the last stanzas :

> So good and bad, sane and mad ;
> The oppressor and the oppressed ;
> Those who weep to see what others
> Smile to inflict upon their brothers ;
> Lovers, haters, worst and best ;
>
> All are damned—they breathe an air,
> Thick, infected, joy-dispelling ;
> Each pursues what seems most fair,
> Mining like moles through mind, and there
> Scoop palace-caverns vast where Care
> In throned state is ever dwelling.

Shelley's view of London recalls, by contrast, Tennyson's inspiriting picture of London as seen by the boy, who

> . . . at night along the dusky highway, near and nearer drawn,
> Sees in heaven the light of London flaring like a dreary dawn,
> And his spirit leaps within him to be gone before him then,
> Underneath the light he looks at, in among the throngs of men. . . .

Page 4.—THE FLOUR OF CITIES ALL. This noble panegyric by William Dunbar, the father of Scottish poetry, was composed by him in 1501, when he came to London with the embassy sent to King Henry VII. to arrange the marriage of James IV. of Scotland and Princess Margaret of England. The ambassadors were Robert Blackadder, Archbishop of Glasgow; Patrick Hepburn, Earl of Bothwell; Andrew Forman, Apostolical Prothonotary; and Sir Robert Lundy, Treasurer of Scotland. These, with their retinue, were entertained at a banquet in Christmas week by the Lord Mayor, Sir John Shaw; it was on this occasion that Dunbar recited his poem, which remains unrivalled as a glorification of London.

Page 6.—HAIL, LONDON! From the *Gentleman's Magazine*, September 1739: "No need of fables to enhance thy praise, no wand'ring demi-god thy walls to raise."—The writer alludes to Geoffrey of Monmouth's mythical account of the founding of London by Brute, a descendant of Æneas, who is declared to have come to England 1008 B.C. and built Troy Novant, or New Troy, afterwards called Caer Lud (under King Lud), and finally London.

"Sublime Augusta rais'd her tow'ry head."—Augusta was the name enjoyed by London in the last half century of the Roman occupation.

Page 14.—TO LONDON. Henry Luttrell, the author of these lines, and of the lines on "A London Fog" quoted on p. 103, was the witty, worldly friend of Byron, Rogers, Moore, and Lady Blessington. In his *Letters to Julia*, first published in 1820, but afterwards greatly improved, Luttrell happily blends descriptions of London in the Season with playful advice on social behaviour, etc. The above extracts are from the third edition.

Page 19.—THE POET'S LONDON. "See the gilt barge, and hear the fated king prompt the first mavis of our Minstrel Spring."—Lord Lytton, in his own note on this couplet, quotes Charles Knight's *London* as follows:

One of the most remarkable pictures of ancient manners which has been transmitted to us is that in which the poet Gower describes the circumstances under which he was commanded by King Richard II. "to make a book after his best." The good old rhymer . . . had taken boat, and upon the broad river he met the King in his stately barge. . . . The monarch called him on board his own vessel, and desired him to book "some new thing." This was the origin of the *Confessio Amantis.*

"Or mark, with mitred Nevile, the array of arms and craft alarm 'the Silent Way.'"—Edward Hall in his *Chronicle* tells how the Archbishop of York (brother to the King-maker), after leaving the widow of Edward IV. in the sanctuary of Westminster, looked out on the river and saw many boatmen, under the Duke of Gloucester, watching that no person went to sanctuary, or passed to Westminster unsearched.

"Or landward, trace, where thieves their festive hall hold by the dens of Law."—This is rather obscure. Lord Lytton's own note places the "festive hall" in Devereux Court, close to Essex Street. Here in the last century were "Tom's" and the "Grecian" coffee-houses, and here died, in 1678, Marchant Needham, one of our earliest newspaper promoters.

Page 21.—THE CONTRAST. Captain Charles Morris was one of the choice spirits of the Beefsteak Club. His lines on Pall Mall have been more quoted, perhaps, than any other verses about London. Less known are his lines "On the Destruction of the Star and Garter Tavern in Pall Mall, and the Demolition of Carlton Palace," yet they have an interesting bearing on "The Contrast." "What art thou now?" he asks, addressing the "Star and Garter":

> What art thou now? a heap of rubbish'd stone :
> " Pride, pomp, and circumstance" for ever gone !
> A prostrate lesson to the passing eye,
> To teach the high how low they soon may lie.
> Dust are those walls, where long, in pictured pride,
> The far-famed Dilettanti graced their side ;
> And where so long my gay and frolic heart
> Roused living spirits round these shades of art,
> Lank are they all, in heedless silence lost,
> Or midst the flames, as useless refuse cast.
>
> .   .   .   .   .
>
> Down falls the Palace too !—and now I see
> The street, a path of deadly gloom to me :
> And, as I range the town, I, sighing, say,
> " 'Turn from Pall Mall : that's now no more the way,
> Thy once-loved ' shady side,' oft-praised before,
> Shorn from earth's face, now hears thy strains no more :
> And where thy Muse long ply'd her welcome toil,
> Cold speculation barters, out the soil."

Page 24.—LONDON LYCPENY. This excellent ballad restores to us the London of the fifteenth century. Whether it was written by John Lydgate is a question ; but it is

attributed to him by the late Mr. Halliwell-Phillips and by
other writers. Two texts of the ballad exist in MS. in the
British Museum; one, in the Harleian MSS., is quoted by
Northouck, and several other historians of London; the other,
in the handwriting of Stow, is in the same collection. The
text quoted is the first. The ballad is often entitled " London
Lackpenny," and the emendation is reasonable. " London
lickpenny" appears to have been a proverbial phrase, indicating
London's capacity for retaining the money of visitors. But
here the visitor had no money; and the burden of the ballad
is London's cold reception of him on this account: hence
" *Lack*penny."

" Hot pescods."—The nursery rhyme says:

> Piping hot ! smoking hot !
> What have I got ?
> You have not ;
> Hot grey pease, hot ! hot ! hot !

" There is more music in this song," says a writer of the last
century, " on a cold frosty night than ever the syrens were
possessed of who captivated Ulysses, and the effects stick
closer to the ribs."

" Cherryes in the ryse."—Cherries on the branch.

" Canwyke streete."—Canwyke, Candlewright, or Candle-
wick Street is the modern Cannon Street. Stow, who refers
to Lydgate's ballad with relish, supposes the name to have
been taken from the candle-makers who throve there.

Page 28.—RETURN TO LONDON. In 1647 Herrick was
ejected by the Puritan powers from his vicarage at Dean Prior,
near Totnes, in Devonshire, and came to London. He had
long bemoaned his " loathed country life"; for although he
sang of " hock carts, wassails, wakes," with unction, his heart
was ever in town. See " Tears to Thamesis," page 194.

Page 29.—THE MAY-LORD. This song is put into the
mouth of Ralph, an apprentice, in the " The Knight of the
Burning Pestle." The May-Day exodus, described with such
spirit, was a very old London custom. Chaucer refers to it in
his " Court of Love ":—" And forth goth all the court both
most and leste, to fetch the flowers fresh, and braunch and
blome." In the reign of Henry VIII. the Lord Mayor and
Corporation went out into Kent on May-Day to gather the

may, and were met on Shooter's Hill by the King and his queen, Catherine of Arragon. It was the London May-Day, too, that Herrick bade Corinna not neglect :

> Come, my Corinna, come, and, coming, mark
> How each field turns a street, each street a park
>   Made green and trimm'd with trees : see how
>   Devotion gives each house a bough
>   Or branch : each porch, each door ere this
>   An ark, a tabernacle is,
> Made up of white-thorn neatly interwove ;
> As if here were those cooler shades of love.
>   Can such delights be in the street
>   And open fields and we not see't ?
>   Come, we'll abroad ; and let's obey
>   The proclamation made for May :
> And sin no more, as we have done, by staying ;
> But, my Corinna, come let's go a-Maying,
>
>   .   .   .   .   .
>
>   A deal of youth, ere this, is come
>   Back, and with white-thorn laden home,
>   Some have despatch'd their cakes and cream
>   Before that we have left to dream.

Page 31.—THE MILKMAIDS' DANCE. The milkmaids' part in the old London May-Day festivities was lively, and dated back some centuries. A French traveller of the seventeenth century, writes, referring to London :

On the First of May, and the five and six days following, all the pretty young country girls that serve the town with milk, dress themselves up very neatly, and borrow abundance of silver plate, whereof they make a pyramid, which they adorn with ribbons and flowers, and carry upon their heads, instead of their common milk-pails. In this equipage, accompanied by some of their fellow milkmaids and a bagpipe or fiddle, they go from door to door, dancing before the houses of their customers, in the midst of boys and girls that follow them in troops, and everybody gives them something.

The Islington milkmaids kept up their May-Day dances to the end of the eighteenth century. At Vauxhall there hung a picture of the " Milkmaids' Dance on May Day," in which two sooty chimney-boys were introduced. Jacks-in-the-Green, usually personated by sweeps, are still seen on May-Day in the London suburbs. The London May-Day is an interesting subject, and it deserves adequate treatment at a time when Maypoles (indoor) are being revived in Bermondsey, Walworth, and other gloomy districts.

Page 32.—THE MAY POLE IN THE STRAND. These spirited lines are probably by Nicholas Breton, who wrote several pieces under the name of " Pasquil."

Page 37.—DON JUAN IN LONDON.   Lord Byron left London, never to return, in 1816. He wrote the London passages in *Don Juan* at Genoa in 1823.

" Through little boxes framed of bricks, to let the dust in at your ease."—See Robert Lloyd's " The Cit's Country-Box," page 291.

" As the party crossed the bridge."—The " bridge " was old Westminster Bridge, built by Charles Labelye, the Swiss, and first opened to the public in 1750.

" The lamps of Westminster's more regular gleam."—Westminster Bridge had been lit with gas in 1814, and on Christmas Day of that year the general lighting of London by gas had been inaugurated.

" The French were not as yet a lamp-lighting nation."—Nor were the English united in their love of gas. Sir Humphry Davy's scoffing suggestion that the dome of St. Paul's should be used as a gasometer was typical ; and the dwellers in Grosvenor Square haughtily burned oil for twenty years after the rest of London had adopted gas.

Page 39.—YE FLAGS OF PICCADILLY.   The late Mr. Locker-Lampson's lines on Piccadilly should be mentioned :

Piccadilly ! Shops, palaces, bustle, and breeze,
The whirring of wheels and the murmur of trees ;
By night or by day, whether noisy or stilly,
Whatever my mood is, I love Piccadilly—etc.

Page 40. — FAIR PALL MALL.   John Gay's poem, " Trivia ; or The Art of Walking the Streets of London," from which these lines are taken, was first published in 1716 by Bernard Lintot. It was printed for that bookseller " at the Cross-Keys between the Temple Gates in Fleet Street " ; and the sign of the cross-keys is emblazoned on the title-page, which bears, also, the motto from Virgil : *Quo te Mœri pedes ? An, quo via ducit, in Urbem ?* Gay makes the pleasant point in his " Advertisement " that since it will be seen that he walks on foot he may be saved from the envy of the critics. He also acknowledges that he had some help from Swift. Perhaps " Trivia " was a direct attempt to emulate Swift's poems "Morning in London" (see page 103, and Note), and "A City Shower" (page 281). Be that as it may, "Trivia," as a plain, rhymed description of the London streets a hundred and fifty years ago, is invaluable. We need a *New Trivia*, a revised "Art of Walking the Streets of London."

Page 41.—ST. JAMES'S STREET. In the late editions of *London Lyrics* Mr. Locker-Lampson appended the following Note to these verses :

I am told that these lines have disturbed some Americans, but surely without cause. The remark in the seventh stanza is natural in the mouth of a rather exclusive habitué of St. James's, who has the mortification to feel that he is no longer young, who is too shallow-minded to appreciate our advances in civilisation during the last forty years, but who is, nevertheless, sufficiently keen to see what is possible in the future. My friends know I have a sincere admiration for the American people.

Page 44.—A SONG OF HYDE PARK. After the Restoration, Hyde Park became the resort of fashion, and a scene of much display. In 1669, only two years before this song was written, Pepys tells how he and his wife drove in Hyde Park, with their servants in new livery : "The people did look mightily upon us."

Page 45.—ROTTEN ROW. Matthew Arnold's lines, in his poem "Summer in Hyde Park," may be quoted :

> Onward we moved, and reach'd the Ride
> Where gaily flows the human tide.
>
> .   .   .   .   .
>
> The young, the happy, and the fair,
> The old, the sad, the worn, were there ;
> Some vacant, and some musing went,
> And some in talk and merriment.
> Nods, smiles, and greetings, and farewells !
> And now and then, perhaps there swells
> A sigh, a tear—but in the throng
> All changes fast, and hies along.
> Hies, ah, from whence, what native ground ?
> And to what goal, what ending, bound ?

Page 49.—WILLY-NILLY IN PICCADILLY. "She clears that gate, which has cleared itself since then, at Hyde Park Corner." The toll gates at Hyde Park Corner were removed in October 1825 ; their appearance may be seen in the picture ascribed, doubtfully, to Dagaty, "View of Hyde Park Corner," in the National Gallery.

Page 51.—KENSINGTON GARDENS. These are the opening lines in Thomas Tickell's "Kensington Gardens." Dr. Johnson said of this poem that it was "unskilfully compounded of Grecian deities and Gothic fairies."

Page 52.—A WOMAN OF FASHION. These lines are often attributed to Thomas Tickell (as in the *Lyra Elegantiarum*), but it is impossible that Tickell, who died in 1740, should have written of macaronies. The first macaroni balanced his cane about 1770. The lines quoted were found among Sheridan's papers by Tom Moore. Sheridan seems to have known Kensington Gardens well; he described them again in his prologue to Lady Craven's "The Miniature Picture." The year was young when this comedy was played, hence we read :—

> What prudent cit dares yet the season trust,
> Bask in his whisky, and enjoy the dust ?
> Hous'd in Cheapside, scarce yet the gayer spark
> Achieves the Sunday triumph of the Park.
>
> .   .   .   .   .
>
> Scarce rural Kensington due honour gains,
> The vulgar verdure of her walk remains,
> Where white-rob'd Misses amble two by two,
> Nodding to booted beaux—how do, how do?
> With gen'rous questions that no answer wait,
> How vastly full !   A'n't you come vastly late ?
> Isn't it quite charming?   When do you leave town ?
> A'n't you quite tir'd ?   Pray, can we set you down ?

Page 56.—A NEW SONG OF THE SPRING GARDEN. The garden referred to by Mr. Austin Dobson was opened at Vauxhall about the year 1661, under the name of the New Spring Garden at Vauxhall, and was afterwards known by the shorter name of Spring Gardens. It must not be confused with the Spring Garden at Charing Cross, the name of which still survives. The New Spring Garden at Vauxhall was leased in 1728 by Mr. Jonathan Tyers, who founded Vauxhall Gardens on the same site.

Page 57.—FARMER COLIN AT VAUXHALL. In 1741, the date of this song, Vauxhall Gardens had assumed, under Jonathan Tyers, the character they were to keep for more than half a century. Mr. Warwick Wroth's account of Vauxhall in his work, *The London Pleasure Gardens of the Eighteenth Century,* is interesting and exhaustive. Mr. Austin Dobson has minutely described the appearance of the Gardens when in the height of their fame in his *Eighteenth Century Vignettes*, first series.

"The king there dubs a farmer," etc. — In this stanza Farmer Colin describes three pictures in the Pavilion, viz.: "The King and Miller of Mansfield," "Sailors Tippling at Wapping," and "A Girl Stealing a Kiss from a Youth Asleep."

Page 59.—VAUXHALL. These reminiscences of Thomas Hood's apply to the time 1826-30. The "taking Kate Stephens" was engaged for Vauxhall in 1826. Blackmore's feats on the rope may have begun later, for he was making his "terrific ascents" as late as 1837.

Page 65.—ON ST. JAMES'S PARK, AS LATELY IMPROVED BY HIS MAJESTY. The interest of the poem is wider than its title; the imperial associations of the Abbey and the Parliament being introduced. This royal park took shape under Henry VIII. and James I.; but Charles II. was the first monarch to lay it out formally. Here he delighted to saunter with his spaniels, and feed the foreign birds collected in Birdcage Walk. He is even said to have been observed swimming in the lake.

"They bathe in summer, and in winter slide."—Some of Waller's vaticinations have not been fulfilled; public bathing and fishing from "gilded barges" have never been among the pleasures of St. James's Park.

"Yonder, the harvest of cold months laid up."—An ice-house was one of Charles II.'s innovations.

"Here a well-polish'd Mall." Charles was fond of the game of pall-mall, and a new mall, 1424 feet in length, was made, and duly kept up by "the king's cockle-strewer."

Page 76.—PHIL PORTER'S FAREWELL TO TOWN, WHEN DYING. "Oh what a Tennis Court was there!" There were many tennis courts in London, and doubtless each had its warm partisans.

Page 77.—MR. POPE'S FAREWELL TO LONDON. In 1715 Pope was beginning his translation of the *Iliad* ("And Homer— damn him!—calls"). The warm-hearted reference to Gay in the last stanza lends interest to Gay's fanciful poem, "Mr.

Pope's Welcome from Greece" (quoted on page 207), when Homer no longer "called." Perhaps Gay never saw Pope's four-line compliment, for, according to Mr. Courthope, his "Farewell" was first printed in 1776.

Page 79.—To Mr. MacAdam. "Down from 'The County' to the Palace Gate," *i.e.* from the "County" Assurance Office to the Waterloo Place entrance of the demolished Carlton House.

Page 81.—Queen Elinor and the Charing Cross. Peele's lines rest on the tradition that Queen Elinor was buried at Charing Cross. The cross was merely raised to her memory.

Page 82.—On the Statue of King Charles I. -This statue, the work of Hubert Le Sœur, a sculptor who came to England in 1630, was set up under the supervision of Sir Christopher Wren in 1674.

Page 86.—The Downfall of Charing Cross. Charing Cross, Cheapside Cross, and other crosses were ordered by the House of Commons in 1643 to be pulled down. For some reason Charing Cross was allowed to stand until 1647. It was then in a decrepit state.

"Tomkins and Chaloner."—These men were hanged in 1643 for participation in a royalist plot. Waller, the poet, was implicated, but his life was spared.

A lament, similar to this on the fall of Charing Cross, was uttered over the old Golden Cross Tavern, which faced the back of the statue of Charles I. It was a great coaching inn:

> No more the coaches I shall see
> 　Come trundling from the yard,
> Nor hear the horn blow cheerily
> 　By brandy-sipping guard.
>
> 　　.　　　.　　　.　　　.
>
> Oh ! London wont be London long,
> 　For 'twill be all pulled down,
> And I shall sing a funeral song
> 　O'er that time-honoured town.

These lines have been ascribed to William Maginn.

Page 89.—Trafalgar Square. The beautiful passages entitled "Trafalgar Square," "Westminster" (page 183), and "Dawn" (page 190), should be read with their contexts in

Mr. Henley's *London Voluntaries*. The poems in this series must be pronounced the most inspired interpretations of the beauty and significance of London in recent poetry. The *London Voluntaries* were written in 1892-3; but the passages quoted follow Mr. Henley's revised text of 1898.

Page 93.—THE FARMER IN LONDON. This poem first appeared in the *Morning Post* of 21st July 1800, and was unsigned. The poem, which usually bears the title "The Farmer of Tilsbury Vale," was founded on fact, but Miss Fenwick's note upon its origin, quoted by Prof. Knight, is not very informing.

Page 98.—HOLY THURSDAY. This beautiful poem is in contrast to the verses on London in Blake's *Songs of Experience*, beginning:

> I wander through each chartered street,
> Near where the chartered Thames does flow,
> A mark in every face I meet,
> Marks of weariness, marks of woe.

In his "prophetical" poem Blake made strange use of London localities. Thus in "Jerusalem":

> The fields from Islington to Marylebone,
> To Primrose Hill and Saint John's Wood,
> Were builded over with pillars of gold;
> And there Jerusalem's pillars stood.

On this day (Holy Thursday) there is a large gathering of the charity schools at St. Paul's, the beadles of various city parishes being present in their official dress.

Page 99.—LONDON WEATHER. "The bookseller, whose shop's an open square." The "open square" type of bookseller's shop is still seen in London.

"How if the festival of Paul be clear."—St. Paul's Day, 25th January, was at one time held to be more critical than even St. Swithin's Day. St. Swithin decided the weather for a few weeks, but on St. Paul's Day prognostications were made for the whole year. The rhyme ran:

> If St. Paul's be fair and clear
> It does betide a happy year—etc.

"Britain in winter only knows its aid, to guard from chilly

show'rs the walking maid."—It was not until many years after the date of "Trivia" that *men*, led by Jonas Hanway, adopted the umbrella.

Page 103.—A DESCRIPTION OF THE MORNING. These lines by Jonathan Swift, in common with "A City Shower," have an interesting bearing on John Gay's "Trivia" (see note to "Fair Pall Mall," p. 328).

Page 103.—A LONDON FOG. Luttrell describes the London fog as a nuisance. Its beautiful effects are, however, being recognised more and more by poets ; as by Mr. Henley, who writes of its "mellow magic," and by Mrs. Marriott Watson, who, in a little poem called "London in October," exclaims :

> Thine are our hearts, beloved City of Mist
> Wrapped in thy veils of opal and amethyst,
> Set in thy shrine of lapis-lazuli,
> Dowered with the very language of the sea,
> Lit with a million gems of living fire—
> London the goal of many a soul's desire !
> Goddess and Sphynx, thou hold'st us safe in thrall
> Here while the dead leaves fall.

"The bill of Michael Angelo," *i.e.* Michael Angelo Taylor's bill for abating London smoke.

Page 108.—THE COMMON CRIES OF LONDON. Some coarse stanzas are omitted from this ballad, to which it is difficult to put a precise date. John Payne Collier has the following helpful note :

The first stanza of the second part shows that the Curtain, Globe, Swan, and Red Bull theatres were then open, but the dates when any of them were permanently closed cannot be stated with certainty; John Shancke, who is mentioned by name, was a popular actor from 1603 to 1635. . . . The allusion to carrying persons to the play-houses by water is also a curious note of time. There were several old actors of the name of Turner ; and W. Turner may have been upon the stage, and may have composed and sung this production as "a jig" for the amusement of audiences. It was "Printed for F. C., T. V., and W. G." in 1662, but that was unquestionably not the first impression of it, although we know of no other : the full title runs thus—"The Common Cries of London Town ; Some go up Street, Some go Down, With Turner's Dish of Stuff : or A Gallymauvery." The tune is the same as "Peg a' Ramsey," mentioned by Shakespeare in *Twelfth Night*, and is at least as old as 1589.

The Cries of London have afforded subjects for many indifferent rhymes.

Page 114.—THE MERMAID. The traditions of the Mermaid Tavern, in Cheapside, used to be set forth with a delightful air of certainty, which is no longer considered prudent. Mr. Jacob Henry Burn, in his usually precise *Descriptive Catalogue of the London Traders, Taverns, and Coffee-House Tokens Current in the Seventeenth Century*, says plumply:

Sir Walter Raleigh established a literary club at the Mermaid in 1603, consolidating such a list of names as its members that at this distant period excite the liveliest feelings of admiration, reverence, and respect. Shakespeare, Ben Jonson, Beaumont, Fletcher, Cotton, Carew, Martin, Doune, Selden, and others—what a galaxy of genius! that nought has exceeded!

Page 115.—VERSES PLACED IN THE APOLLO. The Devil Tavern, the favourite haunt of Ben Jonson, stood in Fleet Street opposite St. Dunstan's Church. Here the wits and poetasters of the age were " sealed of the tribe of Ben." The rules of the Club, *Leges Conviviales*, drawn in Latin by Jonson, and placed over the chimney, were, it is said, " engraven in marble."

Page 117.—THE COFFEE-HOUSE. This song is from Thomas Jordan's *Triumphs of London*, 1675, and is an early and graphic account of coffee-house doings in the time of Charles II. The references to De Ruyter, General Monk, and Lilly the astrologer require no explanation. Booker was a fishing-tackle maker in Tower Street during the reign of Charles I.; he forsook his tranquil calling to decry King and Popery.

Page 119.—THE WITS' COFFEE-HOUSE. From Prior and Montagu's *Hind and Panther Transversed to the Story of the Country Mouse and the City Mouse*. The lines quoted are interesting as showing the later literary importance of the London coffee-houses. The authors ridicule Dryden's influence at Will's Coffee-House. " The great press," says Macaulay in his *History of England*, "was to get near the chair where John Dryden sate. . . . To bow to the Laureate, and to hear his opinion of Racine's last tragedy, or of Bossu's treatise on epic poetry, was thought a privilege. A pinch from his snuff-box was an honour sufficient to turn the head of a young enthusiast."

Page 120.—THE FARMER'S RETURN FROM LONDON. Garrick dedicated this "Interlude" to Hogarth. In his Preface he explains that it was written "merely with a view of assisting Mrs. Pritchard at her benefit"; but its favourable reception, and the fact that Hogarth had made a drawing of "The Farmer and his Family," induced him to publish it. The coronation of George III., and the affair of the Cock Lane Ghost are gently satirised. Hogarth's sketch seizes the moment when his wife exclaims "A Ghost!" In her alarm she is spilling the ale with which she is about to replenish her husband's cup.

Page 125.—IN THE TEMPLE, and THE RED ROSE AND WHITE. Shakespeare could tell of roses in the Temple Gardens; Mr. Symons has to make the most of "slim trees." But the quiet of the old gardens remains to inspire our living poet.

Page 126.—HOLBORN. "I saw good strawberries in your garden there." The garden was attached to the town house of the Bishops of Ely. Ely Place—still a private precinct, where the watchman cries the hours by night—occupies the site.

Page 127.—STREET COMPANIONS. "I walk with mighty Verulam." Lord Bacon lived in Gray's Inn, and dated his *Essays* from his chambers there.

"A blind old man with forehead fair," *i.e.* Milton; but it may be pointed out that when Milton was "a blind old man with forehead fair" he was more likely to have been met in Aldersgate Street and its neighbourhood than in Fleet Street, where he had lived only as a young man.

Page 130.—CLEVER TOM CLINCH. "My honest friend Wild."—Wild, a thief-catcher, and under-keeper of Newgate, who was hanged for receiving stolen goods. (Sir Walter Scott's edition of Swift's *Works*, vol. xiv. 212.)

Page 131.—A CHAMBER IN GRUB STREET. In these lines Goldsmith played with the idea of a "heroicomical poem," when he was himself suffering all the woes of Scroggen.

Page 132.—TIME WAS! "Lisps the French of Hackney boarding-schools." Hackney was noted for these establishments in the eighteenth century.

"Harsh guitars." Did the guitar precede the concertina as the musical instrument of Whitechapel?

"And throw by *Wingate* for the *Art of Love*," *i.e.* throw by Wingate's *Arithmetic* for a translation of Ovid's work.

"Whether at Arthur's, or the Bowl and Pin," *i.e.* at Arthur's fashionable club in St. James's Street, or at the humble tavern.

"Or play at skittles at St. Giles's pound." The author seems to be inaccurate in referring to St. Giles's pound as existing in 1772, the date of his poem; it had then been removed from its (second) position, the junction of the Tottenham Court Road and Oxford Street. See John Thomas Smith's *A Book for a Rainy Day* (1825 ed.), p. 22.

Page 136.—THE MIDNIGHT POMP OF LONDON'S ARTILLERY. In these lines, part of a long poem, Richard Nicolls looks back from 1616 to days when, on Midsummer's Eve, the citizen soldiers of London marched with great pomp through the streets under the eyes of royalty and the nobility. Note the fine picture conveyed in the lines :

> The wanton shine of thy triumphant fires
> Playing upon the tops of thy tall spires.

Page 149.—THE BALLOON: TO MR. GRAHAM, THE AERONAUT. Graham, the aeronaut, made balloon ascents from London in 1825.

"The Eagle's left behind," *i.e.* the "Eagle" tavern in the City Road, formerly a great London landmark.

Page 152.—OF SOLITUDE. In his description of social London under Charles II., Macaulay alludes to this poem : "Islington was almost a solitude; and poets loved to contrast its silence and repose with the din and turmoil of the monster London." (*History of England*, vol. i. 351).

Page 153.—LONDON RENOUNCED. From Dr. Johnson's satire *London*, written in imitation of the third Satire of Juvenal. The poem was probably suggested to Johnson by the intended departure of Richard Savage to Wales, where his friends proposed to maintain him. Johnson was in his twenty-ninth year when he wrote this spirited poem. His later utterances concerning London were very different, and they are perfectly familiar.

Page 159.—SUNDAY IN LONDON. "'Tis to the worship of the solemn Horn."—The allusion is to the famous Highgate oath, which was formerly administered to travellers at the Red Lion and other inns in that village. The chief terms of the oath were these: "You must not eat brown bread while you can get white, except you like the brown best; you must not drink small beer while you can get strong, except you like the small best. You must not kiss the maid while you can kiss the mistress, except you like the maid the best, but sooner than lose a good chance you may kiss them both."

LONDON RIVER

Page 172.—THAMES AND ISIS. "That was to meet the famous *Troynovant.*" See note to "Hail London!" p. 324.

Page 174.—COOPER'S HILL. "O could I flow like thee!" A small volume might be filled with the praises lavished by poets and critics on these four lines. Denham produced no others comparable to them, and even Dr. Johnson, while criticising the passage, allowed that it had not been praised above its merit.

Page 175.—FATHER THAMES. "I see a new Whitehall ascend!" In 1698 a fire, the fourth which had devastated Whitehall Palace, destroyed nearly the whole of the building except the Banquet-hall. Pope wrote in the belief that the Palace would be rebuilt.

Page 182.—ON THE REPORT OF A WOODEN BRIDGE TO BE BUILT AT WESTMINSTER. In 1738, a year after James Thomson's protest, the construction of the first Westminster Bridge, a solid stone structure, was begun by Charles Labelye.

Page 182.—COMPOSED UPON WESTMINSTER BRIDGE SEPTEMBER 3, 1802. The date included in the title of this great sonnet is declared by Prof. William Knight to be incorrect. "He [Wordsworth] left London for Dover, on his way to Calais, on the 31st of July 1802. The sonnet was written that morning as he travelled towards Dover. The following record of the journey is preserved in his sister's Journal :

July 30. Left London between five and six o'clock of the morning, outside the Dover coach. A beautiful morning. The City, St. Paul's, with the river—a multitude of little boats, made a beautiful sight as we crossed *Westminster Bridge*; the houses not overhung by thin clouds of smoke, and were hung out endlessly; yet the sun shone so brightly, with such a pure light, that there was something like the purity of one of Nature's own grand spectacles."

Page 187.—THE CORONATION. The Coronation of Anne Boleyn on Whitsun Day, 1533.

Page 188.—SOMERSET HOUSE. The present Somerset House has, of course, only a local relation to the building which moved Cowley to verse. That building had been founded and partly built by the Protector Somerset, maternal uncle of Edward VI. Throughout the reigns of that monarch, and of Elizabeth, James I., and Charles I., it had a chequered career. There was an idea among the early Quakers of purchasing the building for their meetings, but George Fox forbade it, "for I then foresaw the King's coming in again." In November 1660, Queen Henrietta Maria, who had occupied the palace during the reign of her unhappy lord, again took up her residence here. Her coming, and the repairs by Inigo Jones which she initiated, are the subject of Cowley's poem. Old Somerset House was a fine castellated structure ; its appearance before Inigo Jones had adapted it to Henrietta Maria's requirements is preserved in a painting at Dulwich College, and is engraved in Wilkinson's *Londina Illustrata.*

Page 191.—A SPOUSALL. From *Prothalamion*, Spenser's poem in celebration of the marriages of Ladies Elizabeth and Katherine Somerset.

Page 194.—TEARS TO THAMESIS. Mr. Alfred Pollard notes, in his edition of Herrick in "The Muse's Library": "The references in this poem seem to refer to Herrick's courtier days, between leaving Cambridge and going to Devonshire."

"My beloved Westminster." Herrick was intimate with the organist of Westminster Abbey and his daughters.

"Golden Cheapside." Cheapside was the goldsmiths' quarter.

Page 195.—THE GREAT FROST. The Great Frost, described in the ballad, lasted from the beginning of December 1683 to the 5th of February 1684. Evelyn describes the scene on the Thames in his *Diary*. An engraving after Thomas Wyck, in Wilkinson's *Londina Illustrata*, shows the double line of booths and taverns that stretched across the river from Temple Stairs, called "Temple Street." London Bridge fills the distance.

Page 196.—THE GREAT THAW. Although the ice on the river began to break up on 5th February 1684, Evelyn says "it froze again"; and as late as 4th April he writes in his *Diary*: "Hardly the least appearance of any spring."

Page 199.—BALLADE OF CLEOPATRA'S NEEDLE. This obelisk was presented to England by Mehemet Ali in 1819. Only in 1877 were steps taken for its removal from Alexandria to London. It is 3000 years old, and for 1600 years it stood, with another obelisk, before the Temple of the Sun at Heliopolis. It is said to have been brought to Alexandria by Cleopatra.

"Ye giant shades of Ra and Tum." The hieroglyphs on the "needle" show that it was erected by Tothmes III., who is represented as offering gifts to the deities Ra and Atum.

Mr. Lang's lines may be associated with Dante Gabriel Rossetti's fine poem, "The Burden of Nineveh":

> In our Museum galleries
> To-day I lingered o'er the prize
> Dead Greece vouchsafes to living eyes,—
> Her Art for ever in fresh wise
>   From hour to hour rejoicing me.
> Sighing I turned at last to win
> Once more the London dirt and din ;
> And as I made the swing-door spin
> And issued, they were hoisting in
>   A wingèd beast from Nineveh.

The poet's speculations bring him a vision of:

> That future of the best or worst
> When some may question which was first,
>   Of London or of Nineveh.

Page 200.—SONG TO CELIA. "On the sands in Chelsea Fields." According to Norden, Chelsea derives its name from the circumstances that the strand "is like the chesel which the sea casteth up of sand and pebble stones, thereof called Cheselsey, briefly Chelsey, as is Chelsey (now Selsey) in Sussex."

Page 202.—SHOOTING THE BRIDGE. Old London Bridge obstructed the river to such an extent that rapids were formed in its narrow arches. These were always dangerous. It used to be said that "London Bridge was made for wise men to go over, and fools to go under."

Page 203.—FAREWELL TO OLD LONDON BRIDGE. Old London Bridge was demolished in 1824 to make way for Rennie's structure. The poet has in no way exaggerated the memories of pomp and gaiety which clung to the older bridge.

"On thee the peaceful Pilgrim train." — Many of the Canterbury Pilgrims must have crossed London Bridge to Southwark.

"And laurell'd Kings and Conquerors."—Richard II. was magnificently received here in 1392 by the forgiving citizens. Here Henry V., fresh from Agincourt, was met by the Lord Mayor, the bridge being splendidly decorated.

"The pomp of tourney and of tilt."—In 1390 Sir David Lindsay of Glenesk challenged Lord Wells, the English ambassador to Scotland, to a joust. This was held on London Bridge, Sir David arriving from Scotland in great state. A modern painting of the scene hangs in the Guildhall.

"Thou Moloch of the flood."—The drownings caused by the difficulty of shooting Old London Bridge were a scandal. Thornbury says : "It was rather unfeelingly computed that fifty watermen, bargemen, or seamen, valued at £20,000, were annually drowned in passing the dangerous bridge." See Note to "Shooting the Bridge," above.

Page 205.—A MERRY WHERRY-FERRY VOYAGE. The jingles of John Taylor, the water-poet, may have no charm for the critic of poetry, but Taylor was a veritable son of the Thames and lover of London. "No man," says Professor Masson in his *Life of John Milton*, "knew the town better than he ; and there was not a person of any mark in town or near it, from the King and Privy Councillors down to the Gloucester carrier or the landlord of the inn on Highgate Hill, but had a word for 'The Sculler.' With a fund of rough natural humour, and an acquired knack of writing, he had won his name of 'the water-poet,' and at the same time increased his custom as a boatman, by a series of printed effusions, none of them above a sheet or two in length, and consisting either solely of verse, or of verse and prose intermixed. . . . His plan for disposing of these productions seems to have been to hawk them about personally among his patrons and acquaintances, or to sell them in parcels to those who retailed ballads and other cheap popular literature."

"Or York for My Money."—The voyage was to York, and nearly every knot made is chronicled.

Page 207.—MR. POPE WELCOMED TO LONDON. "Oh, what a concourse swarms on yonder quay !" Fourteen stanzas, omitted in this book, are devoted to the names and characteristics of the brilliant throng which the poet supposes to have gathered to welcome Pope back to England and town. These stanzas are fully annotated by Mr. John Underhill in his edition of Gay's Poems in " The Muse's Library."

Page 210.—HOGARTH'S TOUR. Thornhill's account of the " tour " (in *prose*) is preserved in the Print Room of the British Museum. His story was closely versified by the Rev. W. Gostling of Canterbury. Thornhill was Hogarth's brother-in-law ; Tothall was a draper of Tavistock Street, and had been a seaman ; Forrest was an attorney ; and Scott was Samuel Scott the artist, whose pictures of old London and Westminster bridges are in the National Gallery.

"And this enabled us by ten at Rochester to drink again." —The lines omitted immediately after these lines number some hundreds, and the effect of this enforced abridgment is to make appear that Hogarth and his party, after breakfasting at Rochester, returned to town. Whereas the tour extended to Stroud, Upnor, Sheppy, and Sheerness. It was at Gravesend, on the *return* journey, that the travellers called for tobacco and wine.

Page 214.—THE JOLLY YOUNG WATERMAN. Dibdin's play, *The Waterman, or the First of August,* in which this

song occurs, was produced at the Haymarket Theatre. Its
interest centres in the watermen's race on the Thames for
Doggett's badge and coat—a contest which has been held
annually since 1722—and in the love of Tom Tug, the hero,
for a gardener's daughter.

Page 217.—A WHITEBAIT DINNER. The hotels of
Greenwich and Blackwall were famous for their whitebait,
and it was the height of fashion to dine there. The ministerial
fish dinners and the Lord Mayor's fish dinner lent annual
countenance to the custom.

"Where Lovegrove's tables," etc. In the *Morning Post*,
10th September 1835, the following report appeared:

Yesterday the Cabinet Ministers went down the river in the Ordinance
barges to Lovegrove's West India Dock Tavern, Blackwall, to partake of
their annual fish dinner. Covers were laid for thirty-five gentlemen.

LONDON CITY

Page 223.—LONDON PRAISED AND CURSED. Dryden's
second satire against Shaftesbury, *The Medal*, derived its
title from the circumstance that after Shaftesbury's discharge
in 1681 by a packed grand jury his Whig friends struck a
medal to celebrate the occasion. *The Medal* was Dryden's
reply to this act; and his apostrophe to London, of which only
a portion is quoted, was the more appropriate because the real
medal bore on its reverse side a view of London, with the sun
rising above the Tower.

Page 224.—A LONDON PRENTICE. Chaucer's unfinished
"Coke's Tale" contains little more than this picture of an idle
Cheapside apprentice of the fourteenth century. Other London
characters were drawn by Chaucer, notably the host at the
Tabard, of whom we read:

> A large man he was with eyen stepe
> A fairer burgeys is there noon in Chepe.

The "gentle Manciple" of the Temple is sketched to the life
in the General Prologue, and there are many slight allusions in
the Tales to London life. The following notes are adapted
from Professor Skeat's notes to his edition of Chaucer's works:

" For whan ther any ryding was in Chepe."—This refers to the jousts and other festivals that were so common in Cheapside.

" Al conne he pleye on giterne or ribible."—The ribible was the same instrument as the rebeck.   This line is opposed to the line " Al have he no part," etc., and Professor Skeat paraphrases the two thus: " The master pays for the revelling of the apprentice, though he takes no part in such revel ; and conversely, the apprentice may gain skill in minstrelsy but takes no part in paying for it ; for, in his case, his rioting is convertible with theft."

" And somtyme lad with revel to Newgate."—Disorderly persons taken to Newgate were preceded by minstrels in order that their disgrace might be published.

Page 228.—SIR RICHARD WHITTINGTON'S ADVANCEMENT. The mixture of truth and fiction in this famous ballad has been much discussed : but common sense tells us what we may believe and what we should doubt in the story.   We may believe that on Highgate Hill Dick heard Bow Bells ringing, and taking new heart came back into London to become Lord Mayor.   The ballad has a good deal in common with the Elizabethan ballad, " The Honour of a London 'Prentice," for which space could not be found in this volume.   Therein we read :

> Of a worthy London 'prentice,
>   My purpose is to speak,
> And tell his brave adventures
>   Done for his country's sake :
> Seek all the world about,
>   And you shall hardly find
> A man in valour to exceed
>   A 'prentice gallant mind.
>
> He was born in Cheshire,
>   The chief of men was he,
> From thence brought up to London,
>   A 'prentice for to be.
> A merchant on the Bridge
>   Did like his service so,
> That for three years his factor,
>   To Turkey he should go.
>
> And in that famous country
>   One year he had not been,
> Ere he by tilt maintained
>   The honour of his Queen,

> Elizabeth, his Princess,
> He nobly did make known
> To be the Phoenix of the world
> And none but she alone.

Page 232—PRETTY BESSEE AND THE LONDON MERCHANT. This is the first "Fitt" of the old ballad, "The Beggar's Daughter of Bednall Green." In the Whitechapel Road, near Bethnal Green, there is a tavern named "The Blind Beggar."

Page 237.—LONDON'S SEVEN IMAGES. These quaint lines, quoted by Stow, were inscribed in the porch of the Guildhall, in which the seven statues described in the lines had their place. Stow, writing in 1598, says they were "made some thirty years since by William Elderton, at that time an attorney in the sheriffs' courts."

The idea that London possessed seven virtues is old. In a poem describing the welcome of Henry VI. to London, in 1431, John Lydgate thus exalts London:

> Of seven thinges I preyse this Citee ;
> Of trewe menyng, and faithfull obeisaunce,
> Of rightwysnesse, trouthe, and equytie,
> Of stabilnesse, ay kept in alegiaunce,
> And for of vertu, thou hast such suffiraunce
> In this land here, and othere landes alle,
> The Kynges Chambre, of custom men thee calle.

The "King's Chamber" was a title often applied to the City of London. The spirit of the phrase is plain. Shakespeare makes Warwick say :

> My sovereign, with the loving citizens,—
> Like to the island, girt in with the ocean,
> Or modest Dian, circled with her nymphs,
> Shall rest in London till we come to him.

Page 238.—LONDON'S WELCOME TO HENRY V. These stanzas are part of a long poem accompanying the Harleian MS. of "A Chronicle of London from 1089 to 1483." Sir Nicholas H. Nicholas, editing this manuscript in 1827, wrote : "There can be no doubt of it [the poem] having been a production of the prolific pen of that 'drivelling monk,' as he has been severely termed, the monk of Bury, John Lydgate." It will be allowed that John Lydgate "drivelled" to some purpose when he told the adventures of a Kent yokel in the London that had nurtured Chaucer (see "London Lycpeny," page 24), and when, as in this piece, he described London's welcome to the "happy few" of Agincourt.

Page 244.—THE OPENING OF THE NEW RIVER. These lines are said by Stow to have been spoken during the ceremony of the 29th of September 1613, when Sir Hugh Middleton's New River, brought from Amwell in Hertfordshire, was permitted to flow into the reservoir at Clerkenwell. The Lord Mayor and Aldermen attended in state, and Sir Hugh Middleton's workmen paraded. The poet recited his lines, and when the last was uttered, " The flood-gates flew open, the streame ranne gallantly into the cisterne, drummes and trumpets sounding in a triumphall manner, and a brave peale of chambers gave full issue to the intended entertainment." The opening of the New River inaugurated London's modern water-supply. Hence one William Garbott was justified in lamenting, in 1750, that the event had not been more worthily sung. Not that he greatly improved matters by rhymes like these :

> Had I but skill, how sweetly could I play
> Upon thy *pipes*, Sir Hugh, a roundelay !
> O glorious theme ! equal unto the pen
> Of Dryden great, or matchless *O rare Ben*.

Page 245. — KING JAMES I. AT ST. PAUL'S. The event which inspired this ballad was this. In 1619 the condition of Old St. Paul's Cathedral was forlorn. The spire had not been rebuilt since it fell bodily into the building during the great thunderstorm of 14th June 1561. The nave of the patched-up cathedral had become a promenade under the name of Paul's Walk. After many petitions had been made to him King James resolved to visit St. Paul's. He came with his Queen on Sunday, 26th March 1620, and was received by the Archbishop of Canterbury, the Bishops, and the Lord Mayor and Aldermen. A sermon was preached by the Bishop of London. The scene is portrayed in an old painting, engraved in Wilkinson's *Londina Illustrata*. Both the ballad and the picture contain touches of satire.

"Archie came in gold."—Archie was the Court fool.

Page 248.—THE GREAT FIRE. This calamity began on 2nd September 1666.

"Now day appears, and with the day the King."—Pepys met the King and Duke of York on the river, and accompanied them to Queenhithe, the King giving orders for the stopping of the fire below London Bridge.

"The most in fields, like herded beasts, lie down."—Evelyn says: "I went towards Islington and Highgate, where one might have seen 200,000 people of all ranks and degrees, dispers'd and lying along by their heaps of what they could save from the fire.

"A city of more precious mould."—The rapidity with which London was rebuilt was remarkable. About ten years after the calamity the poets began putting forth their heroics on the new London. The most ambitious pæan was "Troja Rediviva: The Glories of London Surveyed," published in 1674. The author thus exclaims on the speed with which London was restored :

> Nay, what is more miraculous to tell
> It rose almost as quickly as it fell.
>
> .　　　.　　　.　　　.　　　.
>
> When all the town ran to the fields for fear,
> You'd think they on purpose did go there
> Bricks for another building to prepare ;
> 'Twas not for gain their goods they sav'd you'd say,
> But that the rubbish might be drawn away ;
> You'd think they had left their former trade,
> And now all masons were, and bricklayers made !

Page 255.—A Song for the Lord Mayor's Table. From Thomas Jordan's "Pageant," entitled "The Goldsmith's Jubilee, or London's Triumphs," written in honour of Sir Robert Vyner, Lord Mayor, 1674.

Page 258.—The Worshipful Drapers. Lines similar to these occur in most of the City Poets' effusions. These lines by Jordan were in honour of Sir Robert Clayton, Lord Mayor in 1679, and a Worshipful Draper.

Page 260.—The Mercers' Company's Song. This song occurs in the "Pageant" addressed by Thomas Jordan—the most prolific of the City Poets—to Sir John Peakes, mercer, who was elected Lord Mayor in 1686. The Virgin Mary was deemed to be the patroness of the Mercers' Company. The

heraldic device of a maiden's head is still seen on the Mercers'
Hall, in Long Acre, and in other streets where the Company
holds property.

Page 261.—THE MERCHANT TAYLORS' GLORY. Originally
entitled "A Delightful Song of the Four Famous Feasts of
England, one of them ordained by King Henry the Seventh, to
the honour of Merchant Tailors: showing how seven kings
have been free of that Company, and how lastly it was graced
with the renowned Henry of Great Britain." The song is
preserved in a collection entitled *The Crown Garland of Roses,
Gathered out of England's Royal Garden*, 1692.

Page 266.—HYDE PARK CAMP. Some of the consequences
of the Great Plague are described in this ballad, which was
entitled "Hide Park Camp, Limned out to the Life, Truly and
Unpartially, for the Information and Satisfaction of such as were
not Eye Witnesses of the Souldiers sad Sufferings, in that
(never-to-be-forgotten) Year of our Lord God, One thousand
six hundred sixty-five. Written by a Fellow-Souldier and
Sufferer in the said Camp." This ballad is preserved as a
broadside in the King's Library at the British Museum.

Page 269.—LORD MAYOR'S SHOW. J. P., the writer of
these lines, was an industrious city jingler at a period long
after City Poets were petted.
  "Row'd by Nelson's Nobs along."—Nelson was the Under
Water Bailiff of the day, and his "Nobs" the City watermen.

Page 272.—A GOOD LORD MAYOR. In these lines J. P.,
the City Poet referred to in the last Note, turns his long
definition of a good Lord Mayor into a rich compliment to Sir
Peter Laurie. Sir Peter was a saddler, and he was said to be
the original of Alderman Cute in Charles Dickens' story, *The
Chimes*.
  "Let the cat kitten in the kitchen grate!"—There is
a tradition that this event once happened at the Mansion House
under a parsimonious Lord Mayor.
  "And wink at fishing in unlawful ways."—The author
thought the City's rights had been neglected "particularly with
respect to whitebait."
  "And do five hundred, while confin'd for one."—The
reference is to the notorious Carlisle.

Page 274.—THE CURTAIN THEATRE. This theatre, the second built in London, was erected in Shoreditch about 1576. The name, which still survives in Curtain Road, had a local, not a stage origin. In this theatre, it is believed, *King Henry V.* was played by the Burbages and Shakespeare in 1599. The late Mr. Halliwell-Phillipps showed that Shakespeare's "*This wooden O*" referred in all probability to the Curtain Theatre, and not, as has been commonly assumed, to the later Globe Theatre on Bankside.

Page 275.—BARTHOLOMEW FAIR. This annual fair was suppressed as a nuisance in 1855, when it had shrunk to small proportions. Throughout the sixteenth and seventeenth centuries Bartholomew Fair was regularly a scene of riot and dissipation. Ben Jonson's play, *Bartholomew Fair*, records its characteristic features in his day. The literature of the festival has been dealt with by Professor Henry Morley in his *Memoirs of Bartholomew Fair*.

Page 277.—SALLY IN OUR ALLEY. Henry Carey, the author of this charming ballad, stated the source of his inspiration as follows :

The real occasion was this : A shoemaker's 'prentice, making holiday with his sweetheart, treated her with a sight of Bedlam, the puppet-shows, the flying-chairs, and all the elegancies of Moorfields : from whence, proceeding to the Farthing Pie-House, he gave her a collation of buns, cheesecakes, gammon of bacon, stuffed-beef, and bottled ale ; through all which scenes the author dodged them (charmed with the simplicity of their courtship), from whence he drew this little sketch of nature.

Page 279.—THE BAILIFF'S DAUGHTER OF ISLINGTON. Dr. Percy, Mr. Halliwell-Phillipps, and others place the Islington of this ballad in Norfolk. But no lover of London will listen to such a proposition. It is true, as the editor of the Roxburghe Ballads points out, that the distance between Islington and the City hardly accounts for the seven years' separation of the lovers. But they may have been watched and thwarted. A cogent argument against the Norfolk Islington theory is that in the maiden's journey up to London there is no mention of nightfall.

Page 281.—A CITY SHOWER. See note to "Fair Pall Mall " p. 328.

Page 283.—A City Calendar.   "The pride of Hockley-hole, the surly bull."   Hockley in the Hole, a small area to the south-west of Clerkenwell Green, was famous for its bull and bear-baitings.

Page 284.—Marketing.   "And Squirts read Garth, till apozems grow cold."   Squirts was the name of an apothecary's boy in Garth's poetical work, *The Dispensary*.

Page 286.—Summer's Return.   Sir William Davenant's "Long Vacation in London" is a lively catalogue of the humours and amusements of the town, but too long, and sometimes too coarse, for quotation.

Page 287.—The Little Dancers.   The late Miss Mathilde Blind wrote some pleasing lines on the subject of the children's street dances in London.   Mr. W. B. Yeats has written some verses on the same subject, but his modest belief that these are "immature" has led him to withhold permission for their inclusion in this volume.

Page 288.—White Conduit House.   This North London tea-garden was at its zenith when these lines were written.   Its proprietor, Robert Bartholomew, understood how to cater for the small tradesmen and 'prentices from the City.   He provided tea, and milk from the cow ; and cricket was played in an adjoining field.   Oliver Goldsmith was a frequent visitor.   White Conduit House remained merry and fairly rural down to 1849.

Many other tea-gardens thrived in North London in the eighteenth century.   Sadler's Wells still survives in the theatre of that name.   In 1740 it was sung :

> There pleasant streams of Middleton
> In gentle murmurs glide along,
> In which the sporting fishes play
> To close each wearied summer's day.
> And Musick's charm in lulling sounds
> Of mirth and harmony abounds ;
> While nymphs and swains, with beaux and belles,
> All praise the joys of Sadler's Wells.

Bagnigge Wells, the site of which is marked by an inscription in Farringdon Road, also enjoyed long popularity.   In the old song, "The 'Prentice to his Mistress," these lines occur :

Come prithee make it up, Miss, and be as lovers be ;
We'll go to Bagnigge Wells, Miss, and there we'll have some tea,
It's there you'll see the ladybirds perched on the stinging nettles,
The crystal water-fountain and the copper shining kettles,
It's there you'll see the fishes, more curious they than whales,
And they're made of gold and silver, Miss, and wags their little tails.
O ! they wags their little tails, they wags their little tails ;
O ! they're made of gold and silver, Miss, and they wags their little tails.
O dear ! O la ! O dear ! O la ! O dear ! O la ! how funny !

The eighteenth century tea-gardens and pleasure resorts of London have been exhaustively described by Mr. Warwick Wroth.   See Note to " Farmer Colin at Vauxhall," p. 330.

Page 290.—ON THE UNIVERSITY CARRIER.   "Old Hobson " was Tobias Hobson, and the Bull Inn, his London restingplace, stood in Bishopsgate Within, on the site now occupied by Palmerston Buildings.   Hobson is credited with being the first man to let out hackney horses in England, and with being the hero of " Hobson's Choice."

Page 295.—THE POET BAFFLED.   Compare this lament on the northward spread of London with Horace Smith's lines on the building over of St. George's Fields, quoted on page 297.
" For him [the bookseller] he reads on Privy-garden wall." The Privy Garden, behind Whitehall, covered $3\frac{1}{2}$ acres ; and was enclosed by a wall, on a part of which the ballad-mongers displayed their wares.   The poet, doubtless, studied these " to store with images his vacant mind."

Page 297.—THE SPREAD OF LONDON.   St. George's Fields had for centuries been one of London's playgrounds. " O, Sir John, do you remember since we lay all night in the windmill in St. George's Fields ?" asks Shallow of Falstaff. In 1795, nearly twenty years before Horace Smith wrote his lines, a stone on the Goldsmith's Arms tavern was inscribed :

> Here Herbs did grow
> And Flowers sweet,
> But now 'tis called
> Saint George's Street.

Page 298.—RURAL FELICITY.   " I shall be at the old *Bell and Crown*."   This fine old tavern, more familiar as " Ridler's Hotel," is now (in September, 1898) being demolished.

Page 300.—JOHN GILPIN. The original of John Gilpin, according to Mr. Thomas Wright's *Life of Cowper*, was a Mr. Beyer, a linendraper, of No. 3 Cheapside. Mr. Beyer died in 1791, aged 98. In the *Morning Post*, 6th April 1896, Mr. E. V. Lucas showed that the topography of the ballad is weak. For Gilpin came to the Wash before he came to the Bell at Edmonton, which means that he was approaching the Bell from the north, the Wash being a mile further from London than Edmonton. This could only be the case if Gilpin had made an improbable *detour*; and, even then, havoc is made of Cowper's suggestion that Gilpin's runaway horse was making for his stable at Ware (where dwelt the calender), Ware being thirteen miles north of Edmonton.

Page 312.—THE REVERIE OF POOR SUSAN. Prof. William Knight says, in his notes to his edition of Wordsworth's Poems: " I think it probable that the poem was written during the short visit which Wordsworth and his sister paid to their brother Richard in London in 1797, when he tried to get his tragedy, *The Borderers*, brought on the stage. The title of the poem from 1800 to 1805 was ' Poor Susan.' " It was perhaps the sight of the plane tree which still stands at the corner of Wood Street which inspired the lines.

ACKNOWLEDGMENTS

IT will be seen that many copyright poems are included in this book. For permission to print these—most kindly given in every case—I have to return my thanks to the following writers :—

Miss Margaret Armour.	*Mr. Selwyn Image.*
Mr. J. Ashby-Sterry.	*Mr. Lionel Johnson.*
Mr. Laurence Binyon.	*Mr. Andrew Lang.*
Mr. Wilson Benington.	*Mr. E. V. Lucas.*
Mr. Wilfrid S. Blunt.	*Mr. Ernest Rhys.*
Mr. John Davidson.	*Miss Ada Smith.*
Mr. Austin Dobson.	*Mr. Arthur Symons.*
Mr. William Ernest Henley.	*Mrs. Rosamund Marriott Watson.*
Mr. W. H. Hudson.	*Mr. William Watson.*

Several poems by Matthew Arnold and Arthur H. Clough are included by kind permission of Messrs. Macmillan; and a poem by James Thomson, the author of " The City of Dreadful Night," is allowed to appear by Messrs. Reeves and Turner.

For permission to include several pieces by the late Miss Amy Levy I have to thank Miss Clementina Black and Mr. T. Fisher Unwin; and for similar permission in respect of three poems by the late Mr. Frederick Locker-Lampson I am indebted to Mrs. Locker-Lampson, and Messrs. Kegan Paul, Trench, Trübner.

The verses by Mr. Cholmondeley Pennell and the late Mr. Henry S. Leigh are kindly permitted by Messrs. Chatto and Windus. For certain poems my thanks are due to the Editor of the Spectator, *the Editor of* Le Quartier Latin, *and to Mr. Wilfrid Meynell, formerly Editor of* Merry England.

Among books which I have consulted with profit I cannot omit to name Mr. William Ernest Henley's anthology, A London Garland, *and Mr. Henry B. Wheatley's invaluable* London Past and Present.

I am grateful, for assistance in proof-reading, to my friend Mr. Edward Salkeld Burrow; and to my friend Mr. Edward Verrall Lucas for some useful suggestions.

It will not escape the notice of any reader that this book owes its outward beauty to Mr. William Hyde, whose interpretations of the life and streets of London, are recognised as possessing poetic and artistic qualities of a very high order.

THE END

Printed by R. & R. Clark, Limited, *Edinburgh.*

A BOOK OF VERSES FOR CHILDREN

COMPILED BY

EDWARD VERRALL LUCAS

With Cover, Title Page, and End Paper designed in colours by F. D. Bedford.

Third Edition.   Crown 8vo.   Cloth Gilt.   6s.

The Globe.—"Is, we think, the best of its kind —partly because it is so comprehensive and so catholic, partly because it consists so largely of matter not too hackneyed, partly because that matter is so pleasantly arranged. The verse here brought together is full of agreeable variety, it is from many sources, some hitherto not drawn upon ; and it has been grouped in sections with a happy sense of congruity and freshness."

GRANT RICHARDS:

9 HENRIETTA STREET, COVENT GARDEN, W.C.